What Others Are Saying...

AlLee and Richardson craft a unique story filled with humor, mystery, romance, and history. From the gambler disguised as a preacher to the nosy but helpful Pinkerton detective to the good-hearted heroine with a penchant for getting herself into scrapes, these characters will live on in your heart long after the story ends.

—*Anne Mateer*
Author, *Wings of a Dream* and *At Every Turn*

Diamond in the Rough is a delightful romp from beginning to end, including humor, pathos, and romance. Even more than its entertainment value, it carries an important message, one presented in a simple children's song: "Red and yellow, black and white, all are precious in His sight." *Diamond in the Rough* has the potential to turn one's heart toward his Maker. I highly recommend it.

—*Kim Vogel Sawyer*
Best-selling author, *My Heart Remembers*

Diamond
IN THE ROUGH

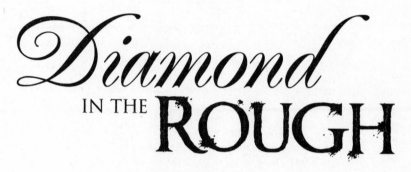

Diamond
IN THE ROUGH

Charm & Deceit

JENNIFER ALLEE *and*
LISA KARON RICHARDSON

WHITAKER
HOUSE

Publisher's Note:
This novel is a work of fiction. References to real events, organizations, or places
are used in a fictional context. Any resemblances to actual persons, living or dead,
are entirely coincidental.

All Scripture quotations are taken from the King James Version of the Holy Bible.

DIAMOND IN THE ROUGH
Charm & Deceit ~ Book One
Jennifer AlLee
Web Site: www.jenniferallee.com
E-mail: jallee725@hotmail.com

Lisa Karon Richardson
Web Site: lisakaronrichardson.com
E-mail: lisa@lisakaronrichardson.com

Authors are represented by MacGregor Literary, Inc., and The Steve Laube Agency.

ISBN: 978-1-60374-742-4
eBook ISBN: 978-1-60374-743-1
Printed in the United States of America
© 2013 by Jennifer AlLee and Lisa Karon Richardson

Whitaker House
1030 Hunt Valley Circle
New Kensington, PA 15068
www.whitakerhouse.com

Library of Congress Cataloging-in-Publication Data (Pending)

1 2 3 4 5 6 7 8 9 10 11   ᵾ   20 19 18 17 16 15 14 13

Dedication

From Lisa
For Crystal and Rachel. You both are amazing,
and I am beyond privileged to spend so much time with you.
Thanks for your support and friendship.

From Jen
To my dad, Henry. I love you.

Acknowledgments

Many, many thanks to Jen, my good-natured and immensely talented coauthor. You are a dream to work with and the sister of my heart.

—*Lisa*

Lisa—words can't say how excited I am to have a book with both our names on the cover! Working with you on this series is a joy and an honor. Thanks for being such a blessing in my life.

—*Jen*

We both give many thanks to the Whitaker House team, especially Christine, Courtney, and Cathy. You have all been wonderful. We also want to offer sincere appreciation to our agents, Tamela and Sandra. You guys make a tough job look easy.

Chapter 1

April 1861
Eureka, California

They're dying, Hodge!" Lily burst through the door of the general store. "I don't know what's wro—*oomph*." She jerked to a stop as her hoopskirt caught in the door. Again.

A handful of choice phrases leaped to mind, but she settled for inarticulate grumbling as she reached back with one hand to wrench the flexible metallic hoops free. As she staggered forward, her skirts belled out, knocking over a display of stacked baking soda tins. She stooped to prevent the cans from rolling willy-nilly across the floor, only to have the back of her skirt swing in the opposite direction and make contact with something solid.

Hodge wiped his hands on his apron as he hurried around from behind the counter. "Just leave it, Miss Lily."

Lily straightened, shifting the cumbersome flowerpot she held in the crook of one arm. With her free hand, she swept the loose tendrils of hair from her eyes and tucked them behind her ear. "You really need to widen that door."

Hodge cocked his head and planted his hands on his hips. "You really need to wear skirts that don't endanger life and limb."

Lily narrowed her eyes and opened her mouth to correct him, but she snapped it shut again when she noticed a man leaning against the counter. His dark hair stood up in spiky patches, as if he'd run his fingers through it repeatedly since removing his hat. His craggy complexion was saved from severity by the quirk of a dimple at the corner of his mouth and the glint of humor in his green eyes.

With a barely perceptible nod, Lily turned away from the stranger's amused glance and squared her shoulders. She wasn't above arguing with Hodge, but she couldn't afford to antagonize him right now. She needed his help.

She thrust the flowerpot she carried at the shopkeeper. A feathery purple peony drooped listlessly over the side, its leaves marred by irregular black spots. "Can you tell me what's wrong with this thing?"

Hodge plucked off one of the saddest-looking leaves and rubbed it between his fingers, then lifted it to his nose and sniffed. "You've got blight." He tossed the leaf back into the pot.

"Blight?" That sounded bad. And pervasive. Whatever it was hadn't afflicted just this particular plant. Half the peonies in the greenhouse looked the same. Mama was going to have a conniption when she got back from San Francisco. "What did I do?"

"Don't flatter yourself. It's caused by a fungus."

"Oh." That was some small consolation. "Is there any cure?"

"Sure, there is."

Lily tamped down her irritation, forcing a smile instead. Getting information out of Hodge was more tedious than pulling weeds from the garden. "And what might that cure be?"

"Steep a handful of elder leaves in hot water with some Castile soap, then rub it on the leaves."

"Castile soap?"

"Yep. I've got some in the back." Hodge held up his hand, halting her attempt to follow him. "Oh no, you don't. Not dressed in them instruments of destruction."

Lily sniffed and raised her chin. Hodge didn't know the first thing about fashion. Granted, she hadn't quite gotten the hang of these hoops yet. But, when she did, all of Eureka would be impressed with her grace and style. And Mama would finally be happy.

With great care, she glided across the room, mindful not to knock over anything else. No use proving Hodge's point. She halted at the counter and picked up a seed catalog. Maybe Mama need never know. Lily could order replacement seeds, or bulbs, or whatever these plants came from. Only, how long did they take to grow?

The black-clad stranger stood only a few feet away, studying a sheaf of paper in his hands. For some reason, his dimple still showed. Lily flipped the catalog page. If he thought she'd come over here to speak with him, he was sorely mistaken.

"You'll need root cuttings to plant peonies." The stranger turned his head and offered her a roguish smile.

Lily nodded once. They hadn't been introduced, but a lady wasn't rude without reason.

"I don't think they'll carry them in that catalog."

"Where might I get some?" The question crossed her lips before she could frame it in her mind. Her hand jerked to her mouth, as if she could catch her words and snatch them back before they reached his ears.

"Special dealers, horticultural friends, botanical gardens." The words rolled effortlessly off his tongue.

Lily blinked. He looked so…rough. What did this sort of man know about frivolities like flower gardens?

He pushed away from the counter and turned to face her fully, giving her an accurate picture of just how tall he was. She was now eye-level with the clerical collar encircling his neck. Her jaw dropped a notch. A clergyman? Mindful of Mama's opinions on good breeding, she pressed her lips together again, but she couldn't tear her eyes away from that stark white square.

Hodge bustled back in from the storage room. "Here you go, Miss Lily. Had to open a new crate." He held out a bar wrapped in paper.

"Thank you." Lily accepted it, then glanced at the stranger again. The way he looked at her made it feel as if the room were ten degrees warmer. Resisting the urge to press her palms against her cheeks, she fumbled with the clasp of her reticule. "How much do I owe you, Hodge?"

"A dime'll do it."

The preacher put on his hat, tipped it at her, and headed outside.

Lily found the coin and handed it over without bothering to quibble about the outrageous price.

"See you were talkin' to Reverend Crew. He's fresh from out East. Sent by some missionary society, think he said."

Lily's head jerked up. "Missiona—oh, no!" Snatching up her flowerpot and bar of soap, she whirled around and strode toward the door, heedless of the destruction she wrought in her pursuit of the stranger.

***

The smell hit him first. Pinkerton Detective Carter Forbes covered his mouth and nose with his handkerchief. His mare, Friday, hesitated, and he patted her neck. "It's okay, girl. Whatever caused this should be long gone by now."

She whickered softly in response, then moved forward with cautious, delicate steps, her muscles bunched and ready to gallop if necessary.

Enormous redwoods stood like sentinels protecting the smaller denizens of the forest. Around the next bend in the trail lay a covered wagon toppled on its side. Carter scanned the area. The horses that had been hitched to it were nowhere in sight. One wagon wheel had caught against a tree. Leaves covered the frame and littered the torn canvas. Nothing moved.

Senses jangling, Carter dismounted and looped Friday's reins over a nearby tree limb. The birds overhead ceased their chattering, and even the breeze stilled, as if the whole forest held its breath in anticipation. The rustle of his footsteps through dry leaves sounded remarkably loud in the hush. His fingers grazed the butt of his pistol.

When he twitched aside the flap of the canvas, the stench redoubled, nearly knocking him off his feet. He staggered back, letting the fabric fall closed again. Gagging, he sucked in a gulp of relatively pure air, but the foulness refused to be purged from his lungs. Over and over he inhaled, pressing his nose against his shirtsleeve in a futile attempt to mask the disgusting odor. At last, he clamped one hand over his mouth and, with the other, wrenched the canvas away with a terrible rip.

The dead man lay on his back. Carter swore under his breath. Why did he always give in to his infernal curiosity? A prudent man would've ridden on by. Minded his own business. But not Carter Forbes. Oh, no; he had to see. The quality made him a good Pinkerton, but it could be downright inconvenient.

He squatted and moved closer to the man. The scurry of tiny, clawed feet against the wood made him flinch. The corpse had lain exposed to the elements and scavengers long enough to make identifying the fellow impossible. Carter shook his head. The poor man hadn't had anyone on hand to mourn his loss.

Sighing, he backed away. The least he could do was dig the man a decent grave. A shovel was still tied to the outside of the wagon. He grabbed it and began digging. The rhythmic thump of the blade biting into the earth sounded a primitive lament.

How much would this set him back? He had made up a lot of time by riding hard. Still, Diamond probably had almost a day on him.

At last, the hole was large enough. Panting, Carter put aside the shovel and scrabbled out of the pit. He removed his coat and vest and slung them over Friday's accommodating back. Now for the worst of it.

He ducked inside the wagon again. He couldn't bring himself to touch the body's decaying limbs, so he grabbed a fistful of pant fabric and another of jacket. The corpse was heavier than he'd expected as he dragged it to the edge of the makeshift grave.

Lord, keep me from such an end. Carter glanced back, and a smear of dark red where the body had lain caught his eye. He rolled the corpse over so that it lay facedown. A small round hole penetrated the back of the jacket at about the level of the heart. The area around the hole was stained with blood, but death must have been nigh instantaneous.

Murder.

He stood and pushed his hat back from his forehead. Why hadn't he passed on by when he'd had the chance? Blast. Maybe God was punishing him for leaving his sister alone for so long.

He maneuvered the body so that it was face-up again and then methodically searched the pockets. He needed to figure out who the victim was. Then he would ride to the nearest town and turn the matter over to the local sheriff.

Inside the inner breast pocket of the dead man's jacket, his fingers found something hard. He plucked out the item—a locket on a gold chain. *Could it be?* He opened the tiny silver clasp to reveal the serious-eyed gaze of a striking young woman.

Triumph tasted bitter—too tangled up with the scent of death. Could it be that he'd finally found Grant Diamond, the murderer?

His search intensified, as though the evidence might begin to vanish if he wasted any time. He turned up a pocketknife, a handkerchief, a twist of string, a pencil stub, and a thin packet of letters. No gun. Carter frowned. A man wanted for murder wasn't likely to travel unarmed. Whoever had killed him had probably stolen his weapon.

Carter sat down on an overturned bucket and took up the packet of letters. He pulled on the end of the faded satin ribbon that bound them together. The pages were scarred with soft, fuzzy creases, as if they'd been folded and unfolded many times.

Grant, my love, I will wait for you in the garden at midnight.

More confirmation that the dead man was Diamond. After three years of near misses, Carter finally had his man. Now he could collect his bonus, return to Emily, and get her started on her new treatments.

So, why didn't he feel any sense of accomplishment? His fingers caressed the worn paper. These letters would be enough proof for anybody. But it was wrong—all wrong. The body was damp, as if it had been outside during the rainfall two days ago. The letters weren't. They were almost entirely dry.

And the body was far too decomposed for the man to have been dead only a day or two. This man must have been killed at least a week ago.

Carter pinched the bridge of his nose. He'd been after Diamond for so long, and he wanted nothing more than to close the case and go home. But he couldn't. Not yet. There was more to this thing than met the eye, and Carter had to see it through, no matter where it led.

Chapter 2

The planks of the crude sidewalk creaked beneath Grant's boots as he stepped out of the mercantile. He ran one finger along the inner side of the stiff clerical collar, pulling it away from his skin. Posing as someone else was one thing—a man did what he had to do to save his skin—but posing as a minister was something else entirely. It chafed worse than the collar.

Grant took another look at the town he'd landed in. Eureka appeared to be a typical boomtown, like so many others he'd drifted through. The recent rains and the constant churning from horses' hooves and wagon wheels had turned the main street into a soupy mess. On either side of the street, rows of wood frame buildings leaned slightly, as if bracing themselves against the breeze coming off the harbor. It took him only a minute to determine the location of what he'd come to consider the most important commercial venture in any new town: the saloon.

Despite the early hour, The Gilded Cage was already open for business. The front door opened and closed continuously as men came and went. Grant smiled. Those exiting the establishment looked considerably less alert than those entering it. He slid his hand inside his pants' pocket, fingering the meager contents of his money clip. If he could assemble a quick poker game, he'd be able to shore up his reserves in no time.

As if conjured by his thoughts, a man rode up to The Gilded Cage on a mangy sorrel mare. He yanked on the reins, bringing the poor beast to a stop, then jumped off and tied her to a hitching post. With a shout, he lofted a dirty canvas bag high in the air. "Watch out, ladies! I've got gold to stay a week!" The prospector laughed, puffed up with his good fortune—however temporary—and propelled himself into the saloon, leaving the pitiful mare standing fetlock-deep in mud.

Grant shook his head. The fellow might find himself broke and heading back to his claim sooner than he thought.

A scuffle behind Grant drew his attention. Something clattered in the store, and a male voice called out, "Dang blast it, Miss Lily!"

He turned just in time to see the woman with the ailing peony come barreling toward him.

"Reverend Crew! Reverend Crew!"

She would have run straight into him, but she jerked to a sudden stop. It appeared that her skirts were wedged in the doorway.

~

Lily didn't know which was worse, her public loss of decorum or the look on the reverend's face. She clutched the ceramic pot tightly to her bosom, the bar of soap resting in the soil next to the limp stem, while yanking on her unyielding skirt with her free hand. Why was this happening? She could feel the metal of the hoop give way, yet the door still held her fast. The skirt fabric itself must be caught on something.

"Reverend Crew." *Yank.* "I'm so sorry for not giving you a proper greeting upon your arrival in our town."

The corner of his mouth twitched. "Were you supposed to?"

Lily struggled to smile while fighting with the voluminous material covering her hoops. "Why, yes." *Yank.* "I'm the one who sent the letter." *Yank.*

"The letter?"

"Yes." *Yank.* "The letter to the Massachusetts Mission Society. Requesting aid for the Indians. I"—*yank*—"sent it."

The reverend closed his eyes for a moment, then opened them, nodding in recognition. "Ah, yes. That letter."

A crowd had started to gather around the entrance to the store, bearing witness to the spectacle Lily made of herself. Why, oh why, did the dictates of fashion doom women to wear such impractical garments? If only she could wear pants, like the men, it would be so easy to sashay out the door and down the street.

Lily Rose, what an unladylike idea.

The memory of her mother's familiar chastisement chased the scandalous notion from her head and sent the warmth of a blush creeping up the back of her neck. Mama would never get herself into a situation such as this.

A grizzled man with a beard in need of trimming stepped out of the crowd. "How long's this gonna take? I need to get me some supplies 'fore headin' back to my claim."

"I'm sorry, sir." Lily set her jaw against the stench that emanated from the fellow. She hoped his shopping list included soap. "I appear to be caught."

The preacher walked up to Lily and lifted the flowerpot from her arm. "Let me take that for you." For a moment, that amazing dimple of his made another appearance. Then, he took a step back, eyeing Lily's skirts and the doorjamb. "You obviously can't move forward. Perhaps, if you tried backing up—"

"Oh, no!" A gravelly voice erupted from inside the mercantile. "There's no way under God's heaven I'm letting that tornado in petticoats back inside my store. No, sir. She's going out, one way or another."

"What?" Panicked, Lily tried in vain to look over her shoulder. "Hodge, wait." She started yanking at her skirts again, desperate to avoid the indignity of being pushed out a door and having her skirt torn into heaven knows how many pieces. With both her hands free, she was able to tug on the fabric while leaning forward. Just then, she felt Hodge's big, beefy palms splayed across the small of her back. "No!"

With a grunt, Hodge pushed, at the same time as Lily pulled harder on her skirts. Then came the sound of ripping muslin. That did it. She was free of the door and hurtling across the sidewalk.

Straight at the reverend.

Lily fought to stay upright and managed to skid to a stop. When she did, her hoops swooshed forward with surprising force, hitting Reverend Crew square in the knees.

He staggered back, till the heels of his worn boots hit the edge of the walkway planks. Lily caught a brief impression of green eyes wide with shock, an arm flailing, and then a flowerpot catapulted into the air.

A moment later, Reverend Crew, the man of God she had summoned to Eureka to share the love of Christ with the Indian population, lay sprawled on his back in the mud, a decidedly unsaintly scowl on his face.

The crowd of folks burst out laughing. Some went about their business, though most of them stayed to see what would happen next. And Lily wished, not for the first time in her life, that she could disappear. But then, she could hardly hope to manage that in these blasted hoops.

Chapter 3

Gritting his teeth, Grant swallowed the curse that sprang to his lips, but he nearly choked on the bitterness. The clumsy lady responsible for his current situation looked as if he'd struck her instead of the contrary. She gaped at him, her mouth forming a wide O, and her head swiveled back and forth. "Oh! Oh! Oh, I am so sorry." She scrambled over and reached for his arm, as if to pull him up.

Before she could touch him, he jerked away, sending mud flying. "You'd best mind that skirt of yours."

The back of her hoops had bobbed up with her abrupt movement. If she wasn't careful, the confounded device would overturn and swallow her whole. Her hands flew around to the back of her skirt to hold it down, safeguarding her dignity, as well as the safety of those around her.

Squelching in the glop, Grant sat up and got a good look at the sorry state of his clothes. Gooey brown muck coated the worsted jacket. Not that he wouldn't be glad to shuck the preacher's itchy suit, but he needed it to complete his ruse.

"Please, Reverend Crew." More sedately, the angel of mercy— or was that misery?—reached out again to help him. "I am so sorry.

I feel just terrible. I wasn't expecting you. I mean, I was expecting you, just not today. The letter said last August, and I was all set back then, but I'd since given up. I expected some word would come, at last, but I didn't expect you, if you know what I mean."

Grant held up a hand to stanch the verbal flood. "Miss, please. Don't help me. Don't even touch me. I'll be fine on my own."

"Oh." The single syllable held a world of hurt and shame. She stepped back, her shoulders hunched a little. A red blotch bloomed just above her modest, lace-trimmed neckline and didn't stop till it met her slightly disheveled hair.

Grant couldn't have felt worse if he'd kicked a puppy. He struggled to his feet as spectators looked on, evidently anticipating Act II. Well, he wouldn't give them the satisfaction. This sidewalk drama was over.

He scraped the worst of the muck from his britches, letting it plop into the street, where it belonged. When he spied the potted peony, he scooped it up and then pulled a relatively clean handkerchief from the inner pocket of his jacket. Using his fingertips, he wrapped it around the pot, then thrust the hapless flower at the girl. "Here."

"Thank you." Her voice was as whispery as rustling leaves, and she clamped her lips tightly together, as if to hold back a tide of words threatening to spill out.

Something in his gut pulled at him. He knew he should walk right back out of this town and head somewhere else—anywhere else. Instead, he turned away from the gawkers and said in a low voice, "Listen. I'm sorry I snapped. Maybe we can start over? I'm Reverend Hubert Crew."

The name felt awkward on his lips, and it didn't fit him at all, but the girl didn't seem to notice. She nodded and offered a smile as delicate and lifeless as the petals of the flower in her arms. "I'm Lily Rose. I'm the one who wrote the missionary society and asked them to send someone to help the Indians."

Grant schooled his features to show none of the confusion he felt—which was just as much as when she'd said it the first time. One rule of every successful con was never to act surprised, no matter how bizarre a turn things took. He needed to conduct himself as if he knew exactly what she was talking about.

Now that the show was over, the audience dispersed, leaving Grant alone with Miss Rose. He extended a hand to help her back up to the walk but quickly retracted it when he saw the mud that still coated his fingers.

She caught his eye, then glanced at her own tattered, mud-spattered attire. Her shoulders began to shake, and for a horrifying moment, he expected her to burst into tears. But when she looked up, a rich gurgle bubbled from her. It was a laugh that compelled those near to join in and drew a body to her, like a poker table drew a gambler.

This was a woman to beware of. In spite of himself, Grant chuckled. "I'm delighted to meet you, Miss Rose. And under such pleasant circumstances." He reached for his hat but found only air. A glance behind him revealed that it was half buried in the mud, right next to a paper-wrapped rectangle. "I would tip my hat, but, as you can see, it's gone the way of your soap."

She laughed harder, her palm pressed flat against her stomach, her eyes wrinkling at the corners. When she finally regained control of herself, she said, "Oh, Reverend Crew. Thank you for not staying cross with me. It's a good thing you're a man of God. My mother tells me I'd try the patience of a saint."

Grant hid a twinge of guilt with practiced ease. "As much as I'd enjoy continuing our conversation, I'm sure you'll agree that I should wash up." He gestured down the street. "Can you recommend an inexpensive boardinghouse?"

"Oh, you're to stay with us, at least until the schoolhouse is built. I arranged everything with my parents months ago."

Blinking, Grant opened his mouth and then shut it again. He had no wish to be under the watchful eye of a jealous papa. On the other hand, staying at a private home could be advantageous. Judging from the costly fabric of Miss Rose's ruined dress, her father must be one of the town's leading citizens. No Pinkerton would think to look for Grant Diamond at a church or among the elite. This could work out very, very well, indeed.

"I'd be honored to stay with your family, Miss Rose. Thank you for your kind offer."

"It seemed the least we could do, since—" She dropped off in mid-sentence, and all traces of humor fled her face. "Hello, Reverend."

Grant glanced behind him and beheld a shortish, balding man with a slight paunch. His scraggly beard did little to hide his receding chin. Bulging eyes gave him a slightly startled air, although that might simply be due to the picture he and Miss Rose presented.

Lily slid past Grant and placed a hand on the newcomer's arm. "Reverend Marsden, allow me to present Reverend Crew. He's the missionary who has come to teach the Indians."

Marsden's nose twitched ever so slightly. "A pleasure." His nose twitched again, as if he'd detected something rank.

Could a true preacher sniff out an imposter by mere proximity? Grant shoved the notion aside. "I'm honored to make your acquaintance, sir. I'd shake your hand, but I'm sure you'd prefer I didn't."

Marsden raised an eyebrow. "Of course." He gave Grant a quick scan, looking more and more displeased by the second. "Funny, when I was at seminary, I gathered that the idea was to help pull poor wretches out of the mire, not to join them in wallowing in it."

Grant loosed a mechanical bark that would probably pass for laughter. "You're quite the wit, Reverend."

"That's our Reverend Marsden." A new voice had joined the conversation.

Lily whirled, her skirts bobbing. Rick Abernathy, tall and thin with a dust-colored mustache and goatee, walked up behind the local cleric. Marsden flinched and seemed to shrink before her eyes as Abernathy set his hands on his shoulders, squeezed hard, and then gave them a dismissive pat.

Lily felt her upper lip curl in distaste. She tried to smooth it out. But really, it was hard enough being polite to Marsden after last year. Must she now bear Abernathy, as well? Between her clumsiness and the bad impression these two would make, her long-awaited missionary would flee for the hills any minute.

Then again, he deserved to know what he was up against. She glanced back and found him looking at her expectantly. Mustering her manners, she offered the appropriate introductions. "Reverend Crew, this is Mr. Rick Abernathy. Mr. Abernathy, the Reverend Crew."

The missionary stepped forward and extended the muddy hand which, moments ago, he'd been hesitant to offer. "A pleasure." His voice was a flat, dead thing, his eyes as rocky as the mountains. It seemed that he had already managed to measure Abernathy's character.

"Lily, here, rustled him up to help her tame the Indians," said Marsden.

At this, Abernathy narrowed his eyes and parted his lips. He then snapped his mouth closed again, ignoring the reverend's outstretched hand. "Now, that is a waste of effort, for sure. They're not even supposed to be here! They're runaways, every one of them."

Lily tightened her grip around the battered remains of her mother's peony. Everyone cowered before this man, just as to the brutal Larabee before him. But she was tired of letting his kind run roughshod over the town, especially the Wiyot Indians. She opened her mouth to say so, but Reverend Crew forestalled her.

"Runaways from where?"

"From the federal government. Nobody wants them here. They've already been rounded up once and sent to the reservation because of all the trouble they've been causing. But they keep coming back." His hand rested on the butt of his holstered side-arm. "Just like vermin."

Rage nearly blinded Lily, and she stepped forward. "They were sent away for their own protection." She flung the words at Abernathy, willing them to open a wound and expose some sign of guilt under his skin.

Instead, he lifted his lips in a smirk. "Then, they ought to know it would be healthier to stay away."

"Why should they have to abandon their homes because men like—"

"I understand the dilemma," Reverend Crew smoothly inserted himself between her and Abernathy. "I'll think on what you've told me."

"Be sure you do," Abernathy said.

Crew turned and touched Lily's elbow with a fingertip of his clean hand. "Come along, Miss Rose. I believe you were going to show me a place to wash up."

Lily nodded, thankful for an excuse to be drawn away. Reverend Crew was probably right. There was a time for every-thing, and now was not the time to give Abernathy a piece of her mind. Father would certainly disapprove if he learned about it. Not because he'd think she was wrong, but because he considered Abernathy dangerous.

Reverend Crew collected the reins of a sorry-looking old mare. That a man of such obvious distinction rode such a pitiful beast was no surprise. It was just like she'd seen in the periodicals sent by the missionary society. What more had he sacrificed for the sake of spreading the gospel? *While he's here, I'll make sure he wants for nothing,* Lily thought as she turned toward home. They both needed a nice cup of coffee to wash away the rank aftertaste of contact with that skunk Abernathy.

"I'm sorry you had to meet Abernathy before I could warn you about him. He's Satan's spawn, as far as I'm concerned. Hank Larabee's protégé...." Miss Rose marched half a pace ahead of Grant, chattering away.

What a puzzling woman she was. Appearances and propriety were obviously important to her, yet she laughed with gusto and looked ready to take on a man more than twice her size. She wasn't the prettiest girl he'd ever met, but there was something quite appealing about her earnest approach to life. Yes, Miss Rose was a walking contradiction, one he would like to examine more closely. But his time in Eureka would be short, and his time in her company even shorter than that.

He picked up his pace to match hers, hoping to insert a word of his own. But the sight of two men across the street stilled his tongue. One he recognized as the town sheriff, thanks to the dull metal star pinned to his vest. And he needed no clues to identify the other. Miss Rose might think herself acquainted with Satan's offspring, but Grant knew the devil himself. Pinkerton agent Carter Forbes had pursued him for the past three years, making his existence a living hell. Now the man stood not ten feet away, speaking to the town sheriff, the sun glinting off an item suspended from his hand, swinging like a pendulum.

Sarah's locket.

A curse shot from Grant's lips, but he managed to catch himself at the last moment and disguise it with a violent cough.

Miss Rose stopped in her tracks and turned to face him, her brown eyes warm with concern. "Are you all right, Reverend?"

He fisted his hand and thumped his chest twice. Mud flew. "Fine. Just fine, thank you, miss. Perhaps you could tell me more about the Indians?"

Her face brightened at his request, and they resumed their walk, she talking, he pretending to listen. Out of the corner of his eye, he studied the Pinkerton, confirming what he'd already sensed: the detective was looking their way.

Grant squared his shoulders ever so slightly. He'd hoped to throw Forbes off his trail by planting his most cherished possessions on the dead man and taking up a new identity. But it must not have worked. The Pink wasn't an easy man to shake, and Grant now knew the man wasn't easily fooled, either.

Bluffing was always a risky move, and it looked like Grant would get called on it this time. Still, if he was sure of anything, it was that a hand is never lost until all the cards are on the table. And Grant still had a few aces up his sleeve.

It was time for the real game to begin.

Chapter 4

It didn't take a detective to realize that something out of the ordinary had gone on across the street. With a slight incline of his head, Carter indicated the couple standing in front of the mercantile. "Who are they?"

Sheriff Van Nest looked in their direction and pushed the brim of his hat back with his thumb. "That's Lily Rose. Her daddy owns Rose Lumber Company, lucky for her."

"Lucky? In what way?"

"Just take a look at her. Plain as the day is long. Wouldn't stand a chance of landing a husband if she weren't rich."

Carter frowned. She didn't look all that plain to him. Dark hair framed a pale face that was as changeable as the weather. In a certain light, it might be called "plain," but a shift of shadows, a quirk of a smile, and she would be stunning.

As much as Carter despised gossip, it was a necessary evil in his line of work. With private apologies to Miss Rose, he nodded and then continued. "Is that how she snagged the muddy fellow beside her? Her beau, I suppose?"

Van Nest laughed, his voice like a braying donkey. "Naw, not Miss Lily. Guess that money hasn't done her much good, after all."

"Then, who's the fellow?"

"Him?" Van Nest squinted. "No idea. Never seen him before."

A tingle skittered from the base of Carter's skull down his neck. A stranger in a town like Eureka wasn't all that unusual. The rush of men come to mine for treasure had died down quite a bit, but there were plenty of hangers-on still determined to find gold in the hills. Besides that, the port was bound to bring in a steady stream of new blood. But something about this particular stranger struck Carter. Perhaps it was the brash way he walked. Or it could have been the almost imperceptible turn of his head to look across the street, as if aware of Carter's scrutiny. He couldn't quite identify it, but something about the fellow was off.

Carter pooled the delicate locket chain into his other palm, then slid the trinket into the breast pocket of his vest. "Thank you for your assistance, Mr. Van Nest." With a nod, he excused himself, then started across the street, mindful of the slop. Halfway to the other side, he caught a piece of Miss Rose's animated conversation.

"I know it's unchristian to feel this way, but he treats them like they're vermin. I simply cannot abide the man."

Hmm. Perhaps she'd already made Grant Diamond's acquaintance. Treating people like vermin certainly fit what Carter knew of the fellow.

"Excuse me," Carter said, stepping in front of the flea-bitten horse the man led. "May I ask you two a few questions?"

The woman blushed, perhaps afraid he'd overheard her complaint. The man, however, did not fluster as easily. In fact, he looked downright annoyed. With a smile stiffer than the mud drying on his suit, he asked, "And you are?"

Removing his hat, Carter turned to Miss Rose and gave a slight bow. "Carter Forbes, Pinkerton agent."

Had Grant been on his own, he'd have been gone before the Pink had time to say his name. Now, he found himself hampered not only by the disguise he'd chosen but also by Miss Rose's exuberance.

"An actual Pinkerton, right here in our town?" She clutched the forlorn flowerpot so tightly to her bosom, Grant was afraid the thing would crack. "Mr. Forbes, it is a pleasure to meet you."

"The pleasure is all mine, miss." He bowed lower, then took her hand and raised it to his lips.

If it hadn't been so long since Grant's last meal, his food surely would have made a reappearance. What a cloying exchange. He opened his mouth to speak, but Lily rushed on.

"I'm Lily Rose, and this is Reverend Hubert Crew."

Now the Pinkerton turned to Grant and held out his hand, giving him his full attention. "Reverend Crew?"

The inflection in his voice called the alias into question. Did the man have any idea who Hubert Crew really was, or was he just fishing?

"Pleased to meet you." Without hesitation, Grant took the Pink's hand in his own, mud-encrusted one, and gave it a hearty shake. Then, as if realizing the error of his ways, he drew back, furrowing his eyebrows in consternation. "Forgive me. I forgot what a state I'm in."

Forbes produced a handkerchief from his pocket and casually wiped his palm and fingers. "Think nothing of it." He looked from Grant's filthy suit to Miss Rose's ripped skirt, and cocked his head. "It appears the two of you have run into a bit of trouble. Nothing nefarious, I hope?"

In other words, *Was this man trying to take advantage of you, miss?* Heat bloomed in Grant's chest, and suddenly his suit seemed two sizes two small. It was the Pink's job to think the worst of people, but Grant was getting mighty tired of having that attitude flung his way.

Miss Rose laughed and then shook her head furiously, making even more hair escape her now precariously loose bun. "Nothing nefarious. Unless, of course, the makers of these dreadful hoops intended them to threaten public safety."

Grant noticed the hard set of Forbes's jaw at the mention of what was underneath the fabric of her skirt. She didn't realize it, but she wasn't helping at all. "Miss Rose, here, got caught in the mercantile door," he hastened to explain.

"And when I finally freed myself, I ran smack into the poor reverend and knocked him into the mud." Miss Rose motioned toward Grant, and some of the merriment left her eyes. "It's all because of my terrible clumsiness. I wouldn't have blamed Reverend Crew one bit if he'd turned right around and left town. Thankfully, he's forgiven me, and we can finally start our work with the Indians."

"We?" Grant yelped, at the same time as Carter's "Indians?"

"Yes, of course," Miss Rose said to Grant. "You didn't think I expected you to do all the work yourself, did you? I'm more than ready to help shoulder the load."

Grant's heart plummeted to the bottom of his muddy boots. It would be much harder to identify the local bumpkins, clean out their pocketbooks, and clear town if Miss Rose intended to be his constant companion.

Lily turned to Forbes, one hand at her side, controlling her hoops. "Reverend Crew was sent by the missionary society to help with the indigenous Indian population. We're going to build a school where we can teach them English and share the gospel. Isn't that wonderful?"

Carter nodded. "Indeed it is, miss."

Building a school? Sharing the gospel? Panic tried to grab hold of Grant, but he shoved it away. He was losing control of the situation, and he wouldn't get it back unless he kept a cool head. "Miss

Rose was just taking me to my accommodations. As you can see, I'm in sore need of a change of clothes."

"Certainly. But first, I would still like to ask you both a question." Forbes frowned. "I'm looking for a man who would have come to town within the last day or so. He goes by the name of Grant Diamond."

Grant scratched his chin and waited for a count of two before answering. "Can't say I've heard of him. But then," he added with a grin, "I'm new here, myself."

The answer seemed to satisfy Forbes. He turned his attention to Miss Rose. "How about you, miss?"

She shook her head. "I've never heard that name before." Her eyes widened. "What did he do?"

Prickles of anticipation danced across Grant's scalp. Never before had he been this close to Carter Forbes. Never before had he heard the charges from the man's own lips.

"He's wanted for the murder of Miss Sarah DeKlerk, of Boston."

Miss Rose recoiled. "Murder! How awful."

The mention of Sarah's name was like a sharp blade cutting through Grant's flesh, and the look on Miss Rose's face was salt rubbed deep into the wound. Steeling himself against the pain, he kept up the charade. "And you think this monster is here in Eureka?"

"Perhaps. If not here now, he at least passed through."

"I see." The wind had started to kick up, affording an excellent opportunity for distraction. Grant began to shiver as blatantly as possible, without making it appear he was suffering a seizure.

"Oh, dear." Miss Rose had noticed, just as he'd expected. "Mr. Forbes, you'll have to excuse us, please. I must get the reverend out of the cold before he catches a chill."

"Of course, Miss Rose. Perhaps I could follow you to the boardinghouse? I'm in need of lodging for the night, myself."

"Reverend Crew will be rooming at my family's home, but I'll be happy to direct you to the boardinghouse. Bertie runs a clean establishment."

Grant was thrilled when Miss Rose pointed in the opposite direction of the way they'd been walking.

Forbes looked down the street. "I see. Bertie's it is, then." He pressed his hat back on his head and turned to Grant. "Reverend Crew, I'd love to hear more about the work you'll be doing with the Indians here. Might we meet tomorrow?"

Not on your life, Grant thought. But before he could gently decline, Miss Rose stepped in once more.

"Oh, I have a wonderful idea! Mr. Forbes, why don't you join my family for dinner tonight? We can continue our conversation, and you can meet my father. He knows everyone in town, so he might be able to help you in your quest."

Forbes smiled with as much satisfaction as a cat that had just swallowed the family goldfish but knew the dog would get the blame. Grant wasn't sure if it was because the Pink was looking forward to spending more time with Miss Rose or eagerly anticipating an interrogation of Reverend Crew. Either way, he foresaw a long, painful evening ahead.

Chapter 5

Grant faltered and came to a standstill in front of the stately house. "This is where you live?" Miss Rose gave him a smile that seemed to say, *And you thought we all were hicks!*

"Welcome to Rose Cottage," she said. "My father owns Rose Lumber. Perhaps you've heard of it?"

Grant's eyebrows shot up. Who hadn't heard of Rose Lumber? The state was being built on the backbone of wood from the Rose mills, the prosperity of the gold fields being channeled into constructing a new land and consequently filling the mill owner's pockets. He should have made the connection as soon as Miss Rose had introduced herself.

Grant's mouth went as dry as Death Valley. Under other circumstances, he'd be as pleased as a tick on a lazy dog to have worked his way so effortlessly into such a household. But he would never become entangled with another heiress. Not even one as intriguing as Miss Lily Rose.

She led him up the path to the enormous Gothic "cottage." Towers sprouted hither and yon, gingerbread trim lined every angle, and a stained-glass window sparkled in the late-afternoon sun.

"I usually enter through the back, but I thought you'd enjoy getting the full effect." She allowed him to open the front door for her, then ushered him in with a little flourish of her hand.

Grant swallowed hard, his Adam's apple rasping against the starched collar of his stolen shirt. He again ran a finger under the edge to loosen the fabric, but to little effect. This house was every bit a match for Sarah's family mansion.

Polished redwood wainscoting anchored and offset the cream tone-on-tone wallpaper. The floors gleamed, except where they were shrouded by the finest Turkish carpets. Before them, a grand staircase opened its scrolling banisters like arms in a welcoming embrace. Paintings adorned the walls, and clusters of knickknacks crowded shelves and tables.

He moved to wipe his feet. A ridiculous gesture, considering that he was head-to-toe mud.

"You can leave your bag here. I'll have Joseph carry it up to your room for you."

Grudgingly, Grant deposited his saddlebag on the polished floor. He preferred to keep it close at hand, in case he needed to bolt, but it would seem strange to refuse her suggestion.

"Are you sure I'm supposed to stay here, miss?" He hoped the answer was no. He wanted nothing to do with this house or its inhabitants.

She smiled at him in the expectant, hopeful way of a little child extending a gift of stinkweed. "Quite sure. My father will be happy for the company of another man around the place. Of course, my mother is gone for the moment; she's down in San Francisco taking care of her cousin. But I know she will be delighted to meet you upon her return. I—oh, here's Joseph."

A dark-eyed servant with the high cheekbones and cinnamon-colored skin of the natives walked up to them. "Miss Lily, you look something terrible. Are you okay?"

"I'm fine, Joseph. Just had a little accident." She waved away his concern, then gestured at Grant. "This is Reverend Crew. He's here to build and run an Indian school. Won't that be wonderful?"

The man eyed Grant with a speculative gaze. It was apparent he intended to make up his own mind about the wonderfulness of the event.

Grant nodded.

Joseph mirrored the gesture ever so slightly.

Miss Rose continued on as if they three were the best of friends. "Would you take his bags up to the garden room, Joseph?" She turned to Grant again. "I thought you'd enjoy the garden room, since you know so much about plants and all." And back to Joseph. "Have you seen Mr. Rose? I was hoping he would be in this morning."

Joseph nodded, but before he could say a word, Miss Rose exclaimed, "Papa!"

A portly man entered the foyer, bearded but as bald as a billiard ball, except for a neat fringe of hair around the periphery of his scalp.

"Lily-belle." He bestowed a beneficent smile upon his daughter. "Child, you're talking a mile a minute."

"Reverend Crew has arrived! Do you recall my writing to the missionary society in Massachusetts and asking them to send someone? He's here, at last! I'm so pleased."

The man turned to Grant. "Sir." He inclined his head politely, but those eyes that had looked at Lily Rose with humor and warmth were more like flint chips aimed at Grant. Mr. Rose raked him over with the shrewd skill of one who knows how to take the measure of a man.

Grant forced his hands to stay where they were rather than attempting to loosen his collar again. He needed to get out of this town, but if he left now, the Pinkerton would be on his trail by suppertime. He would leave tonight, when everyone else had gone to bed. He'd slip away to the saloon, take a few of the drunken miners for all they were worth, and then hit the trail again. Anything to get away from those searing eyes.

⌣⌐

Lily linked arms with her father. He leaned close and whispered loudly, "You sure there's a man under all that mud?"

A hot flush pricked her cheeks. "I'm afraid that's my fault. I bumped into him."

"The mercantile door again?"

Now the prickles were more like nettle stings. Lily nodded.

Her father squeezed her shoulder and then extended his hand to Reverend Crew. "I'll warrant that hoopskirt attacks weren't one of the dangers you were warned about before heading West, eh?"

Lily swallowed hard. She wished she could fade into the wallpaper and disappear. Papa had no appreciation of fashion or propriety or anything of the like.

"They failed to warn me to watch out for my own two feet, as well. It's a wonder I've made it all the way to Eureka."

Lily paused in her intent perusal of the diseased peony she still clutched, and glanced up at the reverend, who offered an infinitesimal wink. Her lips started to curl into a smile, but then she caught herself. Surely, she had been mistaken. He was a missionary. He wouldn't wink at her. But no, he followed it up with an unmistakable grin, one that melted her embarrassment right along with her composure.

Papa guffawed. "Well said! Well said, indeed." He moved to slap the reverend on the back, but his hand stopped short and settled for an awkward pat on the shoulder, avoiding the worst of the mud. "Joseph, here, will see you up to your room and draw a bath for you." He turned to Lily. "Darling, why don't you go on upstairs, too? I'll send Naomi to help you get cleaned up and dressed for dinner."

In a trice, they were all dispersed to their appointed tasks. Lily parted from the reverend and all but flew up the stairs in her eagerness to be free of her crinolines.

In the privacy of her room, she shucked the ruined dress, released herself from the cage of hoops, and flopped on her bed, pinching the bridge of her nose. Reverend Crew was nothing like her long-held image of a missionary. Not that she'd really known what to expect. Someone older, maybe, with a beard, and a very grave and dignified air. Or maybe a reedy, scholarly type of fellow. Reverend Crew fit neither of those descriptions.

He was tall, for one, and she could have sworn that his eyes positively twinkled. Not to mention that wink. That conspiratorial, almost wicked, oh-so-attractive wink. And he had covered for her, dismissing her clumsiness with a few simple words. She shook her head. He was all wrong. And yet, now that she'd met him, she couldn't imagine him being any other way.

The door creaked open. Lily peeked with one eye. Her maid, Naomi, entered with a pitcher of steaming water. "Why are you layin' abed? It's past time to dress for supper." The Indian woman's coppery skin fairly glowed in the waning light of the setting sun slanting through the window.

"Leave me be. I've had a dreadful afternoon."

"I know."

Lily sprang up. "How?"

Naomi eyed her enigmatically. "I always know."

Quite true. Since the earliest days of her memory, Lily had never been able to get a thing past Naomi.

Lily wrinkled her nose. "Then you ought to know that I should be left alone for the evening."

Naomi stooped to pick up the abandoned hoops. "Will you be rude as well as clumsy?"

Sighing, Lily scrunched her eyes closed. There was no escaping the inevitable. "Very well, then."

When Lily opened her eyes, she saw that a knowing smile graced Naomi's lips. "I believe the new violet silk." She nodded once, affirming her own judgment.

Ever efficient, Naomi soon had Lily cleaned and trussed as neatly as a Christmas goose, with her corset cinched tightly enough that her belly button nearly met her backbone, her hoops reinstalled, and her gown draping gracefully. A minute more, and Naomi had tamed her hair into smooth waves gathered in a tidy chignon at the nape of her neck. Naomi even produced a posy of African violets from the greenhouse for Lily to tuck into her waistband.

At last, Lily freed herself from Naomi's clutches, even as the older woman pinched color into her cheeks. She hurried down the back staircase to forewarn the cook about the extra guests, though why she bothered was a mystery. Everyone seemed to know as much as she, if not more.

Lily entered the parlor, moving with utmost care, determined not to knock over anything. Or anyone. A difficult feat, as distracted as she was by the sight of Reverend Crew. He looked like a new man. Not only had he shed his coating of mud, but he'd combed his hair and shaved.

When he saw her, his eyes gleamed, and a slow smile formed on his mouth. "Miss Rose, you look enchanting."

"Thank you, Reverend."

They were interrupted by the arrival of Mr. Forbes, still dressed in his travel-stained garments and scratching at the stubble on his chin, as if he wished to be rid of it. "My apologies for my appearance, miss. Turns out Bertie is full up, so I haven't had a chance to make myself presentable."

Lily gasped. "Then, you must stay here! There's more than enough room, and I would be honored to have a hand in helping bring that murderer to justice."

Reverend Crew gave a strangled gurgle and coughed spasmodically. Papa entered the parlor and clapped him on the back. "Joseph! Get this man a drink."

Lily paused and glanced at Reverend Crew. Although red in the face, he waved a hand, as if to brush off any concern, but her father continued to hit his back. How familiar she was with the desire for less attention. She turned to her father. "Papa, don't you think Mr. Forbes should stay with us?"

"Certainly, Lily-belle." He stopped pounding breath into the reverend and extended a hand to the detective. "Pleased to meet you, Forbes. I've been reading about the exploits of the Pinkertons. I'll wager you have some tales you could tell."

Mr. Forbes glanced down and gave a little laugh. "A few. But I don't want to put you folks out."

Joseph walked briskly into the room and handed Reverend Crew a glass of water, which the missionary accepted but didn't sip from.

"Nonsense. I insist," Papa said to Mr. Forbes. "I'll have Joseph retrieve your bags and see to boarding your horse."

A bell tinkled from the recesses of the house.

"Shall we step into the dining room, gentlemen?" Lily turned and led the way.

The aromas of roast beef, spring vegetables, and fresh bread filled the air. Her mouth watered as Joseph and another male servant carried in steaming platters and set them on the table. She wished she could eat her fill but knew, even before her first bite, that her tight corset would preclude such a possibility.

"Reverend, would you do us the honor of saying grace?" Papa smiled at their guest, and Lily turned to him, as well. A warm glow of pride spread through her like melted candle wax. She was glad that her petition to the missionary society had finally borne fruit. The reverend would do so much good.

"Yes, Reverend." The Pinkerton wore a broad smile as he spread his napkin in his lap. "We sure would like you to say the blessing."

Lily expected him to seize the opportunity to prove his worth, but Reverend Crew wore a bashful expression. "Mr. Rose, I couldn't. This is your table. Surely, you'd like that honor."

"No, I insist."

"Well, all right, then." The reverend bowed his head and clasped his hands together. "Dear Lord...." He paused. The silence lengthened.

Lily was on the verge of opening her eyes when he finally continued.

"Thank You for putting me in the path of such fine folks. Bless them according to the hospitality they have shown. And bless this meal." There was another pause, a jostling of silverware, and then a hurried "Amen."

Papa chuckled as he shook out his napkin. "I like a man who gets to the point. Now, gentlemen, this is our family table, so we eat like a family. No bringing out one dish at a time and picking over a dozen courses. Just help yourselves and pass it along."

For a few minutes, the only sounds in the room were the clink of cutlery and the murmurs of "Please" and "Thank you" as the dishes were passed around. Lily cut a morsel from her helping of roast beef. She closed her eyes and savored the tender, juicy meat.

After dark, when she'd been released from the strictures of her corset, she would sneak down to the kitchen and make a sandwich out of the leftovers. Mmm, with a slice of cheese and a tall glass of cold milk. She cut another dainty bite and chewed decorously.

Mr. Forbes waved his knife over his plate. "This is downright delicious. I haven't eaten this well in ages."

Lily smiled. "Thank you. I shall be sure to tell Cook. He loves to hear when our guests have enjoyed his offerings."

Mr. Forbes nodded pleasantly and took a swig from his glass. "If you're from out East, Reverend, I guess it's been even longer since you had a proper meal."

"Yes, indeed. It has been some time. Travel is often grueling, but I'm sure it will have been worth it now that I'm here." He turned to Lily. "Miss Rose, would you share your thoughts on what must be done first to aid the Indians?"

Lily could scarcely keep from swooning. Not many men would pass up an opportunity to detail all their sufferings on the trail. But Reverend Crew not only tossed the chance away; he asked for her opinion, as if it truly mattered to him.

She glanced at her father, then leaped into a discussion of one of her favorite topics. "If I could, I would say we should leave them in peace, but the settlers aren't going anywhere. The Indians' only chance is to learn how to function within our society. So, I believe a school is needed most—not to force our ways on them, but to give them the tools they need to survive among us."

"Speaking of school, did you attend seminary, Reverend?" Mr. Forbes asked. He smiled around a mouth full of mashed potatoes, but his tone was too tight and hard for mere supper chat.

Lily glanced at the agent, her brow furrowed.

Reverend Crew took his time chewing the food in his mouth. Finally, he swallowed and cleared his throat. "Harvard School of Divinity, actually."

"That's certainly impressive," Papa said.

"What prompted you to become a missionary, then, all the way out here at the backside of beyond?" The agent's tone of voice was sharper than the question seemed to warrant.

Lily put her fork down. "Obviously, God must call one to such a selfless role." Maybe it had been a mistake to invite the detective to stay with them. His questions were rather pointed, which, though it probably made him good at his job, did not make for pleasant dinner conversation.

Reverend Crew smiled and nodded, then shoveled an enormous amount of roasted vegetables into his mouth.

The conversation drifted to politics and the escalating unrest between the Northern and Southern states. The men all weighed in with opinions and pronouncements. Lily was content to nibble at the food on her plate while she waited for a chance to steer the conversation back to more interesting subjects.

At last, the discussion meandered to the topic of travel and how things had changed over the past ten years.

"It's still tough to get to Eureka, though I pay dearly to keep the roads from the lumber mills in good shape," Papa said.

"There's really just the one road into town from San Francisco, isn't there?" Mr. Forbes asked.

Papa nodded.

The detective turned to Reverend Crew. "Then, you must have passed that poor dead man in the road."

Looking up from his plate, the reverend locked eyes with the man across the table, producing an effect similar to metal crashing against flint. "Mr. Forbes, we all appreciate your dedication to your work. But this is neither the time nor the place to bring up such… indelicate matters. Wouldn't you agree?"

Mr. Forbes nodded sharply.

At the head of the table, Papa cleared his throat. "Gentlemen, I believe this would be a good time to share a joke I heard down at the yard." He smiled at Lily. "No worries, Lily-belle. It's suitable for feminine ears."

They finished the meal with amicable conversation, but the air remained thick with antagonism between the preacher and the Pinkerton.

Chapter 6

Saddlebags slung over one shoulder, Grant eased his way down the long, wide staircase. In his previous trips up, down, and back up again, he'd memorized which steps creaked and where he could place his foot without making a sound. Now he wove back and forth, zigzagging like a drunken man, intent on making his escape unheard and unseen.

That infernal Pinkerton. If not for him, Grant might have bided his time at Rose Cottage. A few more days and nights of hearty meals and sound slumbers in a soft, dry bed would go a long way toward making him feel civilized again. But how could he even think of sleep with a Pink across the hall? The second Forbes had mentioned the dead man on the trail, Grant had known his time in Eureka was up.

He reached the foot of the stairs, blinking against the darkness. The front door was mere feet ahead of him, but it was hardly his escape route of choice. Even in the dead of night, there was still a chance someone would see him walk out. The back door was better. Not only was it more secluded, but it also would put him closer to the stables.

With the stealth and soft-footedness of a cat, he made his way through the dining area and down a narrow hall. A faint glow leaked out through the crack under the kitchen door, bringing him to a halt. Had someone left a lantern burning? A shuffling sound, followed by the noise of two solid objects making contact, answered his question. No, someone was in the kitchen.

Grant's forehead wrinkled into a frown. What now? He didn't have many choices. He could leave through the front door, with fingers crossed that no one would spy him. He could abandon the idea of leaving tonight. Or, he could continue on as planned. It took him only a moment to decide. The rest of the household was asleep. He hadn't heard anyone else descend the stairs. So, the person in the kitchen was either an intruder or one of the servants taking a little something to supplement his or her monthly pay. Either way, it was a sure bet that whoever he was about to run into wouldn't discuss the encounter with anyone.

Quietly, he pushed the door open, walked into the room, and stopped short.

At a tall wooden worktable in the middle of the kitchen stood Miss Lily Rose, her eyes closed in rapture as she chewed a bite of the sandwich she held inches from her lips. Seeing an heiress pilfering a midnight snack would have been shocking enough, but that was nothing compared to the fact that she was attired in only a cotton nightgown.

A gentleman would make his presence known, but Grant's mouth had gone so dry, he was afraid of what his words might sound like. Instead, he cleared his throat.

Lily's eyes flew open. At the sight of Grant, she gasped and dropped the sandwich. She was choking, struggling for air, her hands at her throat. Propelled by instinct, Grant dropped his saddlebags on the floor and rushed forward. Standing behind her, he put his arms around her waist and squeezed hard, pulling in and up with such force that her feet came off the floor. A grunt issued from her lips, at the same time as a piece of half-chewed bread shot across the room.

"Are you all right?" Grant leaned forward over her shoulder, trying to get a look at her face.

"I...um, yes, I think so." Her voice quivered like a reed in the wind. She took several deep breaths, trying to steady herself. "Thank you for your assistance, Reverend Crew. You may let go of me now."

Why was he still holding on to the woman, for goodness' sake? He released her and jumped back as if she'd caught fire. Indeed, her cheeks flamed as red as hot coals, but, at the same time, she shivered, her arms crossed protectively over her chest. Had she misread his act as something less than gallant?

"Pardon me, Miss Rose. I had no right to grab you that way."

She turned to face him, wiping tears from her eyes with the back of one hand. "Don't you dare."

Grant's stomach knotted. Any minute now, she'd scream for help, and the conveniently located Pinkerton would come to her rescue.

"Miss, if you'd just let me explain—"

She held her hand out, palm up. "There's nothing to explain. You saved my life. Don't you dare apologize."

Relief settled in Grant's chest. She wasn't angry. Shaken from her ordeal, and embarrassed, but not angry. "I'm afraid I may have endangered your life in the first place. If not for me, you could have finished your snack in peace."

Lily looked down at the remains of the sandwich and shook her head. "If not for my gluttonous self-indulgence, there would have been nothing to choke on."

"I don't think there's anything sinful about eating when you're hungry. In any case, I'm glad I was able to lend a hand. So to speak."

With a quirk of her lip, she asked, "Where did you learn to do that?"

It had been in St. Louis. A sore loser—and very poor poker player—had tried to swallow a gold ring to avoid forfeiting it. As the man had choked and gagged, Grant had watched as the winner casually stood, walked behind him, and squeezed until the ring reappeared. It had been an impressive display, but not something Grant could share with Miss Rose. "I saw someone do it in a restaurant once."

They both nodded. Smiled. An uncomfortable silence enveloped them. Miss Rose clutched the neck of her gown tightly with one hand, as if trying to cover up even more of her skin. In truth, the long, white nightdress was far more modest than most ball gowns. The sleeves came to her wrists, the top buttoned up to the base of her neck, and the bottom flowed down to her bare feet. Her delicate, tiny, bare feet.

Grant jerked his eyes back up to her face, but that wasn't any better. She was smiling at him, the kind of smile you give someone who just saved your life. Someone you respect. If she really knew him, she wouldn't smile like that.

"I'd better go."

"Of course." She bit her bottom lip, then quickly looked down at her toes. Crossing one foot atop the other, she said very quietly, "Reverend, may I ask a favor of you?"

"Certainly." She was like a delicate little bird without those awful hoops. Right now, he'd be hard-pressed to deny her anything.

"I'd appreciate it if you didn't tell my father about this. I haven't used the best judgment this evening, sneaking down for a snack in nothing more than my…." She glanced down at her gown.

Ah. Now, Grant was on firmer footing. Secrets, and the keeping of them, offered leverage. "Your secret is safe with me, Miss Rose."

"Thank you, Reverend. I do so hate displeasing him and Mama."

Grant had no experience with parents, but he was well acquainted with the experience of disappointing those in charge of him. It seemed the sisters at the orphanage had worn constant looks of displeasure whenever they'd focused on him.

"Where are you going?"

Grant drew himself back to the present. "Excuse me?"

"What was it that brought you down to the kitchen this evening?"

An idea sprang to his mind. He might yet salvage his escape plan. "Well, I couldn't sleep. Rather than stare at the ceiling, I thought I might spend some time outside in prayer and contemplation."

Lily pointed behind him. "You brought your saddlebags down with you. Were you planning to go somewhere?"

Drat. How was he going to explain that? "I wanted to have my Bible, as well as paper and pen, to write down anything the Lord might say."

A shot of white light burst through the kitchen windows, followed a few seconds later by the crack of thunder. Grant winced. Was the Lord telling him he'd gone too far?

Rain pelted the house. With a smile, Lily pushed a lock of hair away from her face. "It looks like your evening walk will have to wait."

Indeed it did. Grant sighed as he scooped up the saddlebags and tossed them back over his shoulder. There would be no escape tonight. "If you'll excuse me, Miss Rose, I do believe I should try getting some sleep, after all."

"Certainly. We have a big day ahead of us tomorrow." When he didn't answer, she hurried on. "We'll start making plans for the school. And you must meet the Indians, of course."

"Of course." Grant touched one finger to the brim of his hat. "Until tomorrow, then."

Leaving her in the kitchen, he ascended the stairs quickly, with nowhere near as much care as on the descent. The second step from the top let out a dreadful squeal as soon as he put his full weight on it.

Once in his room, Grant tossed the saddlebags on the bed in disgust. "You're losing your touch, Diamond." There had been a time when nothing, not even an unexpected heiress, could have kept him from his goal. He would have cajoled his way around her. But he'd never impersonated a minister before. And he'd never met a woman quite like Lily Rose.

⟡

The wind howled with a wild banshee cry that froze Drake's blood. Cloaked in shadows, he crouched amid the gravestones. Tonight he would solve the riddle and unmask the fiend who'd been stealing from the dead. He crept closer to the grave where two men dug by the feeble light of a lantern. Slowly, cautiously, Drake reached to pull his pistol from its holster. Out of the corner of his eye, he saw a flutter of white. He whirled around to face the movement. A willowy figure glided from the fog—

Screech!

Carter jerked his head up, lifting his nose out of the dime novel in his hand. With one fluid movement, he set the book down and slid off the bed. The sound had come from the staircase. Crouching in front of the closed door, he put his eye to the keyhole. Chronic insomnia kept him awake reading, but why would anybody else be wandering the halls at this hour?

At first, he saw nothing but darkness. He squeezed his left eye shut and pressed the right one hard against the door, as if that would help him focus. Finally, he saw something moving. A weak halo of light illuminated something pale and ethereal on the staircase. It moved from side to side, as if it were floating. What kind of apparition was this?

Get ahold of yourself, man.

That was the problem with reading novels late at night. They caused him to consider things he otherwise wouldn't. But Carter knew the difference between fiction and reality. The figure ascending the stairs was not some otherworldly specter but a flesh-and-blood person. He stayed at his post until he was able to identify Miss Rose, holding a small stub of candle aloft in one hand, clutching the skirt of her nightgown with the other.

The gentleman in Carter insisted he back away from the door and chase the image from his mind, yet his investigative side wouldn't let him. Something was afoot in this house. Every instinct told him so. Whether Miss Rose was a part of it remained to be seen. The only way to find out was to observe her, as he was doing now. Objectively. Just as any good and honorable Pinkerton would.

She was at the top of the stairs now. She started in the direction of her room, then stopped. Without moving her feet, she turned her head and peered over her shoulder. What was she looking at? In his mind, Carter reviewed the layout of the upper floor.

The reverend's room. She was staring at the door to Reverend Crew's room.

The air was so still, so quiet. Carter nearly held his breath, for fear she would hear him. But she paid no mind to his side of the house. Miss Rose put a hand to her heart, shook her head, and then quickly headed down the hall toward her family's private wing.

Carter lowered himself to the floor and leaned his back against the door. What had Miss Rose been doing downstairs? The creak that had first drawn his attention had occurred well before she could have set foot on the stairs. Had someone else been downstairs with her? And had that someone been Reverend Crew?

If, in fact, the man staying in the room across the hall really was Reverend Crew.

The back of Carter's neck tingled, as if the fine hairs there had all sprung to attention. A young woman in her nightclothes, unchaperoned, with a preacher in the dead of night was suspect enough. But that same young woman, under the same conditions, with a man like Grant Diamond? It was unthinkable.

Carter closed his eyes and saw his sister's face. Emily had been so vibrant, so full of life. But all that had changed at the hands of a heartless man. The same kind of man who had snuffed out the life of Sarah DeKlerk. The kind of man epitomized by Grant Diamond.

With his eyes wide open, Carter pushed himself off the floor. He extinguished the lantern by the bed, pulled back the covers, and crawled beneath them. Sleep might elude him, but he had to try. Tomorrow, he would go wherever Miss Rose went. One way or another, he would discover the identity of the mysterious man across the hall.

Chapter 7

A tapping noise wakened Grant. He flopped over and rubbed at the stubble on his chin. Another knock on the door, and he cracked one eye open. "Yeah?" His sleep-roughened voice sounded harsh, even to his own ears.

"Revered Crew?" Miss Rose sounded tentative. "Are you quite all right? I'm so sorry for disturbing you. We feared you might be unwell. It's nearly noon."

Grant jerked upright. "I'm fine, Miss Rose. I'll be down in two shakes of a lamb's tail."

A swish of retreating skirts was the only response from the other side of the door. He scrambled for some clean clothes, then splashed water on his face in an abbreviated version of his morning ablutions.

He'd spent most of the night trying to figure the best route out of the quicksand he'd landed in. And now, he'd lost his chance to sneak away before dawn. For at least another day, he was stuck playing the part of a preacher, doing good deeds and spouting platitudes.

A peek in the looking glass told him that he at least looked the part, except for his bristly cheeks and tooled leather boots. It would have been better if he could have taken the preacher's more modest footwear, but they'd been too tight.

Regrets. He was so deep in regrets, he could drown.

Grant snatched up the preacher's Bible and shoved it inside his coat pocket. He needed to make his disguise as complete as possible.

Down the stairs he went. He found Lily in the front parlor, looking enraptured as she listened to Forbes's monologue.

"Mr. Pinkerton had me stationed around the back. Since it was my first job, he figured I'd be safer there. But, as luck would have it, the robbers got wind of the trap waiting for them—"

"Morning." Grant stopped in the doorway.

Lily jumped up from the settee, her hoopskirt bobbing. Her action forced Forbes to stand, too.

"Afternoon, more like," the agent said.

"Reverend," Lily faltered, her words coming out strained and slow, "I do hope you'll forgive me…for disturbing you, that is."

It was all Grant could do to keep from grinning at the blush blooming in her cheeks. She was obviously still shaken from their encounter in the kitchen during the wee hours of the night. If he were smart, he would figure out a way to use the situation to his advantage. But all he could think about was putting Lily at ease. "There's nothing to forgive, Miss Rose. I've been on the road so long, I forgot how comfortable a real bed could be. In truth, I hope you'll forgive me."

She beamed. "As you said, there is nothing to forgive." She glanced toward the door to the dining room. "Lunch will be served in a few moments."

Grant nodded. "Thank you."

She sat down gingerly, as if fearful that her hoopskirt might attack. Once she had completed the maneuver, she motioned for the men to be seated, as well.

Forbes took the seat closer to her. Since her skirts took the entirety of the settee on which she was perched, Grant opted for a prim little cane-backed chair, which looked like a relic from the house of the little pig who'd fashioned it from sticks.

Summoning all the false bonhomie he could, Grant turned to the Pinkerton. "I believe you were telling Miss Rose a story of one of your adventures when I interrupted you. Please, continue."

The detective picked up where he'd left off, and Grant watched him closely. Everyone had an Achilles' heel. Even Pinkertons. He just had to pay attention, and it would reveal itself soon enough. Then he'd know the Pinkerton's weakness.

⌒

Lily retied her bonnet strings in a bow for the third time. The ribbons simply refused to fall at an attractive angle. The jingle of harness and the stamp of hooves below signaled that the gentlemen were ready and waiting for her. Sighing, she surrendered to the inevitable and let the bow droop willy-nilly.

She was acting like a woolly-headed schoolgirl. She oughtn't be any more concerned about her looks today than on any other day. With her shoulders set resolutely, Lily marched down the stairs. She would behave as a sober, polished young lady. That would be more attractive than any number of frills and furbelows. At least, that was what Mama had always claimed.

Lily harbored private doubts.

Once outside, she was assisted into the buckboard by Reverend Crew. His hands were warm and strong, providing a brace without clinging too long. He must be the godliest man she'd ever met. Even while performing good deeds, he conveyed an air of humility, as if he'd rather sink through the floor than call attention to himself.

Mr. Forbes scurried around to the other side of the vehicle and hopped in the driver's seat, relegating the reverend to a lonely perch on the second bench. Lily sighed but quickly hid her disappointment behind a pleasant smile. Even if, by some miracle, he was attracted to her, she didn't deserve a man like Reverend Crew. No matter what she might do to make up for her failures, she had no right to taint a man's ministry with the stain of her sinfulness.

Lily fought to rally her faltering mask of cheerfulness as she gave directions to the waiting Pinkerton. Soon, their destination came into view: a scrubby patch of land bordered by a stand of stubborn, gnarled old fir trees that pointed to the sky in defiance of the wind.

She scrambled from the wagon as quickly as her skirts would allow, too eager to wait for one of the gentlemen to hand her down. With her arms spread to encompass the view, she breathed deeply, inhaling the sea breeze. "Here you have it."

"Have...what, exactly?" Reverend Crew asked as he came up alongside her.

"The land for the new school, of course! I convinced Papa to let me purchase it with a portion of the trust my grandmother had set up for me." Lily led the way almost to the edge of the water. "See that island out in the bay? That's Indian Island. The Wiyot used to live there—until last year." Her voice caught, and her eyes stung.

"What happened?" Mr. Forbes asked.

Lily sucked in another breath of salty ocean air. The breeze did nothing to cool her cheeks. She wished she could skim over the revelation. Let the waves suck the past out with the tide until it sank to the bottom of the ocean.

But Reverend Crew needed to know. He had to understand what he was up against.

"A tragedy." She choked on the words, bile burning the back of her throat. She opened her mouth to continue but found she couldn't do it, after all. She shook her head. Another time. She would tell him all of it another time. Whitewashing her emotions with a note of brightness, she pointed to the east. "Most of them live there now."

Just visible over a rise, a tiny village of tent buildings spread out amid the stumpy trees. Smoke drifted in a wispy exclamation point above a single cook fire. Two or three children darted among the tents, followed closely by a pack of mongrel dogs.

"Come on." Lily gestured to the gentlemen, who gazed uncertainly at the camp. "Let's bring the food, and I'll introduce you to everyone."

Obediently, they plucked the heavy baskets from the cart and followed her down the slope.

A pair of children ran to Lily, calling her name. They pulled at her skirts, lightening her heart. She let them take the lead, and an impromptu parade immediately formed. Into the shabby cluster of tents they marched, the children heralding their arrival with calls and halloos.

Despite her pleasure in their company, Lily's heart clenched into a familiar leaden ball. The children cavorted, but they weren't much more than bones with round, protuberant bellies that indicated near starvation.

The cooking fire sat at the heart of the ramshackle village. Lily made straight for it and addressed the oldest mother in attendance. "Greetings, Martha."

Without looking up, the woman motioned for her to sit. "Lily, we're glad to see you."

Lily pulled a bag of sorghum candy from one of the baskets and doled it out to the children. She would have brought something of more substance, but there was the Wiyot people's pride to consider. They didn't mind her bringing a treat for the children, however. The pack of skinny youngsters pounced on the sweets, then ran off to resume their game. Once the last child had been bribed, Lily seated herself on a tree stump overlain with a woven blanket.

A handful of women clustered around her, wearing an odd mixture of their native dress and settler garb—bright skirts, some long and full like Lily's, others shorter and straight; high-necked blouses adorned with long shell jewelry; and flat, basketlike caps resting on unbound hair.

"Martha, I'd like to introduce you to Reverend Crew. He's the missionary I told you about. He's here to build a school and help teach the children, and...."

Lily glanced up at the reverend. She knew what she wanted him to do among the Indians, but perhaps he had additional plans of his own.

The reverend stepped forward, looking distinctly uncomfortable. "Ma'am." He tipped his hat in Martha's direction. "I...uh... hope I can help you folks."

He seemed suddenly shy, so Lily stepped in. "Reverend Crew, perhaps you have a word or a prayer for us?"

He looked around, as if he expected a church complete with steeple to sprout from the sandy soil. "Are you certain? I don't know if it would be—"

Martha nodded. "I want to hear the tales of this Jesus of yours. Miss Lily has told me some things already. Unless this is not the right time for sacred stories?"

"I...no, certainly...if you think it would be wise." He fumbled in his pocket and produced a small black Bible. He leafed through the pages, then glanced up with a weak smile.

Lily chided herself for putting him on the spot in such a fashion. Most ministers liked to have time to prepare their sermons. He couldn't be expected to perform like some dancing bear at the circus.

The lengthening silence was severed by a small boy's shout. He raced up to the assembly of women, panting, and poured out some story in Wiyot. Lily couldn't understand a word of it, but the wide, panic-stricken eyes and high-pitched, breathless tone needed no translation. His fear was plain as day.

She stood and glanced up at Reverend Crew. His expression offered a curious mix of relief and apprehension. Mr. Forbes's hand rested on the butt of his gun, and he spun away from the tearful child to gaze eastward.

Two mounted horses galloped into the encampment, their riders brandishing rifles high in the air. Lily's mouth went as dry as dust. Clods of dirt pelted her skirts as the men reined up hard.

Rick Abernathy's stony eyes peered down at her with the intensity of a ravenous wolf. "Fancy meeting you here."

Chapter 8

He'd met the man only once, but that had been more than enough for Grant to form an impression of Rick Abernathy. Although a smile pushed up the ends of his mustache, his eyes told a different story. They were set close together with lids so heavy, he appeared to be half asleep, yet his pupils were as hard as tiny black pebbles. There was nothing warm or caring about Abernathy. He was a man who took what he wanted without regard for those he hurt. And it was obvious to Grant that, at this moment, Abernathy wanted Lily.

Grant took a step forward and to the side, putting himself between Lily and the riders. Forbes did the same. Grant glanced at him and gave the smallest of nods. Forbes may be a Pink, but the man had good instincts.

"You gentlemen seem to be in quite a hurry." Grant lifted his chin, nodding at their firearms. "Are you hunting game?"

Abernathy held his rifle close to his side, almost cradling it. "That's one way of putting it."

Forbes pushed his hat back with his thumb. "Given your grand entrance, I think it's safe to assume you've chased all the game away."

"Well now, you could be right about that. But my experience tells me that putting the fear of God into the game now will give me a significant advantage later." Abernathy raised his gaze, looking over the trio's heads. "When the real hunt is on, skittish prey is easier to flush out and kill."

Behind Grant, Lily sucked in a great gulp of air. She was shaking so hard that he could feel the sides of her skirts quivering against his calves. She was either terrified or mad as a cornered polecat. A surreptitious glance in her direction settled the issue. It was the latter.

"Mr. Abernathy." She stopped and took another breath, probably to control the fury that had worked its way into her voice. "Mr. Abernathy, I'd appreciate it if you didn't ride in here with guns blazing. These people have done nothing to hurt you."

"On the contrary, Miss Rose, their very existence hurts me."

Lily took a step forward, but Grant's hand shot out, stopping her. "Excuse me, Miss Rose. If I may?"

Lips pressed into a thin line, she jerked her head in controlled agreement.

Grant looked up at Abernathy. "I'm curious, sir. Just what is it about the native people that offends you so?"

A look of pure hatred flitted across Abernathy's face, but he recovered quickly. Leaning forward in the saddle, one hand on the horn, he pinned his eyes on Grant.

"As a man of the cloth, you of all people shouldn't have to ask. They're heathens. Idol-worshipping heathens. They're no better than vermin, living in filth, spreading disease. They're not even human, in God's eyes."

"Who are you to say how God sees things?" Forbes demanded.

In one smooth movement, Abernathy was off his mount and standing in front of Forbes, rifle pointed at his chest. "And who are you to question me?"

At that moment, standing in the midst of crisis, Grant began formulating an escape plan in his mind. It would mean staying in town longer than he'd originally planned, but if all went well, he would be able to shake the Pink off his tail, once and for all.

"Pardon my rudeness, Mr. Abernathy. I forgot that you two haven't met. This is Carter Forbes. *Detective* Carter Forbes." Grant paused a moment to let that sink in. "Mr. Forbes is a Pinkerton agent."

"Is that so?" Abernathy lowered the rifle just an inch.

"Yes. He was just passing through our fine town, but when he heard about the plight of the Indians and the school we intended to build, he insisted on staying to lend a hand."

"He did?" Lily's voice behind him was barely a whisper.

Thankfully, Forbes knew just where Grant was going. "Yes, I did," he affirmed. "You see, Mr. Abernathy, I'm concerned about the Indians, too. About their well-being. And I can't think of a better way to minister to them than by building a school where they can learn to read and write."

"You're wasting your time," Abernathy sneered. "They'll just turn on you."

Grant stepped up to Abernathy and slapped him on the shoulder, almost making him drop the gun. A snicker escaped from the sidekick, still seated upon his horse. "We'll just leave that in God's hands. And if there's any trouble—*any trouble at all*—we've got our very own Pink to deal with it."

Abernathy's neck turned crimson. Without another word, he turned on his heel and remounted. Ignoring the men, he directed a pointed look at Lily. "Miss Rose, you'd be smart to reconsider my proposal. Securing my protection is the only way to ensure your safety—and everyone else's."

Abernathy yanked on the reins, wheeling the horse around. With a kick to the poor beast's side, he was off, his goon close behind.

A sniff drew Grant's attention. He turned to Lily. Her anger had transformed into something else—fear? Sorrow? She held a dainty lace handkerchief to her face, trying to hide the tears that slid down her cheeks.

"What did he mean by that, Miss Rose?" Forbes asked gently. "What proposal?"

"He's such a horrid man." She squeezed her eyes tight and snuffled. "I'm mortified that he brought it up in the presence of such upstanding gentlemen as yourselves."

Grant looked down at his toes. If she only knew. At least he was more upstanding than the snake who'd just slithered away. "Is he demanding protection money?"

"In a manner of speaking. But it's far worse than that. His use of the word 'proposal' was quite literal."

Grant's stomach flopped. If she was saying what he thought she was saying, then Abernathy was worse than just an ignorant ruffian.

"Please, Miss Rose," Forbes interjected. "We need you to be very specific. What are Abernathy's intentions?"

She wiped her eyes and dabbed her nose with the fancy piece of linen. Then, she took a deep breath and pulled back her shoulders. As she spoke, her eyes darted back and forth between Carter and Grant. "Mr. Abernathy is a cruel, vile man who intends for his word to be law in Eureka, no matter the cost. Given my position as heiress to the largest fortune in this town, he sees me as a means to that end."

Lily Rose now focused her eyes directly on the man she believed to be Reverend Crew, silently imploring him to save her. "Rick Abernathy has proposed marriage."

~⁀

Marriage. What ought to be the most beautiful word in the world had turned to ash on Lily's tongue when spoken in the same breath as "Rick Abernathy."

Reverend Crew's eyebrows knit together in a frown. "You refused him, of course."

"Of course. I'd rather die a spinster than marry a man like him."

"And your parents?" Mr. Forbes put a hand to his chest, smoothing the front of his vest. "Do they support your decision?"

A good question, indeed. Lily had seen more than one woman forced into a questionable union by parents who claimed to have their daughter's best interests at heart. "Thankfully, my parents see Mr. Abernathy's true nature. They would sooner have me join a convent than marry such a reprobate."

Not that any convent would have her, either. Sometimes, in her moments of deepest doubt, Lily wondered if perhaps she *did* deserve being joined with Abernathy. Perhaps a life of misery with him would serve as sufficient penance for her past sins.

With a jerk of her head, she shook the thought from her mind. No. Hadn't she done all that she could to atone for her mistakes? Surely, she didn't merit a man like Rick Abernathy. She studied the two gentlemen before her: a Pinkerton and a pastor. Decent, honorable men who had dedicated their lives to seeing justice done and serving others.

No, she didn't deserve a person like Abernathy. But she wasn't worthy to be loved by men such as these, either.

"Enough about me." Lily brushed her palms together, eager to move on to more important things. "Reverend Crew, thank you for putting Mr. Abernathy in his place. Most of the people in this town are too afraid to stand up to him."

The reverend touched the brim of his hat. "My pleasure."

Lily turned to Mr. Forbes, steadying her skirts so as not to bump either of the men. "And you, Mr. Forbes. Thank you for offering to stay and help build the school." She paused. "Did you really mean it?"

He cocked his head slightly. "Of course. You have my word, and my word is my bond."

Heat rushed to Lily's cheeks. Now she'd done it. She'd insulted the man. "Oh dear. I didn't mean to imply...that is, what I meant was—"

Mr. Forbes held up his hand. "There's no need to apologize. The situation called for some quick thinking." He nodded at the reverend. "Good job with that."

The picture of humility, Reverend Crew made no reply. He merely nodded back, hands folded in front of him.

"The fact is," Mr. Forbes continued, "I'm still investigating a murder. Helping with the school gives me an excuse to stay in town awhile. Ask questions." He smiled.

Lily gripped the detective's arm. "With your help, we shall complete the school that much faster." She turned to Reverend Crew. "Isn't it wonderful how God has provided, Reverend?"

To her surprise, she caught the edge of a frown on his lips. "Yes. Wonderful."

The reverend seemed cross. Lily let go of the Pinkerton and then gripped the offending hand with her other, to keep it from reaching out again. "Gentlemen, why don't we continue with the business we came here to do?"

With that, she turned back to Martha and the other Wiyot women.

⌒

Carter waited until Miss Rose was preoccupied, and then he turned to the man beside him. "You handled Abernathy quite well. Have you had much experience with ruffians like him?"

Crew's lips curled up in a lazy smile. "In my line of work, you meet all kinds of people. It pays to be adaptable."

For a pastor, the man certainly was quick on his feet. He hadn't blinked at spinning a lie, albeit a very tiny white one, and the answer he'd just given could mean anything. Perhaps it was time to test him a bit.

"I see what you mean. It's like that Scripture about being as wise as a serpent. How does that one go, again?"

Crew turned away and reached inside his pocket. Instinctively, Carter rested his hand just above the butt of his holstered pistol. The reverend was still looking off toward the cook fire when he spoke. "*Behold, I send you forth as sheep in the midst of wolves: be ye therefore wise as serpents, and harmless as doves.*" He turned back around and waved a Bible at Carter. "Believe me, I live by that verse. Now, why don't we go make some new friends?"

Chapter 9

The church bell tolled in steady rhythm as the Rose carriage approached the steepled building set back from the main road, its whitewashed redwood shingles glowing among the trees.

Lily smiled. She desperately wanted to make a good impression on Reverend Crew. She'd heard of the fancy churches back East, and although there were no paintings on the ceiling of their assembly, it at least had arched glass windows, along with a small rosette window above the main entry made of real stained glass.

Joseph reined in the horses, bringing the carriage to a gentle stop, and came around to help Lily from her seat. She fluffed the jade green fabric of her skirt, her fingers tracing the delicately embroidered lily of the valley pattern along the waistband. As the gentlemen alighted, it dawned on her that the bell continued to ring, now with an uneven cadence. Some young boy playing games, no doubt.

"Excuse me, gentlemen, won't you?"

Both the reverend and Mr. Forbes nodded politely. Bestowing her sweetest smile on them, she hurried away to the rear entrance.

She would give the little scamp the tongue-lashing of his life. She sighed. So much for making a good impression.

Lily yanked open the door to the vestry and bounded up the stairs to the bell tower, her bobbing skirts held high enough to clear the steps. She would not get stuck today.

As she crested the stairs, she stopped short. The culprit was no boy. Instead, the right Reverend Paul Marsden tugged on the ropes with a peculiar, jumping pull, his face scarlet, his protuberant eyes half closed.

Catching sight of her as she stepped hesitantly onto the narrow landing, Marsden beckoned her closer. He gave another tug on the ropes, then bent over and staggered to the side, hands covering his ears. "The bells! The bells!" He collapsed against the wall in a state of snorting giggles.

Lily pinched the bridge of her nose. He'd been doing so well lately. There hadn't been a lapse this bad in nearly six months. For a while, after the massacre, he'd kept himself in a state of perpetual intoxication. He'd somehow managed to clean himself up enough that, lately, it hadn't been affecting him during the Sunday morning services. But now….

She had to get him out of here and figure out what was to be done about the service. If only Papa hadn't been called away to attend to an emergency out at one of the camps. She would have welcomed the opportunity to dump the matter in his lap. He would know what to do.

Marsden flapped a hand at her. "Do you get it? Hugo. Hunchback?"

Lily nodded.

"Why di'n't you laugh at my joke? Nobody ever laughs at my jokes. I can't do nuthin'." He waved a hand wildly, and the action nearly caused him to fall from the loft to the vestry floor below.

Lily grabbed for him. Marsden reared away, falling heavily against the flimsy banister. The bottle of spirits he clutched in his hand spilled out, splattering the front of her gown. She wrinkled her nose. The stuff smelled strong enough to eat right through the delicate fabric. She could only imagine what it did to a person's insides.

Part of her wanted to give him a good push over the edge of the rail. Instead, she backed away, motioning for him to follow her. "Come now, Reverend," she said in a soothing voice generally reserved for small children. "It's time to go downstairs."

He followed her, but his every step threatened to topple one or the other of them down the stairs. When at last they reached the wooden planks of the vestry floor, she exhaled with relief.

"Miss Rose, you are a rose among thorns." At this witticism, he snorted again and then covered his mouth.

Lily shook her head. "Reverend Marsden, you promised."

"Don' you talk ta me 'bout no promises." He thumped his chest with a balled-up fist. "You nest of vipers. Brood of Satan."

Lily gasped.

He leaned toward her. "You think I don't know, but I know. Oh, yes." He tapped the side of his nose.

"What are you talking about?"

"You brought him here to replace me. You think he's better than me."

Lily lifted her eyes to heaven. "Oh, for pity's sake." She then propelled him toward a rickety chair in the corner and sat him down. "No one is here to replace you. But if you don't pull yourself together, someone will have to. Now, sit here and don't move."

His face scrunched up, and he began to cry. "Heartless queen of Babylon."

Lily turned on her heel. In the vestibule, half a dozen ladies surrounded Reverend Crew and Mr. Forbes. The reverend leaned toward each woman in turn as she spoke, flashing a gracious smile that had handkerchiefs fluttering and all the women twittering.

As much as Lily would prefer to avoid the entire situation, there really wasn't any other option. Throwing her pride to the wind, she plowed her way through the press of skirts. "Reverend Crew, I apologize for taking you away from all these lovely ladies, but, if I may, I'd like to borrow you for just a moment. Reverend Marsden is indisposed and would like to see you."

One of the women sniffed, but Lily ignored her and led the reverend toward the vestry.

With his eyebrows pulled down in a deep V, he looked around anxiously. "What's wrong?"

Lily gestured him inside. "That." She pointed to Marsden, who had fallen asleep or perhaps passed out and was sliding from his seat.

Reverend Crew approached the man and reached for his hand. An enormous snore made him jump back.

"Good night! He's drunk."

"Exactly." Lily sighed and twisted the strings of her purse. "Could you...do you think you could possibly...I mean, would you be willing to deliver this morning's sermon?"

He paled. "Oh, no. I couldn't." He glanced down at the prone figure at his feet. "I haven't been introduced to the congregation, and I couldn't take another man's pulpit without his knowledge. It would be like...like stealing someone else's wife. I couldn't, under any circumstances."

Lily slumped, but her corset gouged her, so she straightened again. "Please, Reverend. I know it is a great imposition, and you've had no time to prepare. But the congregation can't see him like this." She waved at Marsden, who by now had a trail of slick drool escaping out one side of his mouth.

The reverend sighed. He nudged the body with one foot, as if in hopes of rousing the man. Sensing that he was softening, Lily pressed on. "He wasn't always like this, you know."

Crew met her eyes, and his shoulders sagged ever so slightly.

"He's suffered great sadness. We all have."

He sighed. "All right. All right."

Lily clapped her hands together. "Thank you!"

"I'll do it, but what are you going to do with him?"

She glared at the snoring, black-clad figure. Yes, that was another problem. At last, she raised her eyes to meet Reverend Crew's. "I'll wait until you start the sermon, and then Mr. Forbes can help me carry him to the parsonage."

A blast of chords from the organ heralded the beginning of the service. They both jumped as if they'd been jabbed by a branding iron.

The color seemed to fade from the reverend's face. Unthinking, Lily put a hand on his arm. "I'm so sorry to put you in this position. I just don't know what else to do."

Something in his eyes turned gentle and warm. "I've been in worse scrapes than this, Miss Rose. And I'll wager I've got worse ahead of me, too. Don't you worry, though. We'll come out on top."

Mesmerized, Lily nodded. An instant later, she realized that her hand still grasped his arm, and she snatched it away. She swallowed. "Do you think you could send Mr. Forbes back here? I don't want to draw any more attention by going out and coming in again."

"Certainly." The reverend doffed his cap and adjusted his collar. "I sure hope they'll enjoy hearing about the wages of sin." With that, he slipped through the door, leaving Lily alone again with Marsden.

The inebriated preacher stirred slightly. "No," he whimpered, cringing.

Lily shook her head. What kinds of demons chased him down in his dreams? Were they the same ones that haunted her?

The vestry door slowly opened, and Mr. Forbes poked his head inside. He eased his tall frame through the door and then closed it with practiced stealth. "Crew said you needed to see me?"

Scrambling for words, she rushed through an explanation. "Do you think you could help me get him to the parsonage?"

"Certainly." He opened the door a crack and peeked out. "All right. Crew's got them eating out of his hand. You hold the door open, and I'll wrangle the parson."

Lily complied, and Carter bent down to hoist Marsden off the floor. As quietly as they could, they maneuvered him into the little foyer, and again, Lily held the door open for Carter. At last, they had him outside, and Lily took his feet. She pointed with her chin. "The parsonage is just there."

Carter glanced over his shoulder. "All right, then."

The preacher was as heavy as a redwood and deadweight, to boot, but, huffing and puffing, they managed to get him into the house. Lily had never been inside before, and she was surprised to see the enormous four-poster bed that took up almost the entire bedroom. Marsden must have brought it with him from out East. Despite the fine quality of the bed, the sheets were gray from lack of washing.

Lily's nose wrinkled. Dirty clothing littered the floor. Using her foot, she nudged it into a heap in the corner and then reached for a broom lying half beneath the bed. "Thank you, Mr. Forbes. I could not have managed without your assistance."

"My pleasure, Miss Rose." He glanced around the room. "Maybe we ought to get back to the service?"

An awkward lift of his shoulders, paired with his refusal to meet her eye, made her realize for the first time the great impropriety of her position.

Her cheeks stung as if she'd been pushed face-first into a nettle patch. "Heavens, yes!"

They practically raced from the house. As they neared the church, Lily slowed to a more decorous pace. She tried to suppress a giggle, but it leaked out.

Carter glanced at her in alarm.

"My mother would have a fit of the vapors if she knew," she explained.

He grinned at her and pushed his hat back a little. "Mine, too." He slowed even more. "But at the reverend's behavior, not yours." He reached for the door handle but stopped before opening it. "Not many folks would show kindness to such a man. You're something special, Miss Rose."

Lily's cheeks warmed at the compliment, but before she could respond, Carter swung open the door and ushered her inside. Cocooned in the haze of his kind words, she vaguely noted the sideways glances of two matrons.

She settled into the back row and tried to concentrate on Reverend Crew's sermon. Instead, her attention was caught by the presence, in the second row, of a half dozen Indian servants.

She blinked. They always waited with the carriages for their employers to come out after the service. No wonder things had seemed odd outside.

Her heart melted a bit. It must have been Reverend Crew. He had already set about his task of reaching the Indians and, beyond that, reconciling the two races. It had taken him a long time to get here, but God had certainly provided the right man for the job.

⌒

Grant almost grinned as he waved his Bible in the air. This crowd was buying whatever he was selling. First, he'd shocked them severely by inviting the Wiyot servants to join them. But he couldn't think of a better way to ensure real interest in the sermon and clear the way for Lily than to do something shocking. Now, several heads bobbed up and down as he spoke. Too bad he was running out of platitudes. The verses he recalled from his days of being drilled in catechism by the sisters at the orphanage would get him only so far.

The main door opened, and Lily sneaked in, followed closely by Forbes. *Finally.* What on earth had taken them so long?

Time to wrap things up. Inspiration struck, so heavy with memories that he could almost smell the cooked cabbage, wood polish, and young-boy stink of the orphanage. "And so, in closing, I would turn your attention to the book of Matthew, chapter twenty-five, verse forty: *'And the King shall answer and say unto them, Verily I say unto you, inasmuch as ye have done it unto one of the least of these my brethren, ye have done it unto me.'*"

The words tasted rancid on his tongue. He'd been reminded every day of his identity as *"one of the least."*

With an effort, he kept his pious mask in place. "Let us stand and pray."

There was a moment of hesitation, as if the congregation didn't believe the sermon could possibly be over yet. Marsden was probably one of those preachers who kept talking because he wasn't quite sure what he wanted to say. At last, there was a wave of rustles and scrapes as the people stood.

The peace of the moment was broken as the main doors flew open, slamming against the walls. Every head in the place swiveled to face the disturbance. Rick Abernathy strode into the church, one hand resting on his holster, as if he expected to have reason to draw his sidearm at any minute.

The gravity of the situation was immediately clear. Abernathy was gunning for the natives. Grant bounded from the pulpit and placed himself at the opening of the pew where the Indians were seated. He might be low-down, but he wasn't going to let these people die because he'd used them as a diversionary tactic.

A handful of other men trooped in behind Abernathy, each one looking more down-at-the-heel than the last. One against five. Grant swallowed, but he held his ground as the rancher approached and stood nose-to-nose with him.

"Who let those heathens in the church with the decent folk?" Abernathy's voice was low and drawling. He might have been asking the time of day, if not for the rage smearing his features. And the gun at his side.

"What's going on here?"

Grant half turned toward the voice of Carter Forbes, who had slipped around the pews and come up behind him. The corner of Grant's mouth twitched. Two against five. Not the best odds, but better than a few seconds ago.

The swish of skirts made Grant look past Carter. Oh, no. Behind him came Lily, her face the color of a newly washed bedsheet. Abernathy noticed her, too. The man clenched his jaw so hard that Grant actually heard his molars collide.

Turning from Grant, Abernathy took a step toward Carter. "I could ask you the same thing, Pinkerton. What's been going on with you and Miss Rose?"

Abernathy's change of focus seemed to confuse his men. They turned to one another, unsure of whom they were supposed to threaten now. Grant seized the opportunity. With a wave of his hand, he motioned for the Indians to head to the back of the church.

Relief surged through him when the last native hurried out the door. But their troubles were far from over. Carter may have saved lives—or, at the very least, averted an unpleasant scene—but he might have sacrificed Lily's reputation in the process.

Chapter 10

If the fire in Rick Abernathy's gaze could have materialized, it would have burned down the church into a smoldering heap around them. Lily put her palms flat against her skirts, determined not to let them betray the trembling of her legs.

Abernathy bounded up to Mr. Forbes and poked the Pinkerton in the chest. "I'll ask you again. What have the two of you been up to?"

The rustle that arose as the congregants shifted in their seats sent Lily's heart plummeting in her chest. Obviously, Abernathy wasn't the only one who wanted an answer to that question. Oh, how she longed to turn and run from the prying eyes, the whispered comments. *Poor dear. Even with all her father's money, she still hasn't nabbed a beau, and now she's sneaking around with a Pinkerton.* But running was out of the question. She couldn't abandon Reverend Crew and Mr. Forbes. Besides, it would only make her look guilty.

Carter pulled his shoulders back. "Reverend Marsden wasn't feeling well, so we helped him back to the parsonage."

Abernathy's nostrils flared as he inhaled deeply. He narrowed his eyes. "Then, how do you explain the fact that Miss Rose reeks of liquor?"

Lily stepped back, glancing down at the damp patch on her dress where the bottle had splashed her. An instant later, she realized her mistake. To the onlookers, she must appear startled and ashamed. She'd as good as confessed. Abernathy's frown deepened to the point that his eyebrows met in the middle, while the congregation was abuzz with shocked whispers. *She finally cracked. She's always been an odd one, but who thought it would come to this?*

Burning with rage against this injustice, she stepped forward to give Abernathy a piece of her mind. What right did he have to question her? He had no claim on her.

Carter glanced over his shoulder at her with the tiniest shake of his head. She halted. He was right. To deny the charge would only make things worse. People would believe what they wanted to. Still, she had a right to defend her reputation.

Willing herself to be strong, Lily met Abernathy's gaze and held it. "I've done nothing shameful. And that's all I will say about the matter."

Abernathy laughed. "That's the most pitiful excuse for a denial I've ever heard. Let me tell you something, Miss Rose. Your father may be the richest man in town, but that doesn't give you free rein to act like a hussy."

Lily reared back to slap him, but Carter caught her arm.

"That's enough!" Reverend Crew roared, eliciting gasps from the congregation. He pushed his way between Lily and Abernathy, his face pale, except for two spots of crimson burning along his cheekbones. Lily had never seen a man so angry, especially on her behalf.

"You are way out of line, Abernathy." The reverend drew up a fisted hand, and, for a second, Lily thought he was going to hit him. Instead, he splayed his fingers and poked them into Abernathy's chest, forcing him to step backward. "You've no right to accuse Miss Rose. She's a fine Christian woman, and if you dare—"

Abernathy swept the reverend's hand away. "Remind us, Reverend, how long you have been in our town. All of three days?

And you've already come to know Miss Rose well enough to vouch for her?"

Reverend Crew lifted his chin. "I'm an excellent judge of character."

Abernathy sneered. "I'm sure it helps that you're living in Miss Rose's home. In fact, I hear the Pinkerton is staying there, too." He leered at Lily. "No wonder you've taken to the bottle. It must be exhausting seeing to the needs of both these gentlemen."

Lily's hand flew to her mouth. She didn't know what shocked her more: Abernathy's vile innuendo, or the pistol Reverend Crew produced from out of nowhere and now pointed at Abernathy's forehead.

⌒

Grant never should have drawn the gun. Not when he didn't know how to put the brakes on this train of events. Next thing he knew, he was staring down the barrel of Abernathy's gun, while Carter aimed his weapon back at Abernathy. His posse of men raised their rifles in an automatic, though somewhat halfhearted, response. A few congregants had pulled their own pistols and now waved them from one man to the other, desiring to protect themselves but unsure from whom.

It was exactly what Grant would have expected—if he'd thought it through. Problem was, he hadn't been thinking about anything but protecting Lily's honor. Now, his impulsive behavior had endangered her life, as well as the lives of all the people in the church.

Judging from Abernathy's smirk, Grant had played right into the man's hands. "It seems we've got a standoff here, Preacher."

"I wouldn't say that," spoke a voice from the back of the church. Although it was familiar, Grant couldn't place it, and he had no intention of taking his eyes off of the snake in front of him.

"Papa!"

It took all the control Grant possessed not to turn his head toward Lily. Her father? When had he slipped in? And just how much had he heard?

"Hold your ground, Lily-belle." The man's voice was calm yet firm, inviting no argument. The sound of his footsteps told Grant he was walking up the aisle. "I suggest that you fellows put down your weapons so we can discuss this like gentlemen. There's no need to shed blood in the Lord's house."

Abernathy's men were the first to comply. Grant heard a click, and, out of the corner of his eye, he saw Carter lower his gun. That left only Grant and Abernathy, and Grant had no intention of being the first to relent.

"Lower your gun, son," Mr. Rose said.

"I'm sorry, sir, but I don't trust him."

Abernathy tilted his head slightly, as though studying Grant. "You drew on me."

Lily stepped around Forbes and into Grant's line of sight. "You're the bigger man. Please, Reverend Crew."

Reverend Crew. The name slammed into him, reminding him what he was doing here in the first place. Grant Diamond would never back down from a fight. But Reverend Crew was a man of God. He'd already made a tactical error by engaging in battle. He had no choice now but to put an end to it.

"You're right, Miss Rose." He lowered the pistol and slipped it back beneath his jacket. "Thank you for bringing me back to my senses."

"Now you, Abernathy."

At Mr. Rose's stern command, Abernathy lowered his side-arm, but he didn't holster it. Instead, he held it against his thigh, his index finger still hovering near the trigger.

It was time to regain control of the situation and to reassume his stolen identity. Grant turned to the congregation. "Services are over for today, folks. You'd best all go on home." The people rose, their faces plastered with fear and confusion. As an afterthought, Grant added, "God bless you."

When the church doors closed behind the last congregant, Lily ran into her father's arms. Mr. Rose held his daughter close, then drew in an exaggerated sniff. "Heavens, gal, did you have another mishap with the Communion wine?" Without waiting for a response, he leveled his gaze at Abernathy. "That would certainly explain the smell of alcohol, wouldn't it?"

For the first time since he'd entered the church, Abernathy faltered. "I suppose it would."

"You'd be wise to gather all the facts before accusing folks of impropriety." Mr. Rose pointed first at Carter, then at Grant. "And the facts are that these gentlemen are guests in my home. When you threaten them, you threaten my family. And I don't take kindly to folks threatening my family."

Grant's admiration for Mr. Rose grew in equal proportion to his own guilt. This honorable man wouldn't be as protective of Grant Diamond, fugitive gambler, as he was of Reverend Crew, selfless missionary.

Abernathy jerked his head toward Grant. "He brought Diggers into this church. Did you know that?"

Mr. Rose nodded. "I'm aware that he invited the Wiyot into the service."

"And you approve?"

"I approve anytime a soul is invited to hear the Word of the Lord, as should any Christian man."

Something akin to a growl rumbled in Abernathy's throat. Abandoning his verbal battle with Rose, he turned his full attention to Grant. "This isn't over, Preacher. If you think you can ride into town and change everything, you're wrong. Those heathens will never reform, and I refuse to sit under the same roof with them."

Grant forced his lips into a calm smile. "It's a good thing you have no say over who crosses this threshold, then."

⌒

Carter was afraid that Crew's last barb would have Abernathy raising his weapon again. Instead, the man holstered his gun, turned on his heel, and stalked out of the church, his lackeys following behind like shadows.

The door slammed with a resounding bang, and Miss Rose hugged her father harder, her head buried in his chest. "Papa, I'm so glad you came. But how did you know?"

"I didn't. Not until I got here. The problem at the camp wasn't nearly as bad as the foreman made it out to be. Joseph saw me riding back into town and told me I was needed at the church." He looked over his daughter's head at Reverend Crew, his eyes blazing. "What were you thinking, man, bringing all those Indians in here?"

Mr. Rose's sudden shift in demeanor caught Carter off guard. From the startled expression on Crew's face, he was just as surprised.

"I was thinking," the preacher answered evenly, "that the Bible isn't just for white men. I thought you understood that."

Miss Rose pulled away from her father and looked up at him, her brown eyes wide and pleading. "Papa, the whole reason we sent for Reverend Crew was to minister to the Indians. You can't be angry with him for doing so."

Mr. Rose muttered something under his breath. "Of course not. What upsets me is his impulsive, reckless action. Abernathy is an ignorant fool, but he's right about one thing: people won't change just because you tell them to. The white folks and the Indians have mistrusted each other for so long, you can't throw them together and not expect repercussions."

The skin above Crew's collar grew red. He nodded. "You're right, sir. I didn't think it through. It won't happen again."

"We'll see about that," said Mr. Rose with a snort.

"Sir?" Carter queried.

Mr. Rose shook his head, refusing to elaborate on his concerns. "No point in looking for trouble before it finds us. In the meantime, you should get busy building them their own church and schoolhouse." He gave his daughter another squeeze and kissed the top of her head. "For now, I say we head home and see what's for lunch."

Lily sighed. "I couldn't agree more." She turned to the preacher. "Reverend Crew, would you mind closing up the church?"

"Not at all. But...I don't have a key."

Lily looked from her father to the reverend and then back again. She cocked her head, and Mr. Rose gave a slight nod. He reached into an inner jacket pocket, produced a big black key, and handed it to Crew. "Don't lose this."

Grant smiled as his fingers closed around the key. "No, sir."

Carter tried not to show his surprise at the exchange. As a lumber magnate, Mr. Rose had undoubtedly constructed more than half the buildings in town—among them the church, apparently. What Crew held in his hand was a skeleton key, which no doubt granted access to every property the man owned.

Carter raised a finger. "I'll help him. We'll be along shortly."

The smile Miss Rose flashed him was full of gratitude, and it warmed Carter to his toes. Without another word, she and her father turned and left the church.

Crew looked around the small space. "Not really a two-person job, is it?"

"That all depends," Carter answered.

"On?"

"On whether Abernathy comes back."

Crew nodded.

"On the other hand, you seem more than capable of taking care of yourself. Can't say I've ever met a pistol-packing preacher."

Crew's mouth tightened for a moment, and then a slight smile graced his lips. "I've learned that, when working on the frontier, it's best to be prepared."

"True," Carter said. "Interesting, though, that you were the first to draw. The act seemed rather...carnal."

"I'm a preacher, Forbes, not a saint." The minister's tone was as smooth and rich as thick cream—the kind of voice that comforted and convinced.

Yet something about it wasn't quite right. Carter had heard that tone too many times in the outlandish promises of hucksters and quacks. "*If used three times daily for three months without fail, this liniment will regenerate the nerves in damaged limbs....*" How many times had such silky-sounding promises raised his sister's hopes? And how many times had he wiped away her tears after the promises had proven to be complete shams?

Maybe Crew was on the up-and-up. Maybe his sole motivation for coming to Eureka had been to minister to the native people. But too many doubts niggled in Carter's gut. Whatever secret was hidden in the heart of Hubert Crew, Carter vowed to uncover it.

Chapter 11

"Heavens, it's good to be home." The minute Lily passed through the door, she yanked on the silk bow beneath her chin and pulled the bonnet from her head. It dangled behind her by the ribbons, bouncing unminded against the side of her skirt, as she trudged into the foyer.

Across from the open door stood Naomi, an empty laundry basket in her arms. "Welcome home, Mr. Rose, Miss Lily." The maid nodded to each of them as she shifted the basket to her hip.

Naomi didn't work on Sundays. She should be home with her family, not standing in the foyer with a laundry basket. Heat crept up Lily's neck as the realization dawned: Naomi must have heard what had happened at the church. She must be in the house now out of sheer curiosity, to find out how it all had turned out. In truth, Lily wondered the same thing.

She'd tried talking to her father after they'd left the church, but not more than a syllable had escaped her lips before he'd shushed her. His terse "At home" had ended her appeal. There would be no discussion until he was ready.

"Hello, Naomi." Papa's smile was tight as he removed his cap and hung it deliberately on the crooked arm of the hat tree. "Shouldn't you be at home with your family today?"

Naomi's cheeks turned a rosier shade of copper, and her fingers gripped the straw basket more tightly. "Yes, sir. But I was at the church, and…I thought Miss Lily might need assistance."

When Lily and her father stared at the maid, she rushed on. "Help with her dress, that is. After the accident with the wine, I thought Miss Rose might want to change before lunch."

A relieved breath whooshed out of Lily. "Naomi, I'd like nothing better than to shed these clothes." While it was impossible to erase the events of the morning from her memory, removing the offensive-smelling dress was a step in the right direction.

Papa's face softened a bit. "Thank you, Naomi. Your consideration is more Christian than most of the people in that church today. If you would, please wait for Lily in her room. We need to speak privately first, but then I'll send her right up."

Naomi nodded. "As you say, Mr. Rose." She shot a concerned look at Lily, then quickly turned and hurried up the wide staircase.

Lily longed to chase right after her. But, as Naomi's calico skirts swished around the corner at the top of the stairs and disappeared, so did Lily's last hope of putting off the inevitable.

Papa cleared his throat. "Join me in my study, daughter."

Daughter. Lily shuddered at the word. A lecture was coming.

Once inside, her father pointed at a low bench in the middle of the room. "Sit, please."

Lily regarded the piece of furniture with the same repulsion she felt for Brussels sprouts. *The scolding bench.* Nobody else called it that, but Lily had always thought of it that way. She'd once overheard her father explain to a business associate that the placement of the bench in the middle of the room, and its nearness to the floor, gave him the upper hand when dealing with troublesome folk. She'd lost track of the times Papa had sat her down on it to give her a good talking-to.

Now, she carefully arranged her skirts, then lowered herself gingerly onto the hard seat. Hands clasped in her lap and spine as straight as a lightning rod, she stared directly ahead, waiting for the inevitable question.

"Lily Gardenia Rose, what am I going to do with you?"

She wished she could give him a satisfactory answer.

Papa paced the floor as he spoke. "I don't for a moment believe you were imbibing. But, blast it all, girl, if that's Communion wine, I'm a Celestine monk. Now, would you care to tell me how you ended up smelling like cheap whiskey?"

"I'd rather not."

"Tell me, anyway."

Lily drew in a deep breath. "I found Reverend Marsden in the bell tower. He was intoxicated. So, I asked Reverend Crew to take over the service."

Papa's eyebrows knit together in concern. "Which explains why all the Indians were in the church. That Crew certainly is an ambitious fellow. But it doesn't explain how you became drenched in liquor." He stopped his pacing, and his face blanched. "Marsden didn't accost you, did he?"

"Heavens, no!" Just the thought of that man's sausage-like fingers on her skin sent a shiver of disgust racing through her body. "He stumbled into me, and his flask spilled. But that was before he passed out."

"Does Crew know Marsden is in the bell tower? I don't want the old fool to be locked in."

"He's not in the bell tower."

"Lily, there's something you aren't telling me. You'd better get to it."

Lily clasped her hands to keep from fidgeting. "I asked Mr. Forbes to help me get him to the parsonage."

"And just how did you transport him there?" Father's voice was low and measured. The calm before the storm.

"We carried him."

"I see. And where did you deposit him?"

Lily swallowed hard. "In his bed."

"You *what?*"

His roar made Lily jump from her seat. She came back down on the hard wood with a painful thud.

"You helped carry a drunken man to his bed with the assistance of another male, unchaperoned and smelling of liquor? Have you lost your mind? Why didn't you find someone else to assist Forbes?"

Why, indeed? If she had, she could have avoided all of this. The town wouldn't be gossiping about her. Again. And her father wouldn't be disappointed in her. Again.

Reverend Marsden had done nothing of late to merit her kindness, yet she'd put her own reputation at stake to save his. A smart woman wouldn't have done that. With tears welling in her eyes, she looked up at her father. "I didn't want to embarrass Reverend Marsden. I'm sorry, Papa." Lily dropped her face to her hands as the tears came.

A moment later, her father settled down beside her, wrapping his arm around her shoulders and drawing her against his chest. "Lily, you have a heart bigger than the great Pacific. But you need to temper your compassion with common sense."

"Yes, Papa," she mumbled into his starched white shirt.

"I believe it's time we sent for your mother."

Lily pushed away from him and looked into his eyes. "Mama? Why?"

"No need to sound so horrified, Lily-belle," he said with a chuckle. "Your mother only has your best interests at heart."

"Can she really leave Aunt Gertrude? Mama's last letter made it sound as if she was still very sick."

"I suspect your mother is enjoying the social scene in San Francisco so much that Aunt Gertrude may seem poorly to her for months yet. I've been thinking it was time for her to return home, but today's events clinched it. Abernathy was right about one thing: it's inappropriate for you to be the only woman in a house with two male guests. Your mother's presence will take care of that."

Lily took in a gulp of air. Oh, her presence would take care of it, all right. It would squelch a lot of other things, too.

The front door thudded shut, and then came the sound of male voices.

"Well, it seems Reverend Crew and Mr. Forbes have returned." Papa slapped his palms on his knees, as if to pronounce the matter resolved, then pushed himself to his feet. Reaching for Lily's hands, he pulled her up, too. "Dry your eyes, now. If you hurry, you can put on a clean dress before we sit down to eat."

He was almost to the study door when Lily called out to him, "But, Papa, what about the Wiyot?"

His shoulders drooped slightly, and then he straightened himself and looked her squarely in the eye. "I'm afraid I don't have an answer for you, Lily-belle. The hornets' nest was shaken today. They're angry and ready to swarm. When and where is anybody's guess. I suggest we all pray for wisdom. And protection."

He closed the door behind him so quietly, it made no sound. Sinking back onto the scolding bench, Lily stared down at the floor. But it wasn't the swirling reds and browns of the Persian carpet she saw. It was a night a little more than a year ago, the sky alight with fire, the air resonating with screams. Would the events of today set in motion a repeat of that horrific night?

What had she done?

Chapter 12

Grant shoved a copy of *The Farmer and Emigrants Complete Guide* under his pillow. He'd borrowed it from the Rose library in the wee hours of the night. Though he had studied it until his eyes had gone, he still had no idea how to go about building a schoolhouse.

He pulled his shirt on. Better to just get it over with. Or maybe pray that they'd be rained out. He flung open the thick russet curtains. Sunlight bullied its way into the room, chasing away the shadows and dashing his hopes for a reprieve. Where was Lady Luck when he really needed her?

Growling and squinting, he turned from the window and went to splash water on his face. They didn't expect him to be a construction foreman. They wanted a preacher. He sighed. Too bad he was neither.

This had all been a very bad idea. He should have ridden right past that wagon. Should have found some way to support himself other than gambling. Should have arrived earlier that night and met Sarah before someone else could get to her. If he had, she wouldn't be dead, and none of this would be happening.

He threw the towel on the dresser next to the washbasin.

He should leave. He should creep away in the middle of the night, and to Hades with Forbes. Yes, the Pinkerton would piece together the facts and figure out his true identity. He finally knew what he looked like, which would give the Pink a distinct advantage. But he wouldn't know which way Grant had gone. He could head back East. Disappear into the crowd in any of its big cities.

That's exactly what he should do. And yet, he couldn't. It was due to his own stupidity that Abernathy was on the warpath. So, Grant would stay, compounding his stupidity and tossing in some dynamite, just for kicks. Because something within him would not leave these people to deal with his mess. That didn't mean he was happy about it.

Avoiding his own eyes in the mirror, Grant dressed in the missionary's dusty black, pulled on his boots, and slapped on his hat. He thundered down the stairs, propelled by his desire to be done with the whole matter and the dark clouds of his foul mood.

Lily looked up from her needlework as he entered the parlor. "Oh, Reverend. Good morning. Would you like some breakfast? I believe it's still laid out in the dining room."

"No," he snarled, instantly regretting it. Then, he was annoyed for feeling badly. Things were simpler all around when he cared for no one and no one cared for him. "Let's just go."

"Of course." She ignored his surliness and tidied up her sewing. "I had Joseph pull one of the carts around. I thought you would want to begin moving materials out to the build site."

"Oh, you did—"

"Morning." Forbes entered, wearing a smirk. That infernal, know-it-all, thinks-he's-perfect smirk.

A growl built in the back of Grant's throat. He turned away from the Pink.

Lily stood and shook out her skirts. The beatific smile she gave him as he took her hand to escort her outside shot a bolt of regret through him. It piled up with all the others he had accumulated.

"I was thinking it might be wise if I accompanied you all today," Forbes said. "Abernathy might turn up again, and we wouldn't want him getting any ideas."

The growl escaped.

Lily scowled, and for one blissful instant, he thought she might tell Carter to mind his own business.

"It's a pitiful shame we have to worry about a thug like Abernathy," she lamented instead. "Our sheriff is about as useful as a lace parasol in a hurricane. Ranchers like Abernathy voted him into office, knowing he wouldn't do a thing to rein them in." She stomped a foot, or at least Grant thought she did. He heard the sound, but her skirt scarcely moved. "Thank you, Mr. Forbes. It would be good to have another person along. One of these days, that man will receive his comeuppance, and I hope I'm there to see it."

Grant decided not to comment. The only things he could think to say would scorch Lily's fair ears.

He stomped out to the cart, all but hoisted Lily inside, and got the horse going while Forbes was still trying to clamber in back.

Lily gave him directions, and they headed away from town. It didn't take long for the forest to swallow them. The redwoods were enormous. Any one would be king of a regular forest. Many of them were well over two hundred feet tall. They stood on tiptoe, their limbs stretching toward heaven. Perhaps, in the ponderous way of trees, they were vying to see which would reach it first.

Sunlight lanced through the branches in shafts of brilliance. Homelier trees and shrubs bowed in the wind before their magnificent comrades. Grant swallowed. Such a place made a man feel suddenly small.

They pulled into the lumber mill yard. Activity swirled around them, as if they'd disturbed a beehive. Lily smiled graciously and nodded to the workmen, who doffed their caps and called out greetings. She was the princess of this land, that was certain.

She gestured toward an enormous shed. "Over there."

Grant stopped in front and set the brake. A passel of workers swarmed Lily's side of the cart. They assisted her down, and she greeted each one by name. "Mr. Forbes?" She nodded at the Pink, and he pulled a huge basket from the bed of the cart. "Gingerbread today, fellas."

Cheers followed her announcement. One of the men took the basket and began doling out the goodies, while Lily motioned for Grant to follow her.

She led the way inside, spreading her arms to emphasize the enormous size of the warehouse. "All this will go to build California."

Grant stood beside her. "Impressive."

She beamed. "Cured logs are this way."

One of the foremen came and carefully noted on a form which logs they wanted. By the time they were ready to leave the shed, a team of men had arrived to load up their order. Next, Lily led the way to a large workshop, where Grant received all manner of tools. Some he recognized; others, he could only guess as to their purpose.

They climbed back in the cart, now loaded with supplies, and took their leave. The workmen all but bowed as Lily rode by.

Grant cast her a sidelong glance. "It seems you're quite popular around here."

Lily flushed. "I think they were trying to show their support. I'm sure word of Abernathy's accusations has gotten all the way to Arcata by now."

"Sorry, I didn't mean—"

She waved a hand. "Think nothing of it. Others will do worse than remind me of the incident, I assure you."

Forbes leaned forward. "They won't say a word while I'm around. Not if they know what's good for them."

Grant slapped the reins against the horses' flanks. The increased pace precluded conversation. It was about all they could do to keep their heads from rattling off their necks.

Soon they reached the build site. High overhead, seagulls wheeled and dived. The tall grass whipped back and forth in the wind blowing off the ocean. Grant inhaled deeply. The clean, briny scent seemed to carry away some of the rankness within him. He raised his face to the sun and let it warm him.

A black-clad figure sat motionless in the middle of the property, facing away from them, apparently oblivious to their approach. As inconspicuously as possible, Grant unbuttoned his jacket for easier access to his sidearm.

The cart ground to a halt, and Grant hopped out. "Stay here, Miss Rose," he murmured.

The Pink was already at his side. Rather than argue with the man, Grant nodded, and they approached the rigid figure together.

Cautiously, they edged around in front of the man.

Grant cleared his throat. "Reverend Marsden?"

The pastor looked pitiful, mopping his forehead with a drenched handkerchief. His face was blotched red and purple, his eyes swollen from tears. Shakily, he stood. "You!"

Grant halted, his hand suspended near his hip. "What can we do for you, Reverend?"

"I knew it the minute I laid eyes on you. You're here to destroy me."

"I have no—"

"Oh, yes. Oh, yes. You want my church. Why build one for the heathen when you'll just allow them in with everyone else? Oh, it was an excuse for you, I suppose. A way to worm your way into town."

"Listen, friend. I want nothing to do with your church."

"Then why would you take my pulpit? I had half the town at my door today, praising you, while the other half wants to know why I *let* you enter my church. Like I had a choice. You took advantage of my weakness."

"Reverend!" Lily marched toward them, her skirts swinging like they'd been caught in a gale. "How dare you! These gentlemen put themselves out to preserve your good name in this town, and this is how you repay their kindness?"

She came as close to him as her skirts would allow and sniffed the air. "Just as I thought. You've been drinking again." She waved a finger under his nose. A dangerous gleam lit her eyes.

Grant took a step back, even though he wasn't the one who was prey to her wrath.

"You'd best take stock of your blessings and avoid attacking people without a thought in your head for what actually happened. Now, you go home and get sober. Eureka needs a pastor, not a drunk. They need a godly man to shepherd them." She poked her finger into his chest for emphasis. "And." Poke. "You're." Poke. "That." Poke. "Man."

He sniffled. "Miss Rose, this fellow is pulling the wool over your eyes."

Grant's throat went dry. How did he know, of all people?

Lily put her hands on her hips. "Reverend Marsden, I suggest you head home right now. I would hate to be unladylike."

The little man's eyes protruded even more than usual, and he drew himself up as tall as he could. "I'll prove it." And then, with as much dignity as he could muster, he turned. Staggered. Steadied himself. And headed back toward town on foot.

"Phew!" Forbes pushed his hat back on his head. "Miss Rose, if you're ever looking for employment, the Pinkertons could use a lady like you."

Lily turned to him, her mouth open to say something, but then she pursed her lips, seeming to think better of it. Some of tension left her posture. "Perhaps, one day, I may take you up on that, Mr. Forbes."

Grant headed for the wagon. Miss Lily Rose was the most spirited young woman he'd ever come across. The way those brown eyes had crackled with fire and bite, she'd been positively...well, there was no other word for it. She'd been beautiful.

He lifted a long saw, a hammer, and a keg of nails from the wagon bed. They ought to make a shed of some kind to store the tools in overnight. No use inviting theft. And it might be good construction practice.

Grant glanced up and froze. Over the rise, half a dozen Indian men approached on foot. There was no way he could get to Lily before they reached her. He dropped the saw and started forward anyway.

Lily looked up and raised a hand in greeting. Air forced its way back into Grant's lungs. The men weren't a threat. He slowed, thinking about returning to the wagon, but instead he walked to meet the Indians.

The Wiyot stopped a good ten feet away. A white-haired man with joints twisted by rheumatism raised a hand. "Miss Rose, it is good to see you. We thank you for driving away the demon."

A shadow passed over Lily's face. She bowed her head slightly. "That was no demon, just a very confused drunk man."

He inclined his head at her words, but it was clear he wasn't buying her story.

Lily waved toward Grant. "John Long Tongue, this is Reverend Crew. He is here to teach the children to read and to teach you all about the Great Creator, Jesus."

"Welcome, Reverend. I have brought men to help with the building."

Grant bowed in greeting. "John Long Tongue, I must warn you that a rancher, Abernathy, is on the warpath. He does not like it that I am here."

"Abernathy does not want peace."

Lily spoke again. "It may be dangerous."

The old man looked at her with an inscrutable expression in his eyes. "Lily Rose, it is dangerous for us simply to breathe in this place. We will not be safe until we can move in the white man's world as more than servants. This is a good thing you do to teach the children. We will help."

"Fair enough." Grant stepped forward and handed over the hammer. "We can use all the help we can get." A twinge in his gut gave him warning. Abernathy and his galoots were going to be as sore as skinned polecats. They wouldn't sit back and allow things to continue on as they were. Trouble was brewing, and he didn't know if there was a thing he could do to stop it.

Chapter 13

Lily pushed her sleeves up to her elbows. She fanned herself ineffectually, sighed, and plucked out her handkerchief. As daintily as she could manage, she dabbed away the perspiration on her forehead. Mama would insist that she call it "dew," but it sure felt more like sweat than anything else. Of course, Mama would also be upset that she was toiling in the sun without a parasol.

Lily would just have to push to get the school completed before her mother returned. She would never understand why Lily had to be involved in a direct manner. Mama didn't mind being a figurehead for a cause, but working alongside a bunch of Indian men would be another thing altogether.

Lily massaged the back of her neck. She hadn't worked this hard since.... She'd never worked this hard.

At least she had something to show for her labors. With her fists planted on her hips, she circled the ramshackle little shed. It was no Sistine Chapel, but it looked like it would keep the tools safe and dry. That is, if the wind didn't blow too hard. Maybe.

The reverend glanced up. "What?" A ferocious scowl shoved away his usually good-humored expression.

"I'm...um...just checking our progress."

"Well, I'm sorry I'm no carpenter." For some reason, the reverend seemed intent on taking offense at her scrutiny.

Lily stepped back. Maybe he was of a like mind with her mother and preferred that she not take a hand in the building.

Carter smiled a peacemaker's smile. "Jesus was a carpenter. I'd have thought it'd come natural."

"He was also the Son of God, and I'm not that, either."

"What kind of theology is that for a parson?" Carter laughed and squeezed Crew's shoulder. "We're all called sons by adoption through the Spirit, aren't we?"

A muscle ticked in the preacher's jaw.

The Wiyot were watching with interest, their hammering and sawing diminishing until a hush settled over them.

For just a second, Reverend Crew closed his eyes. When he opened them again, a charming smile came across his features like jam spread with a knife. "Yes, I suppose we are." He must have been praying for his good humor to return.

Lily reached out to pluck a splinter from the half-formed shed. "Wouldn't it be amazing to own something that Jesus made? To know that His hands had planed the wood and fitted the pieces together?"

"That's an interesting thought, Miss Rose." Carter held a board in place while an Indian man pounded in the nails. "In a way, I suppose we do. The Bible says we are His workmanship. What's that reference, Reverend?"

Now the Reverend's smile was thin, as if someone had tried to spread the jam too far. "Can't recall off the top of my head. Somewhere in the New Testament, I'd say."

"Sure." Carter nodded. "That sounds right."

Lily turned from one man to the other, searching for the source of the hostility between them. She couldn't figure it out. They were both such good men. She couldn't believe Carter's persistent hunch that Reverend Crew might really be that awful Diamond.

Maybe the men were too much alike.

Her reverie was shattered by the clamor of a half-dozen Wiyot children running over the rise. Their youthful voices fluted on the air like the warble of birds.

Lily smiled at their high spirits. Someone around here needed to be cheerful. The children lugged along baskets loaded with clams and roasted wapato.

Her stomach growled at the thought of food. A wonderful idea. If a good lunch didn't put everyone in a better frame of mind, nothing would. Lily retrieved a blanket from the cart and unfurled it on the ground, then spread out their own provisions of roast beef sandwiches, pickles, oatmeal cookies, and a big jar of fresh apple cider.

The Wiyot men hung back, clustering together. Lily waved them closer. "John Long Tongue, you must join us! This schoolhouse is meant to bring the whites and the Wiyot together, not to separate us."

He nodded, then gestured for his men to follow him. They settled awkwardly along the perimeter of the blanket, staring at Lily's delicacies with crinkled noses.

One of the children handed Carter a wapato. He accepted and then, with a startled grunt, tossed it from hand to hand. He looked at Lily. "What is it?"

"Wapato. It's like a potato. Very good. They roast them in the fire."

He nodded, blowing on his fingers.

They made a party of the meal, passing and sampling items all around. The sandwiches were nodded over, but the children screwed up their faces and plugged their noses at the pickles. They devoured the cookies, though, and Lily made sure everyone received at least one.

The tension of the morning relaxed, just as she'd hoped it would. Genuine smiles blossomed on every face, and the men chatted easily with one another. The children's presence helped even more than the food. They were unself-conscious and delighted with their adventure.

Lily watched Reverend Crew with an adorable girl of three or four. He teased her with a cookie, holding it just out of reach. The child grabbed for the treat, and he pulled it back further still. With enormous dark eyes, she watched him as she reached once more. He howled when she succeeded in swiping his snack. The girl fell over in a fit of giggles. He swung her up, tickling her belly.

The other children piled on his back, and he was soon lying prone in the grass.

"Help!" he garbled, breathless and laughing.

"I'm afraid you've made your bed and now must lie in it." Lily's attempt to suppress her smile was only partially successful.

Old John Long Tongue said a few words in the Wiyot language, and the children jumped away from Reverend Crew, then scampered back toward home.

"The children like you, Preacher. But you will need to discipline them to make them respect you so they may learn."

The reverend straightened his severe black coat and nodded gravely.

The shed didn't take long to complete. With great ceremony, all of the tools were placed inside and the door padlocked.

Carter brushed the dirt from his hands. "Well, gentlemen, I feel like we've done a good day's work."

Reverend Crew tilted his head and regarded the shed with an expression of almost paternal pride. "It sure looks like it might be a shed. If you squint."

Carter chuckled. "Aw, now, it isn't as bad as all that. I think we did quite well for our first time trying to build something. Maybe you've got some of the Nazarene Carpenter's skills in you, after all." He clapped the preacher on the back.

During the ride back into town, they chatted about their plans for the following day. Lily mostly listened. She was glad that the tension between the two men seemed to have dissipated, for the most part.

On Main Street, they passed old Mrs. Henderson, and Lily nodded politely. "Good day, Mrs. Henderson."

The woman walked right on by. Lily licked her lips. The poor woman *was* hard of hearing. Surely, that explained her dismissive behavior.

Mrs. Capshaw, a tall woman with narrow shoulders and a fluttery, inappropriately delicate dress, was coming out of the General Store with her daughter.

Lily greeted them both, but Mrs. Capshaw gave her a pointed look and then, cutting off her daughter's polite response, jerked the girl around and started marching her in the opposite direction.

Well, there was no mistaking that.

Lily's cheeks ached from the effort of holding her smile in place. Her throat felt like it did that time she'd had the influenza and had been barely able to swallow for days. She stared straight ahead. Mrs. Capshaw should hardly be one to cast stones. The woman hadn't even been married to the miner with whom she'd moved to Eureka.

What would Mama say when she returned and found the likes of Hester Capshaw turning up her nose at their family?

Carter Forbes touched her shoulder. "Don't pay them any mind, Miss Rose. The truth has a way of coming out."

But he wasn't looking at her as he spoke. He was looking at the reverend.

⌣

Carter tapped the side of the cart. "I'm going to hop off here. I'll walk back later. Afternoon, Miss Rose." He tipped his hat, then stood and jumped out of the lumbering cart.

He waited until his ride had turned the corner before he moseyed across the street to the sheriff's office.

Van Nest didn't bother to stand as he entered, but at least he removed his feet from the desktop. "What can I do for you, Pink?" The words came out in a slow, sticky drawl.

"Afternoon, Sheriff. I'm wondering, is there a telegraph office in town? I need some information from back East."

Van Nest snorted. "Closest telegraph lines to us are down to San Francisco or out Sacramento way."

Carter sighed. He'd figured as much.

"We got a post office. If you can write."

Carter smiled at the attempted barb. "Thought you should know about a character named Abernathy. He interrupted a church service yesterday. Made quite a scene and even tried to sully the reputation of an upstanding young lady."

Van Nest leaned back in his chair. His eyes flickered over the desk, as if he longed to prop his feet back up, but he forbore. "That's unfortunate." He scratched under his armpit. "But it's hardly a matter for the law."

Carter's patience was growing thinner than the hair on the sheriff's head. "From one law enforcer to another, that fellow is trouble. I suggest you keep an eye on him and keep him away from decent folk."

Van Nest's chair legs returned to the ground with a thump. "I've been sheriff around here for a good long while without the help of a fancy private detective. If I want your advice, I'll ask for it."

Carter tipped his hat and banged the door shut behind him. Van Nest was all wrong. That fellow was crookeder than a corkscrew, and he didn't even care if everybody knew it.

Carter marched over to the General Store and bought a pad of paper and a box of pencils. He sat at the checkers table to write out his request. He'd have to mail the letter to the Pinkerton office in Chicago and have them telegraph the request from there. He ground his teeth.

This case had turned into a bottomless pit. He wanted to get home to Emily. And he wanted to work more closely with Mr. Pinkerton. He had so much to learn.

He scribbled out a request that an inquiry be made with the Massachusetts Mission Society about all particulars regarding one Hubert Crew. The man puzzled him. At times, he seemed as genuine as a six-dollar bill, while, at other times, Carter downright liked him.

Would the fellow really go through the trouble of building a school for Indian children if he were a swindler about to blow town? It wasn't like he'd taken up an offering to construct the building. What was in it for him?

The man was truly troubling.

～

Grant rolled out of bed with a groan. Building that shed had taken it out of him, and that had been a mere four-foot square. How did he hope to undertake the construction of an entire schoolhouse?

He whimpered as he splashed some water on his face. He managed to dress, despite his aching muscles, and proceeded down to breakfast. He could leave anytime he wanted. Just up and disappear into the wilderness. He tucked the knowledge up his sleeve like a spare ace and maintained a civilized act through the meal.

When they were all loaded into the cart, he let Carter take the reins and drive them out to the site. Used to be, he could stay up most of the night gambling, then spring from bed as bright as a counterfeit nickel the next morning. Now, here he was, living the blameless life of a preacher, and he was tuckered out.

Leaning against the side of the buckboard, he had nearly dozed off when a gasp from Lily raised the hair on his neck and made him sit up and take notice.

They had reached the building site, and the shed was gone.

All that remained were shattered bits of planking and a few loose nails. It had been pillaged so thoroughly, the structure didn't even remotely resemble a building. The tools were gone. The only thing left intact was the padlock, sitting pristine atop the mound of rubble.

Grant swore under his breath and kicked the padlock a good five yards. Every time he tried to create something good, other people tore it down. Stole the heart right out of it and discarded it. Why did he even bother?

Someone would pay for this.

Lily's tremulous voice pulled him from his seething rage. "Dear God, don't let there have been another massacre." She whirled around and sprinted toward the village.

Massacre? Grant exchanged glances with Forbes. What had they gotten themselves into?

Chapter 14

Lily lifted the front of her skirt to keep from tripping on fabric or hoop stays as she ran. Smoke wafted over the rise, but was it from cook fires or something more sinister? All she could think of was the scene she'd found on Indian Island last year. She blinked madly, trying to erase the pictures from the chalkboard of her mind. The memory of a desperate baby's wail reverberated in her head, merging with the lowing of the wind, blocking out all other sounds.

She crested the hill. Below, children ran around, women tended their meals, and old men sat in the sun. Relief weakened her knees. Her fears had been unfounded. There was nothing to worry about.

Nothing but her blasted, fashionable skirt. Even though Lily had skidded to a stop, the skirt had retained its momentum, its hoop belling forward and thumping into the back of her calves. She bobbled, tilted, then pitched over the embankment.

The world spun as she tumbled down the bluff. The wind was driven from her lungs. Her head crashed against something hard. Flashes of light sparked behind her eyelids. At last, she came to rest at the bottom of the hill. She lay on her side, stunned and unable to move. She tried to breathe, her mouth gaping like a landed fish, but she couldn't seem to draw a breath. A bubble of panic expanded in her chest where air should have been. She clutched her throat. An eternity passed before her lungs recalled their purpose. No sooner had she gulped in a lungful of air than she began to cough and retch.

She rolled onto her back, wincing as a needle of pain shot through her temple. Blurry figures approached her, calling her name. Lily squeezed her eyes shut, blocking out the commotion. Why were they so loud?

Lily managed a smile. "The Indians...they're all right."

"The question is, are you?"

She would have recognized that voice anywhere, but the concern that rumbled in it was something new. Forcing her eyes open, she found Reverend Crew looming over her.

"I did it again," she said mournfully.

"Did what?"

"Ruined another dress." A new, extremely important idea crowded into her brain, and her eyes opened wider. "I've been addressing you as 'Reverend,' but if you studied at Harvard, should I be calling you 'Doctor'? Do you have a doctorate?"

Mr. Forbes now bent over her, as well, kneeling shoulder to shoulder beside the reverend. The Pinkerton turned expectantly, awaiting the clergyman's answer.

Reverend Crew scowled. "I'm certainly not the kind of doctor you need at this moment." He reached out, brushing the hair from her face. She winced as his fingertips touched her temple.

When he pulled away, his fingers were red with blood. Her blood. Lily's stomach lurched, and she moved an impossibly heavy hand to feel the wound.

Carter caught her wrist. "Ah, ah."

She frowned, trying to pull her hand away, but Carter did not relent.

"Your hand is dirty," he said. "Let me." He took a clean handkerchief from the inside pocket of his vest. Though he dabbed gently at the wound, Lily hissed through clenched teeth as spots filled her vision.

Carter looked as pained as she felt, but he continued doing what had to be done. "Do you think you can sit up, Miss Rose?"

"I should be able to."

She shifted her weight, intending to push up on one elbow, but Reverend Crew stopped her with a firm hand on her shoulder. "Not so fast. How many of me do you see?"

"Just one. Why? How many of you are there?" At his sour look, she sighed and waved a hand at him. "Oh, don't look at me like that. I'm teasing. I'll be fine."

A handful of Wiyot children arrived, followed by most of the camp. They chattered and tittered over Lily. Hands reached out—whether the Pinkerton's or the reverend's, she had no idea—and helped steady her until she was able to sit up without toppling back over. Heat flooded her cheeks. Why did everything she touched turn into a disaster? Why couldn't she be dignified and graceful, like Mama?

"You're going to have quite the mouse," said Reverend Crew.

Lily cocked her head.

"A black eye."

"Yes, I suppose so," she mumbled, fending off the efforts of the Indians to make her lie back down.

Reverend Crew touched her arm. "Don't worry about the shed. We'll rebuild it."

"But what if they come to knock it down again?"

"I'll stay here and guard it."

"You can't do that alone."

Carter looked from the reverend to her and then back again. "I'll stay, too. But first, we need to talk. What was that you said—"

"Not now." Lily felt suddenly sick to her stomach, in a way that had nothing to do with her Jack-and-Jill impersonation. "When we are alone again."

The Wiyot women took over, helping her to her feet and supporting her as she walked to the camp, where she was made to sit down and drink some sort of herbal tea. It wasn't unpleasant, but it left a strange tingle on her tongue. Meanwhile, the men went to examine the damage to the shed. None of the Wiyot had seen or heard a thing from the other side of the ridge. But they had learned long ago to stay close to camp at night.

Carter drove the wagon around. Gravely solicitous, he and Reverend Crew helped Lily into the conveyance.

"I'm sorry to put you to trouble, gentlemen," she murmured.

From his seat behind her, the reverend patted her back reassuringly. "It's no trouble. We can't begin work on the school now, anyway. Not until we find more materials. We're just lucky all the wood hadn't been delivered."

"Lucky?" Carter glanced over his shoulder, one eyebrow arched. "I'd expect a man of the cloth to credit the good Lord and His providence, not luck."

Reverend Crew's hand froze on Lily's back, and then he yanked it away. "It's a figure of speech. Of course, the Lord gets the credit."

Lily didn't have to see his face to know he had spoken through clenched teeth. Before another cross word could be said, she changed the subject. "Papa will be furious when he hears what's happened. He'll provide all we require to complete the job."

"Perhaps he will prefer to leave well enough alone," Reverend Crew said.

Lily stiffened. "We must not let evil men have their way. No one believes that more firmly than my father."

"I think you owe us an explanation." Carter angled his head at Lily, piercing her with his gaze. "What did you mean by 'another' massacre?"

Lily sighed. She'd put off the telling as long as she could. The remains of the tea suddenly tasted bitter in her mouth. It didn't help that the jouncing of the wagon made her head feel like it might topple off at any second, and she half wished that it would, as she groped for the words to explain. She opened her mouth, found that she hadn't yet found them, and closed it again.

"Miss Rose, just tell us what happened."

The reverend's gentle voice stilled some of her anxiety. He was right. There was nothing to do but tell the tale. And no better place to start than at the beginning.

"For hundreds, maybe even thousands, of years, the Wiyot lived on Indian Island. They had other villages, but that was their home." She pointed over the water to a green strip out in Humboldt Bay. "But ever since gold was discovered around here, men have been treating the Wiyot like they are less than animals. Just over a year ago, Hank Larabee raised a local militia he called the Humboldt Volunteers. They were more like a gang. A vicious, monstrous gang." Lily wasn't sure she could go on. She stared out at the now-abandoned island.

〜

Unthinking, Grant placed a hand on Lily's shoulder. She did not shrug away, appalled at his immodesty, but instead glanced back almost gratefully.

As if drawing courage from the contact, she continued. "One night, while the Wiyot men were away for one of their religious ceremonies, Hank Larabee led his men to the island and...and slaughtered the women and children, and the few old men who were too weak to leave the camp for the ceremony."

Grant straightened. It was worse than he'd thought. Killers like that wouldn't hesitate to murder a white man guarding a shack.

"It was all my fault."

Grant blinked.

Forbes turned and looked at her. "How do you reckon that?"

"Earlier that day, I had overheard Larabee talking about plans for the Wiyot, but I was too stupid and self-centered to understand. I could have saved them if I had given them a warning, but I didn't lift a finger." Her voice broke, and tears scored paths down her dirty cheeks. Tears. She hadn't cried after nearly killing herself in that tumble down the hill, but the memory of a transgression for which she was not responsible reduced her to sobs.

Forbes patted his pockets, but he'd put his handkerchief to use earlier. Grant handed his over.

Miss Rose wiped her cheeks, smearing the dirt. "I went the next morning to visit one of my Indian friends, and they were all dead. All of them. Murdered brutally with knives and hatchets, so as not to rouse the town with the sounds of gunfire." She trembled, the words growing indistinct as she battled against her tears. Then, she continued, "There was only one survivor. A baby. His mama hid him in some bushes. He was crying so pitifully, and I held him, but I was no help to him at all. When others arrived from town, they took him right out of my arms. They knew what to do for him. But I was so…useless."

"What happened to the killers?" asked Forbes.

"Not a blessed thing." She drew in a deep breath and sniffed, finally stemming the flow of tears.

"They weren't brought to justice?" Forbes sounded shocked.

"Larabee had the local judge, Huestis, in his pocket, and Sheriff Van Nest did anything Larabee told him to."

"Where is Larabee now?" Grant asked.

"He was run out of town over some disagreement with another white man. But Rick Abernathy has set himself up to take Larabee's place. He never misses an opportunity to stir up fresh hatred against the Indians."

Grant winced. A hornets' nest. That's what he'd managed to land himself in this time. A giant, buzzing, stinging mass of trouble. Every time he turned around, things got worse. And, for the foreseeable future, he'd be bedding down next to a Pinkerton. There was no question that God had it in for him.

⌒

Carter drove Miss Rose home and insisted she receive a doctor's care. Yet she refused to send the houseboy for the local medico until she'd penned a letter to her father's foreman at the lumberyard, requesting more supplies.

By the time he and the reverend drove out to the lumberyard, loaded their supplies, and returned to town, it was evening. The journey was largely silent, with the reverend rebuffing all of Carter's conversational gambits. He might have tried harder to pry, but he just couldn't summon any enthusiasm for the task. He didn't much feel like talking, himself. Outside the Rose home, not a single light indicated habitation.

The men exchanged glances. Apparently, the Roses had retired for the night. Crew jerked his chin toward the coast. Carter nodded and flicked the reins, heading back to the building site, where they would bed down until the work was done. He wasn't sure about the reverend, but Carter planned to sleep with his loaded pistol close at hand.

They remained vigilant over the next several days, but no trouble came calling—at least, none but that for which they themselves were responsible as they tried to figure out how to build a schoolhouse.

On the fourth morning, Miss Rose arrived with her father. One of her eyes was ringed by a vivid green-purple, and her exposed skin bore an assortment of other scrapes and bruises, so much so that she looked as if she'd been in a barroom brawl. Before either Carter or the reverend could reach the pair, Mr. Rose had helped his daughter from their carriage. She descended gingerly, her movements stiff, but it seemed there would be no permanent injuries from her fall.

When Miss Rose was safely on the ground, her father clasped his hands behind his back and faced them. "Well, gentlemen. It looks like you're making progress."

Carter glanced back at the scant beams they had placed. Progress, yes, but not much of it.

Mr. Rose seemed to concur. "Am I right in thinking that divinity school and detective work have not provided instruction in the finer points of building construction?"

Reverend Crew scratched his chin. "Yes, sir, I believe that's a fair bet."

"I thought as much." Mr. Rose strolled to the building and began a closer inspection. "I don't see space for a door."

"I—we were trying to make certain the base was strong." Crew turned as red as a brick.

"Did you use the square and a plumb line?" Mr. Rose turned on Carter.

"Papa." Miss Rose sounded agitated.

Mr. Rose waved to silence her.

Carter shrugged. "I wouldn't recognize a plumb line if I saw one, sir."

"Well, gentlemen, I don't want a second set of tools and materials going to waste. If it's all the same to you, I'll be sending a man or two to help oversee this process."

The reverend's eyebrows rose. "Thank you, sir. I appreciate it."

"Protecting my investment in this project, Reverend. That's all."

"Well, I'm not too proud to say the help is more than welcome; it is needed."

Mr. Rose clapped Crew on the back. "I like your attitude. There's no shame in not knowing what you've had no opportunity to learn."

The reverend turned to Lily. "I hope you are fully recovered, Miss Rose?"

A smile transformed her face. "Oh, I'm as fine as could be. I would have come out here sooner, but Papa wouldn't hear of it. I do hope you have at least received the provisions I sent."

Carter patted his stomach. "Oh, yes. Joseph has kept us well supplied."

"That is something, I suppose." She sighed. "I feel terrible that I invited you both to stay with us, and yet you have wound up sleeping out in the open. I do hope you will allow me—us—to help today."

Mr. Rose had already removed his suit coat and was rolling up his shirtsleeves.

Crew stepped in smoothly, placing his body between Carter and the young lady. "Only if you promise not to overdo it, Miss Rose. We don't want you getting injured again."

Her cheeks flushed a pretty shade of pink, and she glanced at the ground. "No fear, Reverend. I even dressed for the occasion."

It was then that Carter realized she wasn't wearing any hoops. Her dress was exceedingly simple, with the skirt's hem almost scandalously high, ending as it did just below her ankles. Sensible boots protected those appendages from prying eyes. She pulled off her bonnet, revealing that her hair was bound up neatly in a scarf. She then wrapped an apron around her waist and fastened the strings with a neat bow in front.

She caught Carter watching her and shrugged in response. "It's an old dress, and I've grown since I wore it last. Now," she put her fists on her hips and surveyed the area, "what would you like me to do?"

They worked through the afternoon, following Mr. Rose's precise instructions. In no time, they settled into a comfortable rhythm, chatting sporadically. For some reason, Lily's reappearance had eased the paralysis that had seemed to grip Carter's voice. Reverend Crew seemed to experience the same palliative effect. And Carter found a revival in his desire to learn more about the reverend, just when he'd begun to think he might be wasting his time here while Diamond was getting farther and farther ahead of him. The reverend hadn't shown the least inclination to make a run for it. Of course, the fellow hadn't done any praying or cracked open that Bible of his, either.

The sun was low on the horizon when Carter stood and surveyed their work. They'd accomplished more that day than in the previous four combined. Behind him, the reverend said something that provoked hearty laughter from Miss Rose, making Carter smile, even though he didn't know what had prompted her merriment.

"Lily Gardenia Rose!" Another female voice rang out in shrill consternation. "What *are* you doing? And *what* are you wearing?"

Chapter 15

Lily's mouth couldn't have gone drier had she been standing in the middle of the Sahara, sipping sand from a teacup. "Mama?"

Dorothea Rose was several inches shorter than her daughter, but, standing ramrod straight, her shoulder blades pinched together and her chin lifted high, she seemed to tower over Lily. Certain of the tongue-lashing to come, Lily steeled herself, but she was greeted with something far worse: stone-cold silence.

Lily tried to swallow as her mind raced. Surely, if she explained the situation, Mama would understand. But where to start? "Mama, I...we...." She wrung her hands, then dropped them at her sides in defeat. "I wasn't expecting you."

Mama inclined her head ever so slightly. "That much is obvious."

The rumble of a throat being cleared sounded behind Lily, and her father stepped up beside her. Hope sparked in her chest. If anyone could make Mama understand, he could. He leaned closer to give her a kiss, and she presented a cheek for his offering. "Dorothea, dear. It's good to have you home at last."

"I wish I could say I'm glad to be home, but, truth be told, I was not at all happy to be summoned, only to be greeted by this… display." Her eyes once again inspected Lily, from the top of her kerchief-bound head to the toes of her scuffed boots.

"Now, Dorothea, don't be too hard on her. There'd be no sense in wearing one of those fancy frocks to work on a building site."

"She shouldn't be present at any building site, let alone working on one. She has no business at all venturing out in public in such a state." She turned on Lily. "You look like a common field hand. And whatever happened to your face?" She reached out to brush a gentle hand over her bruises.

Lily's cheeks burned. She longed to appease her mother, to say something that would erase the worry and disapproval from her face. But it was hopeless. The only thing Mama would deem worse than finding Lily in such a state would be discovering that she had gone full steam ahead with her quest to help the Indians. The best course of action would be to apologize and get her mother away as soon as possible.

"I'm sorry, Mama. I took a tumble down the bluff, but I'll be mended in no time. And there isn't anyone around here to see. I—"

"Good afternoon."

Lily's stomach sank as she turned her head in the direction of the voice. *Oh, no.* Reverend Crew walked toward them, followed closely by Carter. Apparently, one or both of them believed they could reason with her mother. They had no idea who they were dealing with.

Dorothea looked at the men, her mouth pulling up into the faint, polite smile she reserved for barely tolerable company. "And who might you gentlemen be?"

"I'm Reverend Hubert Crew, and this is Mr. Carter Forbes."

"*Detective* Carter Forbes," Carter added.

Lily's father jerked a thumb in Carter's direction. "He's an honest-to-goodness Pinkerton agent."

"How wonderful," Mama said in a voice so flat, there was no doubt as to the depth of her interest.

"Yes. Well." Reverend Crew once again took hold of the conversation. "Mrs. Rose, I'm afraid your daughter's *state*, as you put it, is our fault."

Lily's eyes grew wide. *No! Please, don't say another word.*

Mama looked from one man to the other. "Is that so?"

Reverend Crew must have realized how inappropriate his remark had come across. "Only in a manner of speaking, ma'am. The circumstances being what they are...what we're trying to accomplish here...."

He stammered to a halt, looking completely mortified. Lily wished she could console him, let him know he wasn't the first man Mama had shut down with a look. At least he knew when to cut his losses and stop talking.

"There's a logical explanation, Mrs. Rose." Unfortunately, Detective Forbes hadn't learned that lesson yet. The Pinkerton stepped forward, his hands locked behind his back, as if preparing to present a case before a jury. "The reverend and I are building a school for the Indians. Rather than sit idly by, your daughter has been assisting in whatever way she's been able."

Lily held back a groan. Was there no way to keep these men from saying the wrong things? Forbes undoubtedly thought her mother would be proud when presented with her daughter's determination to assist the Indians. He couldn't know that this information would have the opposite effect. Only one thing would be worse.

"Miss Rose has been quite helpful," Reverend Crew added. "But after she took a tumble down the hill the other day, we're all very glad she decided to forgo those hoops on the building site."

He chuckled at his joke, but the sound died in his throat beneath Mama's withering gaze. "Gentlemen." She dismissed them with a curt nod, then turned to her husband. "Benjamin, I am taking our daughter home. We shall discuss this tonight."

No one spoke another word. Lily's shoulders sagged as she followed her mother to the wagon. It was over. The worst had happened, and now she would have to endure the wrath to come.

⌒

Grant had once found himself stranded in a Nebraska blizzard. The biting, bone-numbing cold was something he would never forget. He'd never been as chilled before or since.

Until today.

As soon as the wagon was out of sight, Benjamin Rose exhaled a long breath. "That, gentlemen, was my dear wife."

Behind him, Forbes gave the appropriate answer. "She's lovely, sir."

That was partly true. Physically, Mrs. Rose was a striking woman. Her rich, amber-colored eyes were emphasized by her pale, smooth skin. She carried herself with grace and dignity, managing her hoopskirt so well that it seemed a natural extension of her body. Grant couldn't imagine her ever becoming stuck in doors or knocking unsuspecting men into the mud.

Carter elbowed him in the ribs. "What are you grinning at?"

"Me? Nothing." The lie flowed easily. It wouldn't do to admit he'd been reliving his first encounter with Lily—or how much he relished the memory. "I was just thinking that Mr. Rose must be happy to have his wife home. It is not good for a man to be alone." Grant couldn't recall whether the quote was from the Scriptures or from Shakespeare. Either way, it sounded like something a preacher would say.

Mr. Rose nodded slowly. "Yes, it's good to have my family back together again. I only wish Dorothea hadn't found Lily here. She's a stickler for propriety, and sometimes I fear she's a bit too hard on Lily-belle." He rubbed the back of his neck and chuckled. "Of course, I'm far too lenient with her, so I suppose we balance each other out. Between the two of us, Lily should turn out just fine."

Or she'd turn out a conflicted mess. The man's logic stirred something in Grant, and he found himself beginning to understand the enigma that was Miss Rose.

～

The twenty-minute ride from the building site to Rose Cottage felt more like a two-hour trek. Mama wouldn't so much as look at Lily, although Lily made a couple of feeble attempts at conversation.

"How was your trip, Mama?"

Silence.

"I hope Aunt Gertrude is feeling better."

Silence.

"Did you get to some nice shops in San Francisco?"

Silence.

"The plants in the greenhou—conservatory are doing just fine."

Silence, accompanied by a suspicious sidewise glance.

Poor Joseph broke into nervous whistling more than once, only to stifle himself. His anxiety must have traveled from his hands through the reins and to the horses, for they tossed their heads and complained more than usual. Lily didn't know which would be worse: her anticipation of the verbal lashing to come or the actual event.

Immediately upon arriving at home, she had her answer.

"I knew it was a mistake to leave you alone!" her mother declared after descending from the carriage. "However, after all the progress we'd made, I truly believed you'd begun to grasp what it means to act like a lady."

Lily took up the rear as her mother breezed into the house. How did Mama do it? Even now, in an obviously agitated state, she carried herself with such grace. Her skirts appeared to hover across the floor, giving the impression that she didn't walk as much as glide. With a delicate tug, Mama undid the perfect bow beneath her chin, removed her bonnet, and hung it on the hat tree. She passed a hand over her neat chignon, although nary a hair was out of place. "Honestly, Lily, what were you thinking?"

Lily opened her mouth to answer, but she didn't have a chance to utter a syllable before Mama ranted on.

"Clearly, you weren't thinking at all. This is yet another instance where your enthusiasm has gotten the better of you. You rush headlong into things with no consideration of the consequences."

Regret churned in Lily's stomach. Mama had no idea how often she stopped to consider the consequences of her actions. But, no matter what she did, however carefully she thought things through, the results were always wrong. "On the contrary, Mama, I haven't rushed into anything. You opposed my desire to teach the Indian children, and so we agreed that I would request that the missionary society send someone. That someone is Reverend Crew, Mama—a kindly preacher who doesn't know the first thing about construction. Why, he'd never even framed a door before. I was just doing what I could to help with the building. And I knew I'd be of no help in a hoopskirt. I just can't manage them like you can. I'll have you know that this was the longest old gown I could find."

Mama ignored the rush of words, removing her gloves with a dainty tug on each fingertip. She gripped Lily's chin and turned her face toward the light. "Has the doctor come to see you?"

"Yes, Mama."

"How long did he say it would take to clear up?"

"A week or two."

"We shall have to make do until then, I suppose." She sighed. "Naomi!" Somehow she managed to project her voice without screaming.

A moment later, Naomi hurried into the room. "Welcome home, missus." Naomi smiled at her mother, and then her eyes grew wide when she caught a glimpse of Lily standing in the doorway.

"Thank you, Naomi."

The maid looked back at Mama. "Are you hungry, missus? Thirsty? Would you like me to draw you a bath?"

"A bath is in order, but not for me." Mama turned back to Lily, her brows drawn together. "You'll have to soak in buttermilk for days to erase all the freckling." She reached out and unrolled Lily's sleeves so that they covered her arms entirely. Well, almost entirely. Even at their full length, the sleeves were a touch short and left a band of wrist showing. Mama shook her head. "First, we need to scrape off all this grime. I know my handsome daughter is under there somewhere."

Naomi looked over Mama's shoulder, communicating silent sympathy to Lily. "Of course, missus."

Lily knew exactly what "handsome" meant. It was the word used for someone who wasn't pretty but who could, with much work and concentration, become passably attractive. It was a word with which Lily had become well acquainted over the years.

"Come along, Lily."

Mama swept past Naomi and strode upstairs, expecting her daughter to follow close behind. Which is exactly what Lily did.

For the moment, at least, all of her fight was gone.

Chapter 16

Carter leaned back against the seat of the cart, removed his hat, and wiped his forehead with his arm. "It was kind of you to invite us to stay with you folks again."

Mr. Rose nodded. "Certainly, certainly. And don't you worry about the site. Those men of mine are good guards. They won't let anything happen to the schoolhouse."

Carter suspected that Mr. Rose's invitation had been strategic, designed to dissuade Mrs. Rose from interrogating him too eagerly. But, all the same, a hot bath and a soft bed sounded mighty good after three nights of roughing it. His mouth watered at the idea of another supper from the Roses' cook.

As the first straggling evidence of Eureka came into view, it occurred to him that he hadn't gone to town to see whether he'd received a response to his query about information regarding the reverend. And, come to think of it, the reverend had been mighty quiet ever since being put so firmly in his place by Mrs. Rose. It seemed that few ladies could resist his charm, and her blatant disregard must have come as a rude shock.

Carter grinned.

Crew angled him a glance, but Carter just broadened his grin and adjusted his hat.

Yep, it was early yet, but he'd need to come into town in the next day or so to see if there was any word about the reverend.

⌒

Lily's scalp hurt from the too-tight chignon pulling her hair at the roots, held in place by at least two dozen hairpins, all bent on drawing blood. She reached with a hand, trying to adjust the worst offender. Mama caught her and smacked her hand away.

"Honestly, Lily! You act as if you're still six."

Lily glared at her mother's reflection in the glass, watching her deftly unwind another strand from the curling iron and strategically position it against Lily's cheek.

"Don't sulk, Lily."

"I'm not sulking, Mama." Yet her voice undermined her efforts and sounded sulky, even to Lily's own ears.

Mama stepped around the chair and sank to her knees, her skirts puddling in graceful folds around her. "Lily-belle, I know you think I am too harsh. But I worry about you. What will become of you if I let you run wild? You'll never find a husband and have a home of your own. I don't want you to end up lonely. Or worse. Helping the Wiyot is dangerous. Your father's money can provide a great deal, but it can't stop evil men from doing evil things. I don't want you getting hurt."

Lily met her mother's eyes, and her anger dissolved into shame. She struggled to find a way to articulate her feelings. "If only I could make you understand. The men in Eureka aren't interested in the things that interest me. They see me only as the Roses' daughter. The few who have come around did so only because of Papa's prestige. They view me as a straight path to wealth, but they don't want me for my own sake."

"That's just what we're working on, dear. We want men to see you as a refined, cultured young woman of style and grace."

Lily sighed. "But I don't want any of them, either."

"We just haven't focused on the right one yet. But I had an idea on the ferry." Mama's excited smile made her look like a schoolgirl. "We're going to have a ball."

"A ball! In Eureka?"

"Exactly. They're all the rage in San Francisco. Since Fort Sumter was attacked, folks have been lining up to show their support for Federal soldiers. We're going to do the same. We'll have a ball and invite all the folks in town and the officers from Fort Humboldt. There's sure to be a strong, handsome young army officer who'll take a shine to you."

"Mama! What a ridiculous way to find a husband."

"No, it isn't. If we lived in San Francisco or out East, you would have attended a dozen debutante balls by now. And you would have had your own, as well."

"But a ball seems so frivolous when we're facing war and the Wiyot—"

Mama raised a hand. "Do not talk to me about those Diggers. They have nothing to do with this."

An idea zipped across Lily's mind with the brilliant pop and flash of a firework. She sat up straighter. "Fine. I will go to your ball. But only if you will allow me to continue working on the schoolhouse."

"I don't think so." Mama stood and began attacking her hair again.

Trembling within at her own audacity, Lily raised her chin. "Then I shan't attend the ball."

"Of course, you will."

Lily kept her voice even. "No." She met her mother's eyes in the mirror. "I will not."

"Lily, you will go if I tell you to go, or you'll be out of the house. I won't tolerate a disobedient daughter."

"In which case, I will not only go and help build the schoolhouse; I will offer my services as a teacher, as well. And everyone in town will know that you cast me out because I declined to attend a fancy ball."

Mama's eyes narrowed, and she turned two shades paler.

Lily bit her lip to keep from blurting out that she didn't mean it and that she took it all back.

"What has gotten into you?"

Lily turned to face her mother directly. "Nothing, Mama. But this is very important to me. I owe the Wiyot."

"Lily, we have discussed all that. What happened was not your fault."

Tears scalded Lily's eyes. Furious at her weakness, she blinked them away. "Oh yes, it was. All of us are to blame—everyone in Eureka. We all knew the monster Larabee was, and what he'd been doing. He'd killed before, and we didn't do anything about it. We kept silent and minded our own business. And people died."

Mama's lips parted slightly, and she looked stricken. For a moment, she stood as still as if she had put down roots. Then, she turned woodenly. "You look quite presentable now. I must go get ready for dinner." Her voice sounded taut, as if it had been stretched thin and dried in the sun.

"Mama?" Lily twisted in her seat.

She gave no response, except for a single pat on Lily's shoulder as she departed, closing the door behind her with a soft click of the latch.

Lily stared at the door. Another black mark against her name. Another disappointment. She hadn't meant to hurt her mother. She'd merely wanted to make her understand why she wanted—no, *needed*—to be part of this project.

She heaved as much of a sigh as she could in her corset, which had been tightened until black dots had swum in her vision. If she could just be more like Mama, life would be so much simpler.

Too restless to stay cooped up in her room, she wandered down to the greenhouse. She could at least check to make sure the plants were as healthy as she had implied to Mama.

A quick scan was all that it took to confirm that several of them were in need of watering. She went out to the back and filled a large watering can at the well, glancing around the whole while to make sure no one caught her at it in her dinner gown.

On her return, she found Mr. Forbes sitting on one of the ornate iron benches available for visitors wishing to enjoy the blooms. "Good evening, Detective."

He jumped to his feet. "Miss Rose. I hope I'm not intruding."

"Not at all. Mama loves to share her flowers. They're her pride and joy." Lily poured water over some sort of feathery-looking fern.

Mr. Forbes stepped forward, his hand outstretched. "Let me do that for you. Just tell me what to water."

Lily waved a hand. "Anything that looks withered or droops."

Mr. Forbes glanced around him and then focused again on the can in his hand. "I think we're going to need more water."

Lily's laughter was heartier than the joke deserved, but she couldn't help it. He was good company and easy to talk to. And he didn't make her feel as if her every action was an embarrassment.

They made a slow circuit around the greenhouse, returning several times to the well to refill the watering can. As they worked, they chatted about inconsequential matters, until Lily's curiosity got the better of her.

"Mr. Forbes?"

He paused at the changed note in her voice and looked up. "Yes?"

"Why do you dislike Reverend Crew so much?"

He blinked twice. "I don't dislike him. But I'm afraid I must be suspicious of him."

"Because of the dead body you found on the trail?"

Forbes nodded.

"You can't possibly think he had anything to do with that."

"Why can't I?"

"Well, why would a preacher attack and kill a stranger? It makes no sense."

"Ah, but we have only his word that he is a preacher."

"I sent for a preacher months and months ago, and he's finally arrived. That can't be suspicious in the least. It's not as if he was just passing through. He had to have been sent from out East when I requested a missionary. So, he can't possibly be the fellow you've been tracking."

"Excellent observations, Miss Rose." He went back to watering.

Lily could tell from his voice that he was humoring her. So, she continued making her case. "Besides, he certainly acts like a preacher. Why would a murderer bother to build a schoolhouse for Indian children?"

"Now that is a good point. I'd have expected a skunk like Diamond to flee for greener pastures the minute I came within hailing distance. But the reverend's stayed."

Lily suddenly thought of the night in the kitchen when she would have choked to death, had the reverend not stepped in and saved her life. He'd had his saddlebag with him. Had he meant to leave? She shoved the idea away. If departing had been his intention that night, there had been nothing stopping him. It would be disloyal to start questioning the man's integrity now, when he'd done so much.

⌒

The first thing Grant noticed upon entering the greenhouse was neither the warmth nor the scent of the blossoms; it was Lily and the Pink, looking very cozy with their heads together. A pang zipped through him. It wasn't jealousy, he assured himself, merely concern that he might be the topic of their tête-à-tête.

As he approached, he cleared his throat, and they jumped apart. "Evening. Did you get rid of that blight, Miss Rose?"

She looked at him blankly. He didn't blame her. It did seem an awfully long time since her biggest concern had been her mother's flowers.

He waved a hand toward a row of potted peonies, and the light dawned.

"I think they're going to pull through. Except perhaps this one." Her fingers brushed the last in the row. "This poor thing went through rather more than blight, I'm afraid."

Grant smiled as he moved to examine the plant. The pot bore traces of dried mud and had a chipped rim. Ah yes, this sad little flower had seen its share of trouble. "It's still rather young. I suggest that you stake it and apply mulch."

"Then, it's not a lost cause?"

Grant looked down into her wide, trusting eyes, and something inside him cracked, like a new seedling breaking through its protective shell, ready to spring to life. "Yes, Miss Rose, it would appear that both of your victims will survive to a ripe, old age, despite everything."

Her sharp intake of breath told him she understood his meaning. The slight upward quirk of her mouth told him it pleased her.

"Now that's interesting."

Grant turned to Forbes, irritated at the interruption. "What?"

"How did you come to know about plants, Reverend?" Forbes held himself unnaturally still, like a hunter trying to get a bead on his prey without spooking the animal.

Grant focused on making sure his face revealed nothing. In his attempt to impress Miss Rose, he'd made a grave mistake. Before his life had fallen entirely to pieces, he had been a gardener. A good one. Of course, the Pink would know that about Grant Diamond. And while it wasn't unheard of for a man of the cloth to dabble in gardening, Grant had tipped his hand.

"It's something I picked up in seminary," he said with a shrug of his shoulders. "I found great comfort among the plants."

Lily sighed. "I imagine you did. Strolling in the garden with the Lord, just like Adam and Eve before the fall. How wonderful that must have been."

For a second, Grant hesitated. He didn't want to lie to her. And, for reasons he couldn't fathom, he didn't want to pretend he'd walked with the Lord when that was the furthest thing from the truth. But then, he noted the expectant look on the Pink's face, and his survival instincts took over.

"Wonderful doesn't begin to describe it," he said smoothly. "I was in the garden so often, the caretaker began teaching me about the plants." At least that part was true. The caretaker at the orphanage had shared everything he knew, opening Grant's eyes to the possibility of a life beyond the swindle and a deck of cards.

The tinkling of a bell sounded. A moment later, one of the servants appeared in the conservatory doorway. "Miss? Sirs? Dinner is ready."

Lily looked at Grant, her eyes expectant. Of course, she thought him the kind of man who would escort her to the dining room, maybe even pull out her chair.

After a few seconds with no movement from Grant, Forbes threw a scowl in his direction, then took a step forward and offered the crook of his arm to Lily. "If I may, Miss Rose?"

Still looking at Grant, she faltered ever so slightly, and disappointment flashed in her eyes. Then she turned away, inclining her head toward Carter. "Thank you, Mr. Forbes."

Her hand slid around his arm, and the two walked from the hothouse. Carter leaned in slightly to hear what Lily was saying, and then they both shared a laugh. Bringing up the rear, Grant told himself this was a good thing. In fact, the more attention they paid to each other, the less they would pay him. From now on, he would do what he could to point them toward each other. At least until he could finish what he'd started with Abernathy and hit the trail.

It was a good plan. The fact that it made his stomach clench and the back of his neck burn was immaterial. For years, he'd done what he had to in order to survive, no matter how distasteful. This was no different. No matter what his heart told him.

Chapter 17

Lily had worked up quite an appetite at the construction site, but now, presented with an array of sumptuous food, she could scarcely eat a bite. It was bad enough that her tightly laced corset crushed her ribs and constricted air flow to her lungs. But the events of the day had left her stomach fluttering as if a rabble of butterflies had taken up residence there.

Papa held court at the head of the table, cutting into an oyster patty as he pumped Detective Forbes for information about life as a Pinkerton. Lily snuck a glance to her right. From his relaxed posture and good-humored replies, Carter certainly didn't seem to mind Papa's questions. Lily sent up a silent prayer of thanks. If not for Carter, the mood at the table would be strained to the breaking point.

Across from Lily, Mama was uncharacteristically quiet as she cut her food into bite-sized pieces. Beside her mother, Reverend Crew appeared fascinated with his soup, which he stirred, scooped up, and then spooned back into the bowl. Lily lifted her water glass and took a sip. Even flavorless liquid had a hard time sliding down to her stomach.

"Are you feeling well, Miss Rose?"

Carter's voice broke into her thoughts. She put down the glass, taking care not to slosh water over the side and onto the linen tablecloth. "Excuse me?"

Without lifting his hand from the table, he motioned to her plate with one finger. "You've hardly touched your food."

"I'm afraid I don't have much of an appetite."

"After all the time you spent in the sun today, it's no surprise." Mama had found her voice, and it had an edge to it.

Lily bristled. She would gladly gobble up half the food on the table if she thought it would make its way into her stomach and stay there. But she couldn't very well say that out loud. However, she thought there might be a way to turn the conversation and use it to her advantage.

"I believe you're right, Mama." Lily folded her hands primly in her lap. "The next time I'm at the building site, I shall wear a wide-brimmed hat."

Reverend Crew's head jerked up. At last, his soup bowl had lost its appeal. "The next time?"

Lily smiled sweetly. "Yes. Mama and I talked, and she understands now just how important it is to me to assist the Indians."

"She does?" Papa looked from Lily to his wife. "You do?"

Mama's nostrils flared. "Yes, we spoke." As she answered her husband, she glared across the table at Lily.

So far, so good. While Mama had no problem making her opinions known, she would never engage in a full-out confrontation at the dinner table. Buoyed with confidence, Lily rushed on. "She's agreed that I should continue my work on the schoolhouse, as long as I am appropriately attired."

Proud of herself for giving that concession, Lily turned a smile on her mother. The look that came back could have burned holes through a stone wall. Then, Mama took a deep breath. She dabbed daintily at her lips with her napkin before smoothing it out on her lap again. The corners of her mouth lifted slightly upward. Her brow relaxed.

Lily knew that look. It did not bode well. Mama was back in control.

"Yes, Lily and I had a wonderful talk before dinner." She speared a potato with her fork, just a tad too forcefully, and lifted it to her mouth.

Papa looked from Lily to her mother. "Excellent news."

Mama swallowed her food, took a sip of water, and nodded. "Yes, it is. I see now how important it is to Lily to help the Indians, and she has my full support."

The tension in Lily's shoulders lost some of its grip. Had Mama really heard her this time? Did she finally understand Lily's heart?

"Thank you, Mama." She reached again for her water glass.

"No, thank *you*, dear one, for reminding me how crucial it is to put the needs of others before our own. Which reminds me," she put her hand on Papa's wrist. "Lily had the brilliant idea of organizing a charity ball. Isn't that wonderful?"

Lily gasped at the unfortunate moment when the water hit her lips, drawing it into her windpipe. She sputtered and choked, and would have dropped the glass entirely, had it not been for Carter Forbes's quick reflexes.

Papa reached over and pounded her back with his broad palm. "Easy there, Lily-belle."

"Breathe through your nose." That dry bit of advice had come from Reverend Crew, but his concern for Lily seemed short-lived. He turned his attention quickly to her mother. "You're planning a ball?"

"We are." She lowered her chin and gave him her best Southern belle simper. "Please don't tell me you object to dancing, Reverend."

"Not at all. There are several references to dancing in the Bible. If the good Lord finds it acceptable, then I have no qualms about it."

"What a very reasonable attitude." A note of true admiration undergirded Mama's words. "Several of the spiritual leaders in San Francisco found reason to complain about the balls there, even though most of them are held for the purpose of supporting charitable causes."

Reverend Crew nodded. "And where will you direct your benevolence with the funds you raise?"

"Why, the war effort, of course. For that reason, I think it appropriate to invite the soldiers based at Fort Humboldt."

Lily had just about gotten her breathing under control, but Mama's latest revelation threatened to choke her again. "All of them?" she sputtered. "Where will we put them all, and the townsfolk, too?"

Mama dismissed her concern with a wave of her hand. "No need to worry. Naturally, not all the soldiers will be able to attend. Someone needs to mind the fort. Isn't that right?"

Papa's voice cut through the tinkle of Mama's laughter. "There really isn't anyone out at the fort right now, Dorothea. They're all in town because the rains have been so bad."

"Even better—they shall be close at hand. Although there's no reason we couldn't invite the men from the other forts around the county, as well. It will be the biggest event of the year."

Lily's mind raced. How would she ever get herself out of this scrape? She had no desire to spend her time planning something as frivolous as a ball. Mama might purport to organize it in the name of charity, but Lily knew her ultimate aim: to parade her in front of the soldiers and townsfolk in the hopes of her catching the eye of some poor, unsuspecting officer.

As if to confirm the thought, Mama looked from Reverend Crew to Mr. Forbes. "Of course, you gentlemen are invited, as well. But don't think that because you're guests in our home, you'll get a place on our Lily's dance card. She'll be highly sought after, I guarantee it."

Lily's cheeks flamed. She dared sneak a glance at Reverend Crew, praying he would understand that Mama's machinations were not her own. For his part, the reverend appeared to be trying very hard to hold back a grin.

"Yes, ma'am," he said. "I believe all the gentlemen will want a turn on the floor with Miss Lily."

Her stomach jerked again, and a burning sensation rose in her throat. No. Not now. She couldn't be sick right here at the table.

"I need to be excused." Lily pushed back her chair and stood up quickly, completely misjudging the distance between herself and the table. Her skirt jammed into the side with such force, it set the dishes rattling and the crystal goblets teetering. She watched in horror as the glasses in front of Mama and Reverend Crew tipped at a slower-than-natural speed, then toppled over toward them. The reverend managed to block the flood with his napkin and, in the same motion, smoothly stand up. But Mama was slower to react. Hands lifted in surrender, she emitted a shriek as the water cascaded over the edge of the table and into her lap.

Just when Lily thought things couldn't get any worse, blackness crept in around the edges of her vision, and the room began to tilt. Too fast. She'd stood too fast. Gripping the edge of the table, she concentrated on breathing. She was not a woman who swooned. She wasn't. She…. "Oh dear," she murmured, just before her legs buckled beneath her.

⟲

For a large man, Benjamin Rose was surprisingly agile. As soon as Lily began to faint, the man was up and catching her in his arms. How he managed to carry a full-grown woman plus her voluminous skirts was a mystery, but Grant supposed this wasn't the first time he'd done it. Undoubtedly, Mr. Rose had been presented with many opportunities to rescue his daughter over the years.

"If you gentlemen will excuse me," he said over his shoulder, "I'll see to Lily. Finish your dinner, please. Someone should enjoy it." A chuckle punctuated his statement, showing that he found his daughter's antics more amusing than vexing.

Mrs. Rose, on the other hand, looked thoroughly vexed. "I'll come with you." She huffed as she stood up, shaking water from her skirt, then stalked out of the room.

Now it was just Grant and Forbes. The two men looked at each other, sizing up the situation.

"Never a dull moment at the Rose Cottage," Carter said lightly.

Grant shook his head. "True enough." He sat down and motioned to Carter's plate. "I suggest we do as he said and finish. No guessing what might happen at the next meal."

Carter snorted in agreement.

Off to his right, Grant caught sight of a maid carrying two full water goblets. "Thank you, my dear. You are an angel sent from heaven."

Dark spots stained the woman's coppery cheeks. "Thank you, Reverend."

She set the glasses on the table and removed the overturned ones, as well as the plates abandoned by the Rose family.

"Is there anything else you gentlemen need?"

Although she addressed them both, she looked only at Grant as she spoke. Good. He'd succeeded in making an ally. If she was ever forced to side with either him or Forbes, the Pink would be out of luck. "That's kind of you, but I think we have everything we need. Thank you."

The woman turned and hurried from the room, a girlish titter trailing behind her.

Shaking his head, Forbes ripped off the end of a roll and spread it with butter. "You certainly have a way with people, Reverend."

Grant moved his wet napkin to the side and scooted his chair to a dry portion of the tablecloth, buying time to design his next move. He'd caught the change of inflection when the Pink had said "Reverend." Despite the days they'd spent working together on the schoolhouse and enduring the trials and tribulations of Miss Rose, the detective still had doubts about his identity. Grant would just have to show him the error of his ways. "Understanding people is an important part of my vocation," he finally said.

Forbes chewed thoughtfully, his head cocked to the side. "I'm not sure it's that simple. Your powers of persuasion go beyond what I've witnessed in most preachers."

"Detective, it sounds like you're implying that I manipulate people."

"Your words, not mine."

"I simply treat other people the way I'd like to be treated. Just as the Good Book says."

The men stared each other down. This was crucial. Grant needed to stand his ground but not come across as defensive. He needed to assure the detective that he really was the godly man of the cloth he claimed to be. Normally, this part of the swindle was not a problem. He found it easy to slide from one alias to another, becoming whoever he needed to be, depending on the situation. But he'd never pretended to be a preacher before. Much to his chagrin, the deception chafed.

Grant leaned forward, his elbows on the table. "If there's something you'd like to say to me, Detective, I wish you'd do it plainly. I have nothing to hide."

His invitation seemed to take the Pink aback. He paused, as if weighing the wisdom in laying all his cards on the table. Then, he nodded, apparently ready to play Grant's game. "Then, you won't mind showing me your credentials."

"Credentials? I'm sorry, Pink, but preachers don't get issued badges."

Carter returned a thin-lipped smile. "No, I suppose they don't. Nor do they usually call me 'Pink.' You must have something in your possession that can help corroborate your identity."

"I can give you my letter of introduction from the missionary society. But tell me something. What do *you* have on hand that would corroborate your identity beyond question?"

The Pinkerton blinked, and Grant seized the advantage. "That's right." He nodded as if Forbes had just made some sort of significant admission. "There's an element of faith in everything, Detective. I've taken you at your word that you're a Pinkerton. And I sure haven't made up any wild stories about how you must have murdered a stranger on the road, just because you arrived in town the same day I did."

The maid entered the dining room again with a serving tray laden with platters of savory roasted rabbit, some sort of stuffing, and a mound of fluffy mashed potatoes.

Grant stood. "Let me help you with that." He took the heavy tray from her and placed it on the table. Once again, she blushed furiously at his attention, but she seemed pleased. Which was just as well. He was playing the biggest bluff of his life, and if the detective ever caught on to the truth, Grant would be tied up and dragged back to New York so fast, they'd probably beat the cable announcing his capture.

A stray query slipped in and twanged his conscience: Lily seemed to cry only for others. Would she cry for him if he was caught, or would she curse his name? The thought of causing her sorrow pinched like too-tight boots.

Forbes spoke the instant the maid closed the door behind her. "Reverend, there's no reason for me to fabricate a story about being a Pinker—"

Grant plucked the letter of introduction from his pocket and slid it across the table. He'd taken it from the dead man's body, just like he'd taken the fellow's clothes. It had named the man and given an account of his credentials, which had proven helpful to Grant in assuming his identity. And now it just might save his life.

Forbes scanned the letter, then looked back at Grant. Clearly, he wanted to believe that the man sitting across from him really was the Reverend Herbert Crew. But some part of him, some gut instinct, held him back. He needed a nudge in the right direction.

Grant smiled. "Have a little faith, Forbes."

The Pinkerton narrowed his eyes as if trying to peer beneath Grant's skin. Then he nodded, slowly and contemplatively. "Very well, Crew." He picked up his fork and knife. "Let's enjoy our rabbit, shall we?"

Chapter 18

Lily could not bear to meet the eyes of Reverend Crew or Detective Forbes at breakfast the next morning. It was all too humiliating. Thankfully, they seemed to take pity on her and acted as though nothing unusual had happened the night before.

Mama insisted they leave early for church, and she spent most of the morning greeting friends and acquaintances as they arrived. Before long, the same women who had been snubbing Lily for the past week were seeking her out to chat about the upcoming patriotic ball. As dismayed as she felt about being forced to participate in Mama's scheme, she had to admit the positive attention felt good.

"I was just saying to Edward that what Eureka needs is more culture!" Mrs. Walters puffed out her ample bosom, as though the ball had been her idea all along. "This is just the ticket. Finally, a respectable opportunity for the single young women of our town to mingle with the fine young soldiers!"

She looked over her shoulder, and Lily followed her gaze to Anna Walters, standing by the family buckboard. Short and nearly as round as her mother, she should have been swallowed up by her hoopskirt. But she carried it in a way Lily never could.

"Yes," Mama said with a whisper of a smile. "Your Anna will surely be the belle of the ball." She looked past Mrs. Walters and motioned with her chin toward the church building. "It looks as though the service is about to start. We should go in."

They walked through the door, and Lily's eyes took a second to adjust from the bright sunlight to the dim church interior. She blinked once, twice, then saw Carter Forbes sitting at the end of the very last pew. Reverend Crew sat in the same position across the aisle. He looked up, caught her eye, and nodded. From the somber expressions both men wore, she suspected they were keeping guard, in case there was another incident with the Indians and Rick Abernathy.

They needn't have worried. Walking up the aisle, Lily noticed with a tinge of sadness that there were no Indians in the building. On the other hand, Abernathy and a few of his ranch hands sat rigidly in the pew immediately behind her parents. Just ahead of Lily, Mrs. Watson harrumphed loudly, trumpeting to one and all that her seat had been usurped. The woman turned and brushed past Lily, in search of a different pew. Fire burned in Lily's gut. It was unfair that Abernathy was permitted to come in and sit among the faithful, even though he made a mockery of everything the church stood for, while the Indians who truly sought to know the Lord were unwelcome.

Pushing and pulling on her skirts, Lily wedged herself between her mother and father. Papa smiled and moved his leg to make room. Mama scowled and didn't move a whit. Lily settled down as quickly as possible, ceasing her fidgeting. But her mind continued to whirl. Things needed to change. They had to. But how could she alter the opinion of an entire town?

At the front of the church, a side door opened, and Reverend Marsden entered. Narrowing her eyes slightly, Lily took a good look at the man who was supposed to be Eureka's spiritual leader. His expression was hard to read—a blend of boredom, resignation, and irritation—but at least the man didn't appear intoxicated. That was a step in the right direction.

He turned to the congregation. "Please stand and open your hymnbooks to page twenty-four."

They began a shaky version of "Just as I Am, Without One Plea," growing stronger as more voices joined in. The words filled Lily's spirit, washing over her like a balm. And then, in the fifth verse, they convicted her.

> Just as I am, Thou wilt receive,
> Wilt welcome, pardon, cleanse, relieve;
> Because Thy promise I believe,
> O Lamb of God, I come, I come!

That's how the Lord accepted her—just as she was, with all her imperfections, sins, and shortcomings. And that's how He accepted everyone else—the Wiyot, Reverend Marsden, and even Abernathy. They needed only believe, and every spot would be washed away. How hypocritical of her to think that anyone didn't belong in this worship service.

Behind her, deep voices rumbled the words of the hymn. Whether Abernathy and his men believed or not, they were here. They were surrounded by God's love and listening to God's Word. There was no telling how it would affect them.

Lily continued mouthing the words, but she was no longer singing. She was saying a silent prayer, requesting forgiveness for herself, and grace and mercy for those men, who had no idea how badly they needed the Lord's love.

⌒

Grant was positive he'd heard this sermon before.

Standing in front of the congregation, Reverend Marsden rattled off words that sounded well-rehearsed and well-used. Even if Grant hadn't remembered hearing it preached before, the man's monotone delivery would have provided a clue.

Lily had approached Grant more than once, wanting to know when "Reverend Crew" would be ready to preach to the Indians. He'd continued putting her off, positive that if she heard him preach more than once, he would be exposed. But if Marsden's sorry performance passed for real preaching in Eureka, Grant had nothing to worry about.

Fifteen minutes later, the congregants sang the last note of the final hymn, then quickly exited the church. Looking down the aisle, Grant spotted Abernathy standing in front of the Rose family.

What on earth was he up to? Like a salmon fighting its way upstream, Grant weaved through the sea of people.

"Mr. Abernathy," he said, drawing up beside the man. "How are you this blessed Sunday?"

The corner of Abernathy's mustache twitched, indicating how little he appreciated Grant's false bonhomie. "Just fine, Reverend. Particularly now that I've been informed of the upcoming ball."

Mrs. Rose smiled broadly. Lily's mouth tipped up just a bit. Mr. Rose looked as though he was waiting for an opportunity to escape. What could Abernathy be scheming that had anything to do with a charity ball?

"Mr. Abernathy has promised a generous donation to the cause." Mrs. Rose beamed.

Grant stared Abernathy down. "I'm sure his generosity knows no bounds."

Abernathy didn't squirm like most men would. Instead, he matched the intensity of Grant's glare without blinking. "It's the least I can do for our fair town. And it's not entirely selfless. What's good for Eureka is good for us all."

Too bad Abernathy's idea of what was good for Eureka was as twisted as he was. Grant had known men like him all his life— power-hungry bigots who believed their way was the only way and assumed the right to inflict their opinions on everyone around them.

With a glaze of indifference in his eyes, Abernathy looked away from Grant and glanced past the Rose family. "Excuse me, folks. Have a pleasant day." He walked over to Reverend Marsden, who had been cornered by several parishioners. As soon as Abernathy approached them, they scattered, giving him Marsden's full attention. For the first time that day, the minister showed an emotion other than boredom. Now he looked downright scared.

Interesting.

Mrs. Rose craned her neck as she looked up the aisle. "Oh my, there's Major Raines." She grabbed her daughter's hand. "Come, Lily. We must speak to him about the ball."

Lily pulled back slightly. "But Mama, I—" A sharp look from her mother ended the protest. "Yes, ma'am. Excuse us, Reverend Crew."

Grant bit back a smile as Lily trudged away dutifully. Dorothea Rose may claim that the charity ball was Lily's idea, but he knew better. Lily was giving her mother something she wanted in exchange for permission to work with the Wiyot. It was the only explanation for Mrs. Rose's sudden change of heart. And also why Lily looked like she was being led to prison.

⌒

Marsden was one unhappy man. Certain he'd been cast in the role of a modern-day Job, he'd never expected anything good out of life. The best he could hope for was to lessen the severity of his miserable existence in whatever way he could. It made him a terrible pastor but an excellent lackey.

Rick Abernathy headed to the rear exit of the church building, motioning for the mouse of a man to follow him. Once outside, the bright sun highlighted the dinginess of the pastor's wrinkled shirt and coat.

"Have you no pride, Marsden? When was the last time you had your laundry washed?"

The preacher's shoulders curved in as he shrugged. "What difference does it make? Half the miners in this town don't even know what soap is."

Being downwind from Marsden, Abernathy could tell the preacher wasn't well-acquainted with the product, either. But he had more important things to discuss than personal hygiene. "What do you know about Reverend Crew? Did he travel out here with someone else?"

Marsden frowned, his face puckering up like a lemon that had sat in the sun for too long. "I don't think so. I don't know much about him at all. Heard he was sent by the Massachusetts Mission Society. Can't say I'm impressed."

Of course, he wasn't impressed. It wouldn't take much to be a better preacher than Marsden, and the sloppy little man knew it. Naturally, he was jealous of the new clergyman and the attention he was getting.

Marsden rubbed his bleary eyes. "I went to seminary with one of the members of that missionary society. I wrote him to make inquiries, because the fellow seems suspicious to me. What kind of minister pulls a gun during a church service?"

Abernathy nearly chortled with glee. This was all too perfect. He didn't even have to manipulate the pastor into doing what he wanted. He made his voice as smooth as velvet. "I think that was a wise move. You've got to keep an eye on your parish."

Marsden straightened his narrow shoulders and stood a little taller. "He says he's here to preach to the heathens, but there's more to him than he lets on. I need to know what it is."

"He's certainly not helping with the Digger problem." Abernathy shook his head. "Building a school, inviting them into service with everyone else...he's stirring the pot."

That he was.

"I'll let you know when I hear something from the missionary society. I'm sure my friend will help us get to the bottom of all this. I made my dissatisfaction known, so maybe they'll recall him. Either way, we'll get rid of him."

Abernathy let his grin surface this time. Marsden had no idea just how right he was. One way or another, Crew would be dealt with.

Chapter 19

Carter yawned as he tightened the girth strap beneath Friday's barrel. He'd much rather be in bed, but the only way to avoid explaining his errand was to leave while the rest of the house slept. The simple note he'd left behind would reveal nothing. At least, nothing he didn't want revealed. After a final check of Friday's bridle, he led the mare from the stable and swung up into the saddle. Riding out of the yard, he took a quick look over his shoulder. Was it his imagination, or had the curtain in the upper left window dropped hastily back into place? He reined Friday to a halt. There was no other hint of movement in the predawn gloom. Not a soul stirred anywhere as he glanced up and down the street. With a squeeze of his knees, he nudged Friday into a canter, but he couldn't quite shake the uneasy sense of someone drawing a bead right between his shoulder blades.

He rode into town, passing the post office for now. Unfortunately, other than the saloons, nothing was open at this hour of the morning.

Friday tossed her head, reveling in the fresh, humid air. Soon enough, the muddy paths and clapboard buildings of Eureka gave way to the forest, with its sense of hush. Normally, the thump of Friday's hooves on the soft earth seemed irreverently loud. But today, Carter felt in tune with the noises of the woods. The wind hustled through the treetops with as much bustle as a gossip to a crime scene, then left the trees chattering in its wake.

The trek to the abandoned wagon didn't take as long as he'd expected. Whoever the dead fellow was, he'd been only an hour's ride from the sanctuary of town when death had caught up to him on the trail. With the removal of the dead body, it seemed that passersby had overcome their shyness. The abandoned cart had been picked clean. All four wheels had been removed, even the two that had been broken. All that remained were shattered bits of wood and tattered remnants of the canvas cover.

Carter dismounted with a sigh. He should have paid more attention the last time he was here. Examining the area now would likely prove an exercise in futility. He eyed the bald mound of the grave he'd dug and briefly considered exhuming the fellow to see if the body might yield further clues. But he just couldn't bring himself to do it. Once he'd spotted that bullet hole, he'd made a thorough inspection of the corpse. And he didn't think he could stomach that smell again.

He shuddered. Nope, it was time to beat the grass. Literally. He tethered Friday and began combing through the underbrush. He found a number of things, mostly rocks, moss, moldering leaves, and an invasive thorn bush that tore at him mercilessly until he scrambled free.

A miserable drizzle started, sending a chill right down his back. He pulled his hat lower on his head and hunched into the warmth of his jacket. As the rain intensified, he sought cover under the bedraggled bits of canvas that still hung together on the cart frame, defying the odds. Huddled in the questionable shelter, he wondered if he shouldn't cut his losses and head on back in the rain. Sure, he'd be soaked, but at the rate things were going, he'd get soaked sitting here, too. He touched a bit of the splintered wood. Was it dry enough to start a small fire, even in this deluge? The next thing his fingers felt was something altogether smoother. He plucked at the object, working it free of the debris.

It was a ferrotype featuring a family portrait: a man in clerical garb, a matronly woman in a stiff-looking dark dress with an old-fashioned bonnet, and a pretty young lady with delicate features, challenging eyes, and a subtle smile that could hold a man's gaze for a lifetime.

Settling back on his haunches, Carter pondered his discovery. The fellow in the picture was more than likely the corpse rotting away underground. And he appeared to be a pastor. Just like Crew.

Carter flipped open the cover of the ferrotype. Embossed on the back was the legend: Freeman and Sons, Boston, Massachusetts. Crew was from Boston. At least, that was where he had attended seminary.

Questions niggled at Carter's brain. If the man he knew as Reverend Crew was who he claimed to be, then what were the chances of the dead man hailing from the same town and practicing the same vocation? And if the pastor in the picture was the murder victim, then he most certainly was not Grant Diamond. Which meant Diamond was still on the run. Was there any choice but to conclude that the man he knew as Crew was really Diamond?

After spending an interminable amount of time staring blankly at the image, he finally tucked it in his pocket. The picture proved nothing, one way or the other. But Crew had certainly emerged again into the limelight of suspicion.

Carter rooted through the rest of the rubbish but found nothing else of interest. At last, he gave up and decided to head back to town, in spite of the rain. It would be better than crouching in the cold all day. At least he could look forward to a good, hot meal at the Rose Cottage.

Stiff from being hunched over for too long, he made his way from under the shelter, but a sound stopped him—a sound that was distinctly out of place in the forest. It sounded like someone trying to sneak past, without success.

Pistol drawn, Carter stood and ordered the intruder to stop.

The mousy figure of Reverend Marsden halted and froze, his hands in the air, as rain trickled down his sleeves.

Carter lowered his weapon. "Sorry to startle you, Reverend. I thought you might be someone up to no good."

The fellow gave a weak smile and lowered his hands in jerky little spasms. "No, no. I'm just on my way to visit some of my flock."

"All the way out here?"

"Yes, Mr. Abernathy asked me to call. The path to his house is just up ahead there a little ways." He pointed through the rain, and for the first time, Carter noted a crude track perhaps a hundred yards distant. There wasn't much to it, really; just some flattened underbrush and the traces of a rut where a cart had passed.

The minister didn't seem all that enthused about his pastoral visit. Carter frowned. "It's early for a call, isn't it?"

Marsden sniffed. "He won't be my only visit today, Mr. Forbes. There is more to a pastor's work than most people believe."

"No offense intended. I was just surprised."

With a nervous wave, Marsden continued on his way. As Carter watched him go, speculation sprung to life. Abernathy lived very close to the site where a man had been murdered. To get to town and back, he would have to pass right by the wreckage. Why had he done nothing about it? He could have buried the fellow, or at least notified the sheriff. Maybe Crew wasn't Diamond, after all. And maybe Abernathy had some explaining to do.

❧

Grant finished washing up and then smoothed his damp hair back from his face. He'd worked late at the building site and had missed supper altogether. Forbes's cryptic note had been the start of an excessively trying day; until now, he hadn't fully appreciated how much it meant to have the extra hands helping around the site. He never would have expected it, but the two of them actually made a fairly good team.

The Pink couldn't have picked a better day to absent himself from the job. The steady drizzle throughout most of the day made progress grind to a near halt. At least the thing had started to look like a building now, complete with a door and windows, and even a slat floor. The last major step was the roof, but that couldn't be done in the rain.

He put on a dry shirt, wishing as always for one of his own, rather than the preacher's scratchy garments. But at least it wasn't sopping wet. He rubbed his hands together. Now it was time to go see what sort of supper he could charm out of the cook at this time of night. His stomach gurgled as he made his way downstairs, encouraging him to do his best.

As he passed the parlor, Mrs. Rose's clear voice floated out through the half-open door. "Benjamin, I don't see how you can even think of taking Lily's side in all this. She's hardly getting any younger, and soon she will lose what looks she has. At that point, all she'll have to attract a suitable husband really *will* be her inheritance."

Grant slowed to a stop. The comments stung as if they'd been intended for him.

Mr. Rose's voiced waxed and waned, which suggested that he was pacing. "Our Lily is a very attractive young woman. She has a great deal to offer any man."

"She has a tender heart, I'll give her that, but that girl gets in more scrapes than all the other young ladies of Eureka combined. She is utterly reckless, without the slightest semblance of grace."

"She is also kind, and brave, and genuine. There's no fakery in my Lily, unlike those other girls you cast up to her all the time."

Grant found himself nodding in silent agreement, even making additions to the list: resourceful, forgiving, compassionate, unselfish…. She didn't take herself too seriously. And that laugh of hers…remembering it brought on a smile, and a pang sliced through his chest.

"There is such a thing as being too earnest. It's a wonder she hasn't completely tossed away her reputation. And her obsession with the Indians is so off-putting. What man wants to be saddled with a wife who courts trouble?"

"I don't know, I've been thinking that the rever—"

"That man. I'll grant you, he is a pleasant enough fellow, and easy on the eye, but what could he offer Lily beyond a life of drudgery and turmoil? A missionary's wife? When he gets bored with the Wiyot, who knows what even more backward places he might drag her to!"

Something brushed the backs of Grant's legs, and he jumped. Red-faced and bright-eyed, Lily stood close enough behind that her skirts touched his calves. "They say you never hear good of yourself when you eavesdrop," she hissed.

He couldn't imagine how she'd managed to creep up and catch him. Usually the sound of breaking glass heralded her arrival, as surely as trumpet fanfare announced a king. Then he realized that the brightness of her eyes was on account of unshed tears. If he'd been able to hear her parents' conversation, she must have, too. But how much? Grant instinctively held out a hand to her. "I'm so sorry, Lily."

At first, it seemed she would take it, but then she recoiled. Pain creased her face. "I don't need your pity." She spun on her heel and hurried away, skirts swinging. Miraculously, she didn't collide with anything.

There was a rustle at the parlor entrance, and Grant turned to find Mrs. Rose standing with the door fully open. She didn't look as if she'd heard his exchange with Lily. He stole a glance back the way Lily had gone, thinking he might catch her and try to explain, or apologize, or comfort her, at least.

"Reverend Crew, good evening," said Mrs. Rose. "We missed you at dinner."

"Thank you, ma'am. I was delayed at the site today. Hoping to be done there soon, and out of your hair."

Mrs. Rose patted his arm. "Don't be foolish. We enjoy having you as our guest."

"Thank you again, ma'am. The hospitality has been very generous. Would you excuse me, please?" Knowing he should try to further ingratiate himself with her, he nevertheless hurried away. He couldn't leave things like this with Lily. If nothing else, she had to know he didn't share her mother's biting opinions.

He searched the grounds, doing everything but call for her. As he rounded the corner of the house for the third time, he spotted her, closeted once more with Forbes in the greenhouse. He watched through the curved glass panes as she stood, engaged in animated conversation with the blasted Pink. She leaned into him, so close that their shoulders nearly touched. Were they discussing Grant? Lily's mother?

Grant clenched his jaw. This was exactly what he'd wanted. If Lily and the Pink were distracted with each other, they'd have no time to scrutinize him too closely. Still, the sinking feeling in the pit of Grant's stomach told him he'd just lost something precious.

～

Lily examined the ferrotype Carter had handed her with even more care than it warranted. She welcomed the distraction of his company and his tale of the day's adventures. In truth, she would have welcomed just about any diversion at the moment. But Carter's investigation did interest her, and it helped push the dreadful scene with Reverend Crew from her mind.

"I'd say this couldn't have been taken any later than last autumn," she finally posited. "That was when the kind of bodice the younger woman is wearing came into style. And she's dressed for cooler weather."

Carter blinked. "That's very helpful, Miss Rose. Is there anything else you notice about the picture?"

"This preacher obviously didn't frequent the same fancy cobbler as Reverend Crew." She smiled ruefully and handed the image back to him. "You said the place you found the body is near Abernathy's homestead?"

"Yes. The track to reach his place is within sight of the spot."

Lily nodded. "I've been that way, and I know the area, though I've never been out to his ranch."

"I gave Marsden a good head start this morning, then followed him. Abernathy's house is maybe half a mile from the main road. It looks more like a fortified outpost than a homestead."

Lily sat down on the conservatory bench. "You have to understand, Mr. Forbes, there has been trouble with the Indians in the past. Not the Wiyot, but some of the other tribes, especially those up in the mountains. A small number of them have taken to attacking whites—usually in retaliation for some atrocity committed by Hank Larabee's 'Knights,' and now Abernathy's gang of toughs. But every attack and counterattack only escalates matters further. In truth, most of us—whites and Indians alike—are peaceable enough and just want to live our lives."

"That may be, but the fellow even has guards on duty. The place looked as polished and professional as a military fort."

Lily shuddered. This boded well for no one. "How many men?"

"I'm not certain. More than ten, probably fewer than twenty. Plenty enough to make trouble."

Lily nodded, chewing on her lower lip as she tried to assimilate the facts and figure out what Abernathy was up to. There hadn't been an Indian attack in months. Why were they on edge?

Did it have anything to do with the Wiyot? How could it not? And why was Abernathy so interested in helping with Mama's ball?

She stopped herself in the middle of her train of thought. She couldn't afford to go running around half-cocked. Besides, hadn't she decided just last Sunday that she would try to act more charitably toward Abernathy? She ought to be showing him a better way. Plus, she recalled a quote from an ancient Chinese general on the importance of knowing oneself and knowing one's enemy if victory was to be achieved. Maybe it was time to get to know Abernathy.

Chapter 20

With her back against the wall, Lily squeezed her eyes shut, steeling herself for the conversation to come. She took a deep breath, popped her eyelids open, and twisted to peek around the corner and see whether Reverend Crew was still staring out the window. He wasn't. He was right in the doorway, and her nose was about two inches from his shirt.

"Oh!" She stepped back hastily.

He leaned against the doorframe, arms crossed over his chest. "Looking for me?"

Her carefully prepared speech slipped away. "I…uh, yes. I…."

He studied her with a strange, hard light in his eyes, his lips pressed into a thin line.

She had the sudden urge to turn and flee. Instead, she moved forward with the plan she'd concocted. Standing a bit straighter, she folded her hands together gently at waist level. "Yes, Reverend. I was hoping you would accompany me to Mr. Abernathy's home."

"Abernathy?" He moved away from the wall. "Why would you want to see that skunk?"

"Why, Reverend, I'm surprised at you! We're talking about one of God's children."

"Some of His children are less lovable than others."

"To you and me, perhaps. But not to God." The words of the hymn came back to her, bolstering her courage. "I've not treated Mr. Abernathy with an ounce of Christian charity, and it's time I remedied that."

Another indecipherable look crossed his face, and red splotches appeared on his cheekbones. "And when did you receive this revelation?"

"In church, as we were singing. It's as if God spoke directly to my heart."

His head tilted slightly, and a muscle in his jaw twitched. "I don't recall hearing a voice from heaven instructing you to go visit Abernathy. Believe me, that's something I wouldn't forget."

Should she tell him the whole truth? That, besides extending a hand in Christian fellowship, she also intended to gather information for Mr. Forbes? What would the reverend think of her duplicity? "Very well. I shan't trouble you again." She spun around to leave.

His hand on her arm stopped her mid-flounce. "But you're still going to see Abernathy?"

"Yes."

"Not a chance in—" He sucked air through clenched teeth. "I'm coming with you."

Lily wanted to insist that she would be just fine on her own. But she heard her mother's voice in her head, upbraiding her for her impulsiveness, and she held her tongue. In truth, she did not want to brave Abernathy's den alone. "Thank you. We will depart in thirty minutes."

Reverend Crew was waiting for her in the wagon when she came down, but he didn't move to assist her. Instead, Joseph gave her a disapproving frown as he all but tossed her into her seat, then climbed up in front. Hunched forward, his elbows touching his knees, with the reins threaded between gnarled, dark brown knuckles, Joseph was as irritable as a mountain lion with a thorn-pierced paw.

Brooding became their traveling companion all the way through town. When she found that she couldn't bear it another minute, Lily leaned forward and spoke to Joseph, since she had no desire to engage Reverend Crew. "Is something wrong?"

"I don't like it, Miss Lily."

The reverend's glower of agreement burned between her shoulder blades, even though he remained silent.

Lily sighed. "It's just a neighborly gesture."

"Nothing neighborly about Rick Abernathy."

She couldn't argue with him on that point. Abernathy had done unspeakable things to Joseph's people. There was no excusing his actions, and she wouldn't insult the Wiyot's memory by trying. "Joseph, remember that passage of Scripture you asked me about the other day? About doing unto others as you'd have them do unto you?"

The wagon hit a rut, bouncing Lily and jostling the plate she held in her lap. She peeked beneath the corner of the clean cotton napkin covering it, as if the lemon cake beneath might have disappeared. But all was well.

Joseph made an unintelligible noise in reply.

"Well, that's what I'm doing. I'm treating Mr. Abernathy with kindness, because that's how I want to be treated. I hope that, by sharing this cake with him, I will soften his heart at least a little."

"Best not tell him a Wiyot made it, or he's likely to shoot you."

"I have every intention of telling him who made it," Lily said. "That's the point. I want him to start seeing the Wiyot in a positive light."

"And you think a lemon cake will do the trick?"

"As Mama is fond of saying, 'The way to a man's heart is through his stomach.'"

Beside her, the reverend shook his head slightly.

Joseph snorted. "Man's got to have a heart to begin with."

"Really, Joseph. I...." They rounded a bend in the path, and thick trees gave way to a large clearing. They had arrived at Rick Abernathy's. "Please now, be on your best behavior."

"Only for you, Miss Lily."

She exhaled a sigh of relief. Bringing Joseph along had been a calculated risk. Abernathy had been known to shoot an Indian for setting foot on his property. But, with her and the reverend there, he ought to be safe. Movement out of the corner of her eye caught her attention. She turned to her right and held back a gasp. "Mr. Forbes wasn't exaggerating. This place really does look like a fort."

Reverend Crew looked at her askance. "You knew about this?"

"Oh, well...yes." Lily fidgeted in her seat. "That is, Mr. Forbes indicated that he suspected some questionable activity going on here, and I thought...well, I thought it would be good to see for myself."

"And you thought you'd hide behind Christian charity and charm your way in with a lemon cake?"

Joseph glanced over his shoulder with a crestfallen look that pierced her heart with guilt.

"No, that's not it at all."

"Isn't it?" The reverend voiced the question that had flashed across Joseph's features.

Lily blinked against the heat building in her eyes. She really had wanted to show Mr. Abernathy a bit of kindness, in hopes of helping him to see just how wrong he'd been about the Indians. But she'd also wanted to get onto Abernathy's property to see for herself what was going on. She didn't want to let another opportunity to help the Wiyot slip by. In her haste, however, she hadn't thought through the potential consequences of her actions.

"Joseph, I'm sorry. I shouldn't have tried to sermonize or make this seem like a holy mission."

"Doesn't make a lick of difference now, Miss Lily." He motioned at the three men riding toward them, rifles held at the ready across their saddles. "I hope that God of yours is real, 'cause it looks like we need His help right now."

⌒

Rick Abernathy had made a point of filling his home with fine things. From the look on Lily's face, Grant could tell that it was far from what she'd expected.

She sat perched on the edge of a red velvet settee, her hands clasped so tightly in her lap that her knuckles had gone white. Grant stood next to her, and, in the corner of the room, Joseph stood as still as a redwood. No doubt, Abernathy would have preferred the native stay outside, but Lily had refused to come inside without him.

Standing by the fireplace, his elbow propped on the mantel, Abernathy ignored the two men and inclined his head toward Lily. "I must say, Miss Rose, your visit today is quite a surprise."

"I'm very sorry to have interrupted your day," she said in a rush. "It's just that our cook baked so many treats for us, I was afraid they'd go to waste. And I recalled hearing you express a fondness for lemon cake at the last church social."

Abernathy's jaw tightened. "You didn't make it yourself?"

Grant felt his own jaw clench tight. They should leave now. In fact, they never should have come. This man was dangerous.

Lily chuckled, fluttering her fingertips just below her throat. "Me? Oh, no. Believe me, you wouldn't want to eat anything I might bake. But our cook is a wonder. His cakes simply melt in your mouth."

From Abernathy's expression, it would seem that the piece of cake he'd pinched off before his servant had taken it away had soured in his stomach.

Now that Lily had spoken, she seemed more at ease. She chattered on, extolling the virtues of the Wiyots, but Abernathy wasn't interested. He held up a hand, cutting her off.

"Miss Rose, your dedication to helping the less fortunate is greatly misplaced with the Wiyot brutes."

She took in a deep breath. "Mr. Abernathy, I'd ask you to mind your words, especially because they are untrue."

Abernathy barked out a laugh. "Come now, Miss Rose. Face the facts. They steal. They lie. They murder. *Brute* is a complimentary designation for those Diggers."

She pursed her lips, as though holding back sharp words, and looked over her shoulder at Joseph. Save for the lowering of his eyebrows, he hadn't moved. Abernathy sneered as if he wished he would. One step forward, one hostile movement, would be all the excuse Abernathy needed to draw his pistol.

Grant cleared his throat and shifted, positioning himself between the two men.

When Lily's gaze returned to Abernathy, her eyes had taken on a hard glint. "Jesus calls us to love our fellow man, Mr. Abernathy. If the Wiyot are indeed ungodly, as you say, then all the more reason for us to share the love of our Savior with them."

"The Good Book also tells us to put no evil thing before our eyes, and to destroy the idolater." Abernathy took a step forward. "Miss Rose, we are not so different, you and I. We both want to see God's will be done."

Considering his own masquerade, the idea of a wolf dressed in sheep's clothing shouldn't have surprised Grant, but he couldn't restrain his grunt at the way the man had twisted the Scriptures.

Lily stood, her hands pressed against the sides of her skirt. Her jaw was set, her back rigid. "We are nothing alike, Mr. Abernathy. I believe in abolishing evil by spreading God's Word. You believe in calling good 'evil' and destroying it."

From the quaver in her voice, Grant knew she was afraid to stand up to Abernathy, and yet she'd held her ground. She possessed admirable inner strength and courage. The color that rose in her cheeks, the fire that snapped in her eyes, made her radiant. But Grant wasn't the only one who noticed. Interest flashed in Abernathy's eyes, followed by an almost faraway gleam. The fellow was spinning possibilities.

Grant had a very bad feeling about this.

He could envision the calculations, even as Abernathy added up the tally in his head. The Rose family fortune and name were exactly what he needed to cement his status in Eureka. No doubt he was wondering how to make Lily reconsider her rejection of his suit. It sickened Grant that he found it so easy to follow the train of thought of such a monster, for it meant that he thought the same way, himself.

"Coming here today was a mistake." Lily turned and started for the door. Grant followed her, trailed by Joseph.

"Miss Rose, wait."

She stopped at the door, her back to Abernathy. No doubt she wanted to ignore him and continue outside, but proper breeding and good manners would not allow her to be so rude. She turned slightly, her skirts twisting as she did so.

"Obviously, you have very strong beliefs. So do I. But I'm willing to rethink my position. I'd welcome the opportunity to discuss this further with you."

Grant thought furiously, trying to figure out what game Abernathy was playing. In the fellow's eyes, Lily's least desirable quality was her blind devotion to the Wiyot. It was also her greatest area of vulnerability, and something Abernathy would know exactly how to exploit.

Her brow furrowed, confusion apparently warring with caution. "Really?"

Abernathy grinned. "Perhaps you can show me the error of my ways."

A heavy exhalation came from Joseph. He stood as close to Lily as he could, arms at his sides, hands fisted. His eyes, dark and menacing, shot arrows at Abernathy.

Joseph knew exactly what was going on, too, but he'd made a crucial mistake. He'd alerted Abernathy to his knowledge. The jackal might consider that a problem.

Lily, however, was not as wise to the ways of deception. She wanted to believe people were good; therefore, she would take Abernathy at his word. The hint of a smile tugged the corners of her lips upward.

"Then, I would enjoy talking further with you, Mr. Abernathy."

A nod of agreement from him, a few words of good-bye, and then Abernathy escorted them to the door. Grant was certain Lily had bought the humbug Abernathy was selling. She would continue the conversation, and Abernathy would do whatever was necessary to make her come around to his point of view.

And Grant would do everything in his power to make sure that didn't happen.

Chapter 21

Even though she felt that a patriotic ball was a completely frivolous thing to focus on with the town on the brink of turmoil, Lily couldn't deny her sense of accomplishment as she surveyed the ballroom. She had convinced Mama to employ several Wiyot women to help prepare for the festivities, and, under Mama's auspices, the native women had done a marvelous job making sure the house shone from top to bottom. Tall candles glimmered softly in wall sconces. The chandelier overhead was completely aglow for the first time since its installation. Flowers from the conservatory had been arranged with swags of bunting and silk ribbons of red, white, and blue. The floors gleamed, patiently awaiting dancers. Better yet, the wages the women earned would go a long way toward providing for the needs of their village.

Mama bustled in, looking regal in her gown of bone-colored silk with a trim of black velvet vines. She looked Lily over with a critical eye. "I do wish we could make that corset a little tighter, dear."

"Any tighter and I won't be able to speak, much less dance with anyone."

"At least the color becomes you." She made a circle with her forefinger, and Lily twirled obediently. Mama had ordered the periwinkle blue silk gown based on a fashion plate she'd seen in San Francisco. It was supposed to be the height of style. Lily had to admit it was a beautiful dress.

Mama nodded. "Very nice." She fluffed the little puffs of sleeves, pulled a curl around from the back of Lily's coiffure to lie across her collarbone, and tugged the cuffs of her long white gloves further up on her arms, despite her certain knowledge that her efforts would be undone within a matter of minutes. Probably as soon as Lily blinked, and certainly as soon as she moved. "Now, remember to walk slowly. Ladies do not gallop. Move gracefully. Think of yourself as being fluid, like water."

Lily nodded. "I'll try, Mama."

"I know you will, sweetheart." Mama reached up to pat her cheek. "Don't think of the crinoline as a cage. It should be an extension of your person. It moves with you."

"Yes, Mama."

"Good. Smile, dear. Try to look welcoming."

A clatter announced the arrival of the ragtag orchestra Mama had managed to assemble. They'd been practicing in the garden all week, and they weren't terrible. Perhaps the evening wouldn't be so terrible, either. Music would be welcome, and Lily's gown did complement her coloring.

Anna Walters and her mother were the first to arrive. In cream silk, Anna looked as sweet as an apple dumpling, and about as tall. Her gown featured swags and bows and lace and trim, and her crinoline was wide enough to comfortably hide a goat and two donkeys. Even though she was half buried in cloth, her smile was bright, and she managed to embrace Lily without causing either of them to topple over. As graceful as she was, Anna drew a reproachful glare from Mama. Luckily, neither Anna nor Mrs. Walters seemed to notice.

"Oh, Lily! Everything looks just beautiful. I can already tell this is going to be a wonderful evening, and none of the handsome officers has even arrived yet." Her unfettered happiness made Lily feel like a stick-in-the-mud. As usual.

She smiled and squeezed Anna's hand. "I hope it's the best evening you've ever had."

Anna leaned forward eagerly. "Do you really think an officer might propose? Which one?"

Taken aback, Lily floundered, "I...uh, I'm not—"

"Oh, I hope it's Lieutenant Collins. I find him so very dashing. Don't you?"

"He's certainly—"

Anna scrunched her eyes shut and let out a little squeal, her hands clasped to her bosom. "It doesn't matter who. They're all dashing, and it's going to be a divine, romantic, wonderful night."

Lily smiled and glanced at her mother. She and Mrs. Walters exchanged a glacial nod of greeting and a terse acknowledgment.

"Dorothea."

"Harriet."

It was as if they each backed a different champion and couldn't bring themselves to be friendly until a victor was declared.

Lily felt a little sick to her stomach.

Papa took his place in the receiving line as guests began to arrive in earnest. They crowded in until Lily thought the room would burst and her lips had grown stiff from smiling. And still more came. The enormous, double glass doors leading to the garden were flung open, and guests spilled outside, chattering and laughing with the good humor of partygoers.

Naomi appeared and whispered something in Mama's ear, after which Mama raised her hand and made a gesture. The orchestra struck up "The Star-Spangled Banner." Joseph and the other Wiyot men who had been hired to wait on guests for the evening cleared a path, and the officers and other men from Fort Humboldt filed in, parade style.

The guests erupted into applause and cheers. Right in front, Anna Walters waved her handkerchief like mad. In spite of herself, Lily felt a glow of pride, but it was tempered by the bitter reality— these men would likely be shipped off soon from Fort Humboldt to fight against their own countrymen. They might never return.

Lily caught sight of Reverend Crew. It was the first she had seen of him in several days. He'd stayed out at the building site, insisting that even though the school was almost finished, someone needed to keep watch. His hair was neatly combed, and he had shaved, but those seemed to be his sole concessions to the festivities. He wore the same black wool suit as always, and he appeared to be the only person in the room not smiling.

His gaze was on Lily, and she realized that she wasn't smiling, either. She didn't think she was even breathing. He looked so solemn and intense. Had she done something to offend him? Heaven knew it wouldn't be the first time. She resolved to apologize for her behavior, whatever it had been.

The orchestra swept into a bouncing, rollicking version of a waltz, which teetered on the edge of becoming a polka. Lily covered her lips with her hand to conceal a smile.

Reverend Crew crossed the few feet of distance between them and held out a hand. "May I have the honor of this dance, Miss Rose?"

Lily blinked. She must have been mistaken. "Oh, Reverend, I wish I could, but"—she held up her dance card—"this dance has already been claimed."

"Miss Rose, you're looking lovely. I hope you remembered to save me the first dance."

Lily looked up at the too-loud voice and found Mr. Abernathy at her elbow. He had been surprisingly helpful with the preparations for the ball. Rumor had it he had even coerced many of the local ranchers to purchase tickets. With more exposure to the Wiyot, Lily felt certain it was only a matter of time before he changed his attitude, as well. He was a work in progress, but then, so was she.

Abernathy held out his arm and offered a surly smile to Reverend Crew. Somewhat hesitantly, Lily placed her hand on the rancher's arm. She had promised him the dance, after all. She held her card out to Reverend Crew. "I have several other dances open." Before he could accept it, Abernathy covered her hand with his and swept her out onto the dance floor.

Mr. Abernathy was not the most uncoordinated man in the room, but he was far from graceful. He tugged Lily around in jerky circles to the rhythm of the waltz, and she counted it a blessing that he mostly refrained from treading on her toes. As he droned on about his views on the war, Lily scanned the crowd for Reverend Crew. At the opposite end of the ballroom, the wide-open doors allowed the cool evening air to sweep in and refresh the dancers. Reverend Crew stood in the doorway, and for a moment, Lily's eyes locked with his. He was such a hard man to read, but if she wasn't mistaken, he looked almost disappointed.

Before she could ponder his mood further, Mr. Abernathy swung her around with such force that a pin became dislodged from her hair. By the time she'd danced a full circle, the reverend had left the ballroom, taking some of Lily's joy with him.

⁓

Leaning against a tree, Carter pulled the thick wool blanket more tightly around him. From his position on the rise, he could see most of Eureka. The hulking shadows of ship masts and steamboat smokestacks bobbed on the bay. Main Street was abnormally quiet, save for the vicinity of The Gilded Cage, which welcomed its usual mix of those down on their luck and those of newfound prosperity in a raucous party. A few streets away, an entirely different kind of soiree set the evening aglow—one Carter had planned on attending.

He should feel better, knowing that Rick Abernathy was at the ball—as long as the man was dancing and socializing, he couldn't cause trouble—and knowing that the schoolhouse had not been left unattended. In an uncharacteristic show of selflessness, Reverend Marsden had volunteered to stand watch that night. Yet Carter hadn't felt reassured. In fact, allowing Marsden to guard the schoolhouse was a bit like putting a snowman in charge of a furnace. He might look good for a little while, but in the end, he would be useless. Hence Carter's taking it upon himself to guard the guard.

He imagined the music playing in the ballroom; the couples, dressed in their finest, skimming the dance floor. Carter had never been much of a dancer, but Emily would love it. The image of his little sister as a child, dancing and twirling around the drawing room while Father puffed out a tune on his harmonica, drew a chuckle from Carter. But his mirth was short-lived, thanks to the intrusion of reality. Emily hadn't danced in a long time—not since sustaining the gunshot wound that had changed her life forever.

Carter's life had changed that day, too. His desire to see justice for his sister had driven him to pursue a career in law enforcement and, eventually, had led him to the Pinkertons. Impressed, his superiors had expected him to move quickly up the ranks. But three years of chasing the same man across the country had derailed that plan. Three years of being just a little too late, riding into town a day—or, in one annoying situation, an hour—behind Diamond had taken their toll on Carter. He missed his family, especially his sister.

He wriggled as a jagged piece of tree bark bit through the blanket and into his back. He missed sleeping in his own bed.

Maybe it was time. He'd found a body and, with it, evidence that suggested it was Grant Diamond. What more did he need?

Perhaps the nagging feeling that there was more to this case was simply because he'd been on it so long. Maybe….

A flash in the distance caught his eye. *What in the world?* He grabbed the binoculars by his side and peered down the hill. Minutes ago, Marsden had been sitting beside his makeshift tent, poking at the campfire with a stick. Now, the reverend was nowhere to be seen, and glowing embers were all that remained of the fire. The flash hadn't come from there. Carter swept the area. He muttered under his breath when he saw Marsden lying facedown on the ground not more than ten feet from the tent. The man was probably drunk again.

Carter continued surveying the area, stopping to focus on the new schoolhouse. It required a few finishing touches but was done for the most part. It was the first project Carter had taken on and seen to completion in over three years, and it filled him with pride. From the roof to the foundation…wait a minute! Jutting his head forward, Carter zeroed in on the base of the schoolhouse. Piles of something were stacked all around it. The workmen had already removed the excess building materials. Carter had helped. What was he looking at?

The next flash, magnified by the binoculars, knocked Carter backward. His head hit the tree, and he dropped the glasses. But he didn't need them anymore.

The schoolhouse was on fire.

Chapter 22

Lily's feet screamed in agony. Whoever had designed the torture devices disguised as shoes must surely have been a man, for no thought had gone into the comfort of the wearer. Lily limped her way across the ballroom, hoping that her huge skirt would work in her favor, for once, and mask her gait.

"Drink, miss?" Joseph smiled at her, a silver tray of crystal punch glasses in his hands.

Lily stopped cold. "That would be divine."

"If you say so, Miss Lily."

The sweet liquid slid down her throat, providing a moment of sweet relief. A couple came toward her, fresh from dancing, the woman giggling behind a silk fan, the man smiling down at her. As they passed, the man lifted two glasses from the tray. He didn't offer a word of thanks; he didn't even look Joseph in the eye. He simply took the drinks and moved on.

The proud Indian remained stoic. "Work to do, miss."

"Joseph, I—" But before she could finish, he was gone.

The punch lay heavy in Lily's stomach. She'd been so happy when Mama had agreed to hire on the Wiyot to serve at the ball.

The more the people of Eureka interacted with the Indians, the sooner both sides would realize they had nothing to fear. But they weren't really interacting. The Indians were hiding their resentment as they served the White Man, and the White Man was taking from the Indians without a smile or a thank-you, solidifying the roles they'd played for years. Lily sighed. In her desire to help, she had yet again failed to anticipate the ramifications of her actions.

A slightly salty ocean breeze swept through the open ballroom doors. Lily looked outside. Was Reverend Crew still in the garden? Her dance card finally empty, she wanted nothing more than to sit on a bench in the cool air and spill her heart to the preacher.

The crush of partygoers outside was nearly as great as that indoors. Lily made her way through the crowd, manipulating her skirts with her hands to keep from knocking anyone over. She felt as if she'd run the gauntlet when she finally spotted Reverend Crew. He stood by himself at the far end of the garden, his hands in his pockets, gazing out into the darkness. The man was a million miles away.

"A lovely evening, isn't it, Reverend?"

She'd obviously taken him by surprise. When he turned, she saw something on his face she'd never seen before—a mixture of anger and frustration that hardened his features and made her want to slink back into the crowd. But the expression was fleeting. As soon as his eyes locked on hers, he changed; his mouth lifted in a lazy grin, his eyes crinkled at the corners, and he was his normal, congenial self. "Miss Rose. It's a lovely evening, yes. And it just became a little lovelier."

He was probably just being polite, but the thought that Reverend Crew found her attractive brought heat blooming in her cheeks and spreading down her neck. Suddenly, the pain in her feet was just a minor distraction.

He leaned forward, his eyes narrowed a bit. "What brings you out here? I would have thought you'd be inside, charming the eligible young men and dancing until the wee hours."

"My dance card is empty." Lily thrust out her arm to show him the card, suspended from her wrist by a satin cord.

Removing one hand from his pocket, he reached out and opened the folded card. "So it is. Well then, might I interest you in a dance, Miss Rose?"

This was a time for action, not questions, but Lily couldn't stop herself. "Is that allowed? You're a preacher."

He chuckled and let go of the card. "Yes, I'm a preacher. But I'm also your friend. I believe it's appropriate for two friends to dance, especially at a charity ball. What do you think?"

She thought she was in deep trouble, because what she was starting to feel for Reverend Crew went beyond friendship. "I think—"

Two shots rang out, silencing Lily and everyone else in the garden. Reverend Crew spun around, facing the same direction as before, and started counting: "One...two...."

"Reverend, what—?"

He held up a hand to silence her as he continued his count. "Three...."

Lily squinted, following the reverend's gaze. And then she saw it. An orange glow. It began low and bled up against the velvet backdrop of the sky, higher and brighter.

"Four...."

Fire.

"Five...."

Another shot sounded.

A curse broke from Reverend Crew as he turned to Lily. "That's the Pink's signal." His fingers grasped her upper arm. "I need you to summon everyone you can to help, and send them to the schoolhouse. Do you understand?"

Lily nodded, then watched him run—not into the ballroom but toward the stables. "Where are you going?" she called after him.

"To help Forbes!"

Carter. He was by himself, facing an unknown number of ruffians. And now, Reverend Crew was going to help him. It would be two against…how many? Without a care as to whom or what her skirts hit, Lily raced into the ballroom. After all their hard work, this couldn't be happening. They couldn't lose the school. And she couldn't lose the two men she'd come to care so much for.

⌒

With a kick of his heels, Grant spurred the horse to a gallop. He rode faster than was safe in the pitch dark, but time was of the essence. Anybody in town who would miss him was at the Rose Cottage, and that bulldog of a Pinkerton was busy up at the schoolhouse. It was the perfect time for Grant to make his escape.

So it made absolutely no sense that he was heading in the other direction.

"Why did you have to go and grow a conscience now?" Grant mumbled under his breath as the horse pounded up the hard-packed dirt road. The old Grant Diamond would have reached the city limits by now. But leaving wasn't an option. Not to the new Grant Diamond. Whether it was from posing as a minister or being influenced by Miss Rose, he didn't know, but something had changed him during his time in Eureka.

The closer Grant got to the building site, the greater the feeling of dread grew in his chest. Sliding his hand beneath his jacket, he fingered the butt of his pistol.

The wind shifted and began to gust, enveloping Grant in smoke, ash, and flying embers. The mare shook her head, whinnying in protest. Patting her neck, Grant urged her forward, but now that the burning building was in sight, she refused to go any further. Grant swung from the saddle, tossed the reins over a nearby bush, and sprinted forward.

Flames licked the walls of the white frame building. There was no saving it—at least, not by himself.

"Forbes!" Grant hurried on, shielding his eyes with his arm. "Carter! Where in blazes are you?"

Grant cringed at his poor choice of words. Out of nowhere, a prayer came to mind: *Please, Lord, don't let him be anywhere near the flames.* A moan sounded over the crackling and whooshing glow. Two man-sized lumps lay beneath a tree not twenty feet away from the fire. Grant ran over, knelt beside them, and rolled the first one onto his back. It was Marsden, smelling of cheap whiskey. There was no sign of injury on the man; he must have passed out in a drunken stupor. Another groan called Grant's attention to the second man.

There was no doubt that Forbes had been attacked. Blood had matted the hair on his left temple and spattered his shirtfront.

"What happened to you, man?"

With a bestial roar, the beams of the schoolhouse gave way. The roof crashed in, sending up a shower of sparks. Grant instinctively leaned over Forbes, protecting his face. Nearby, a patch of dry grass lit up, the flames snaking closer and closer.

"That's our cue to leave." Grant looked from Forbes to Marsden. There was no way he could drag them both out, and Forbes was in worse shape. Grant shook Marsden's shoulder, trying to rouse the preacher, but was rewarded with only indistinguishable grumblings. This was no time to be delicate. He pulled back his hand and slapped the man across his pudgy cheek. His eyes flew open, and he looked around in confusion. "What? Where am—" A wall fell with another fiery burst, and Marsden's eyes grew as round as a hoot owl's. "Sweet Lord in heaven, I'm dead! I've gone to hell! Forgive me, Lord! Forgive me!" The man dissolved into hysterical sobs, rocking on his knees, his face in his hands.

With a growl, Grant grabbed him by the shirtfront, pulling him up to look at him. "You're not dead, you fool, but you will be if you don't move." He pointed away from the burning building. "If you want to stay out of hell, get over there. Crawl, if you have to. Just move."

Marsden's lips quivered and sputtered, but he sat still.

"Now!" Grant roared.

With a whimper, Marsden scrambled to his feet, teetered, then fell. A second later, the preacher was indeed crawling along the ground, away from the fire.

Grant shook his head. Once they got through this, something must be done about Marsden. The people of Eureka deserved better.

As do you.

The voice in his head was so loud, Grant thought someone had spoken in his ear. There was no time to ponder what it meant. He had to move Forbes.

He hunkered down beside the Pinkerton. Forbes moaned in pain as Grant pulled and maneuvered him over his shoulders. "Sorry, no time to be gentle." He pinned Forbes's legs beneath one arm and anchored his upper body with the other. Jaws clamped together, he rose with a determined grunt. Legs shaking, Grant moved as quickly as he could away from the fire.

He'd almost made it to the spot where Marsden had taken shelter when he stumbled and fell, landing hard on his knee. Pain sliced through his leg. The weight of Forbes on his back pushed him forward into the ground. He lost his grip, and Forbes rolled off of him, landing on his back. Pushing himself up on one elbow, Grant looked at the Pinkerton. His face, contorted with pain, became gruesome in the flickering orange light of the fire. He wasn't in good shape, but at least he was alive.

From a distance came the sound of pounding hooves and men's voices. Grant turned just in time to see the remaining bit of the schoolhouse topple over. Reinforcements were coming. But they were too late.

There was nothing left to save.

Grant's eyes burned, but not from the smoke or the heat. For the first time in his life, he'd been part of something truly good, something that would help others. Now evil men had destroyed it out of hatred and ignorance, and they'd nearly killed his friend. They wouldn't get away with it.

Not if Grant Diamond had any say in the matter.

Chapter 23

"Fire!" Lily's panicked cry drew plenty of attention. Conversations stuttered to a halt all around her, and everyone's eyes followed where she pointed, toward the orange flicker on the horizon.

Major Raines barked a command, and his men scrambled to set down cups of punch and offer hasty bows to dance partners. Less than a minute later, not a single soldier remained in the house. Several of the civilians followed suit, tumbling out into the garden.

Lily hurried through the yard, trying to find Papa in the crowd. When she spotted him, he was already mounting a hastily saddled horse. He was gone before she could fight her way through the gabbling crowds to the stable. Many guests seemed to be unsure whether to shriek, leave, or stay put. Lily's fingers clutched at her skirts. The dreadful crinoline would make it impossible to ride. She was losing precious minutes.

As if he'd read her mind, Joseph brought the cart to a stop beside her.

"Oh, Joseph! Bless you!"

He didn't look pleased at the sentiment. "Miss Lily, I don't know if your m—"

A hand gripped Lily's arm, and she turned. There was Mama. "You're not going to gawk at a fire. It's undignified."

"You're right, Mama. I'm not going to gawk." Lily set her chin. "I'm going to help."

"Help? What can you possibly do?"

"I can pass a bucket as easily as anyone else."

"You'll just be in the way."

"I won't be in the way, and I won't be in danger."

Mama sighed heavily, and, for the first time, Lily could see lines of age and fatigue creasing her face. Lily patted the hand still clutching her arm. "I have to go, Mama. I *have* to."

Shoulders sagging as if she were too weary to fight anymore, Mama nodded.

Joseph reached down to give Lily a hand up.

Many of the partygoers had gone back to drinking punch and chatting. If anything, the fire had spiced up the evening, as the guests now had something interesting to speculate about. Lily looked back at the crowd. How could they be so complacent? She wondered if there was anything more she could do to spur them to action. Her gaze found Mr. Abernathy standing at the bottom of the front stairs. His eyes locked onto hers, his lips twisted in a mirthless grin, and he raised his glass in a tiny salute.

Joseph snapped the reins, and Lily grabbed the edge of the seat as the cart lurched forward. How could Mr. Abernathy be so cold? So uncaring? He'd seemed to be making progress, but perhaps it had been nothing more than a show. And to what purpose? Lily could think of no benefit he'd gain from such a ruse. Maybe she was being judgmental again. In truth, he hadn't behaved any worse than the hundred other guests who could not be bothered to leave the festivities.

The cart hit a rut, jostling Lily's thoughts back to the task at hand. What would they find when they arrived at the site? How much of the schoolhouse would need to be rebuilt? Taking a deep breath, she squeezed her fingers into fists and murmured the words of her favorite psalm: "*God is our refuge and strength, a very present help in trouble.*"

As the school came into sight, Lily could see the soldiers from Fort Humboldt and a half-dozen other men. But there was none of the frenzy of activity she'd expected. They stood on the perimeter of the destruction, where dying flames consumed the last of the schoolhouse. Part of her knew there was nothing to be done—the school was already lost—but a larger part wanted to scream and throw things at the men. To make them stop the greedy blaze from devouring the hope of the Wiyot people.

She stumbled from the cart without waiting for Joseph's assistance. Her dress caught on something. She pulled away, ignoring the sound of ripping fabric. Blind to any danger, she pushed her way through the outermost ring of men. Before she could draw too close, someone caught her and held her back.

"Turn me loose." She croaked the words through the lump of emotion in her throat.

"Can't do that, miss. It's too dangerous. We don't want an errant spark singeing that pretty dress of yours."

The man chuckled, no doubt to lighten the mood, but his effort had the opposite effect. Tears of bitter disappointment spilled down Lily's cheeks. She sank to her knees, her face in her hands.

A groan of anguish arose from deep within her. "God, how could You let this happen? Will You let evil win?" She bent under the weight of the question, until her corset so constricted her airflow that the edges of her vision grew black.

She dropped her hands, her fingers digging into tufts of grass turned brittle by the heat of the flames. Staring silently into the fire, she was aware of men shuffling around her, their talk guarded and hushed, until it finally petered out, and only the crackle of flames, and the distant murmur of the ocean, could be heard.

Lily closed her eyes. *The ocean.* Ever constant, ever present. A testament to the power and majesty of its Creator.

A wave of resolve straightened her spine and snapped her eyes open. "God, please…I don't understand what You're doing, but I know You have a plan. Please reveal the good You will bring from this, in Your time. May Your will be accomplished." Her voice choked off into a dry sob. "Please, Lord. Let there be no more bloodshed."

⟶

Aside from the occasional, incoherent moan, Forbes hadn't made a move since Grant had dropped him like a sack of potatoes. A hand beneath the Pinkerton's nose confirmed he was still breathing.

"Excuse me, Reverend."

Squatting on the balls of his feet, Grant looked up into the face of one of the soldiers. Any other day, Grant would have laughed at being caught between a Pinkerton and a soldier, but today, it was about as normal as anything else. "Yes?"

The young man motioned behind them. "Sir, Miss Rose is taking the fire badly."

Grant frowned. "Miss Rose is here?"

"Yes, sir. Major Raines wondered if you might be able to help."

He should have known Lily wouldn't stay away. "Of course. Keep an eye on Mr. Forbes, would you?" Feeling as creaky as a hundred-year-old house, Grant fought to stand without help.

Lily was on her knees, her hands in the dirt, her head bowed, her shoulders heaving from the power of her sobs. Didn't she realize how dangerous a fire could be? Had she no regard for her personal safety? He wanted to throttle her and wipe away her tears at the same time.

He approached quietly, the other men watching him as if he were a lion tamer approaching a beast. As he came alongside her, she sprang up, and a prayer tumbled from her lips. The simple words stopped him cold. Yes, she was devout, but how could anyone trust God that deeply? How could she expect to find anything good in an event that had so devastated her? He couldn't imagine being so...passive. Then again, there had to be immense peace in possessing that kind of assurance. What would it be like to know he didn't have to carry every burden on his own? To know that he didn't always need to have an answer?

Grant knelt beside her and placed a hand gently on her shoulder. "Miss Lily."

Turning to him, she blinked a few times, as if trying to register who he was. "Reverend Crew?" For a fraction of a second, one corner of her mouth quirked up, as though she tried to force a smile, but it was for naught. Her lips twisted, and a cry escaped. "It's all destroyed."

He wasn't quite sure how it happened, but seconds later, she was in his arms, a fresh torrent of grief surging from her. Poor little bird. One moment, she was as resolute as an eagle; the next, as frail as a sparrow. Grant made comforting sounds and patted her back, reminding himself that to those who stood around and watched, he was a pastor offering consolation to a good Christian woman.

"We'll get through this, Lily," he whispered, trying to ignore how her lavender-scented hair tickled his nose, despite the thick odor of smoke around them.

Her sobs subsided into sniffles. With a hand on each of her shoulders, Grant gently pushed her away from him. As he looked into her eyes, he wanted to promise her that everything would be all right, that he would protect her, but those were promises he couldn't make. Instead, he said the one thing he knew to be true. "Evil will not win."

Lily blinked, took a gulp of air, and shook her head. "No. It won't."

She still seemed dazed and in shock. Grant needed to get her focused on something else. And he had just the thing. "Forbes has been hurt, and I could use your help."

She gasped, a hand flying to her throat. "I didn't know." For an instant, he feared she'd descend into sobs again. Instead, she waved over a couple of the men who'd been standing around. "Joseph and I brought the cart. If we can load him into it, we can get him back to the house and send for the doctor."

Grant nodded and watched as she ran off to get Joseph. There was the Lily Rose he'd come to know and love.

No, not love. Respect, admire…but not love. She deserved far better than anything he could offer.

With the help of several soldiers, Grant maneuvered Forbes into the cart. Lily cradled the detective's head in her lap to keep it from jarring against the wooden seat. Grant hopped up into the front next to Joseph, but he turned around to keep hold of Forbes and make sure he stayed anchored over the bumpy track back to town.

Grant had managed to stanch the bleeding from Forbes's head wound, but the movement had started it going again. Blood seeped down his face and onto Lily's skirt, where it spread out in a slow stain. Grant frowned. One more thing ruined today. Lily looked up at him, a sad half smile on her lips. "It's only a dress, Reverend Crew."

As if to prove her point, she reached down and, after much tugging, tore a swath of fabric from the hem. She held it to the wound on Forbes's forehead. Looking down at him, she moved her lips in a silent prayer.

At the Rose Cottage, Joseph started steering the cart toward the back.

"Drive to the front, please, Joseph," Lily requested.

"Miss?" Joseph pulled the horse to a stop and looked over his shoulder. "If we go in the back, we can get Mr. Forbes upstairs with no one seeing."

Lily shook her head. "That's exactly the point. I won't let the complacent people of Eureka ignore what's going on right under their noses. They will face the consequences of tonight's atrocities, whether they want to or not."

Joseph raised his eyebrows and nodded slowly, respect shining in his eyes. "As you say, Miss Lily."

"You don't think the party is still going on, do you?" Grant asked.

"No, Reverend, I don't think it is. I know it is."

Joseph brought the cart to a halt directly in front of the porch steps. The wheels had barely stopped turning when Lily eased Carter's head out of her lap and descended from the conveyance. She went ahead and opened the front doors, after which Grant and Joseph carefully carried Carter inside.

Grant was shocked to discover she'd been right. Most of the partygoers were still assembled, dancing, laughing, and partaking of refreshments.

"Excuse me. Pardon me." Lily cleared a path, loudly announcing their presence. Gasps went up and whispers raced around the room as the guests took in her bloodstained, sooty, grimy appearance. But she ignored them all with magnificent aplomb. Grant was certain he looked no better, but almost no one spared him a glance. Their eyes moved from Lily to Forbes and back again.

Mrs. Rose pressed through the crowd and stopped short when she reached her daughter, sucking in a huge gasp. "Lily, your beautiful dress! What happened?"

Lily kept moving as if she hadn't heard. At the stairs, she turned. "Joseph, once he's in bed, please take the cart and fetch Dr. Paul."

The Wiyot nodded.

She mounted the first step and turned to face the crowd. "Ladies and gentlemen, thank you so much for coming and showing your support for our brave soldiers. As I'm sure you know, the money raised tonight will go toward purchasing new, quality boots for them all and ensuring they have adequate winter garments as they face the prospect of battle. But now, as you can see, we are facing another battle, right here in Eureka. It's a battle against hatred and ignorance, and tonight, it resulted in a tragedy. The new school for the Wiyot was burned to the ground, and Mr. Forbes was gravely injured as he strove to protect it. Now he needs quiet and rest. Although I hate to cut short your evening of gaiety, I'm afraid we must tend to the wounded men."

Though Lily hadn't shouted, Grant had heard her speech all the way upstairs and down the hall in Forbes's room. He bit the inside of his cheek to keep from smiling. She had more of her mother in her than she realized.

There was a general rustle and murmur among the crowd as they moved to follow Lily's directions.

Grant and Joseph lay Carter gingerly on the bed, and Grant began removing one of Carter's boots, but Joseph stopped him. "I'll tend to Mr. Forbes. You'd best go down and check on Miss Lily."

Grant chuckled. "Sounds to me like she's got the situation under control."

"She does." Joseph looked up from their patient, his dark eyes pinning Grant. "But she shouldn't have to handle it alone."

No, she shouldn't. With a nod of agreement, Grant left the room and descended the stairs. He found Lily standing with Naomi in the ballroom. Though his plan had been to support and assist her, he instead positioned himself on the other side of the doorway, behind a large clump of festive bunting, from whence he could watch and listen.

Lily rattled off a list of detailed instructions, ticking them off on her fingers as she did so. "The water will cool quickly, so make sure it's boiling when you bring it. There are clean bandages set aside in the linen closet. Bring those, and the creosote, and perhaps some laudanum, though we won't dose him until Dr. Paul arrives. I'm not sure one ought to sedate a man with a head injury."

Naomi scurried away, and Lily saw to the last of the departing guests. She shooed away the musicians, who were demanding payment, and instructed them to return on the morrow, when her father was home. Then, she walked over to her mother, who stood forlornly in the entrance to the ballroom, wringing her hands.

Lily put an arm around the older woman and guided her toward the stairs. "Mama, you look done in. Why don't you go up to bed? I can manage here."

Mrs. Rose shook her head. "I declare, Lily, you do beat all." But she started up the stairs without further protest.

This was a side of Lily that Grant had not fully appreciated before. It seemed that in real crises, she was calm and sure of herself—and of her God. Was that the source of her sudden wellspring of confidence? Or was it simply that when she didn't have time to analyze everything as it happened, she didn't question her every move?

Whatever the cause, her adroit handling of the situation caused his heart to swell with pride. Even greater was his respect for her determination to stand up for what was right. And then, with a sinking sensation, Grant realized that his feelings went far beyond mere pride and respect. He'd done the one thing he'd known he should never do—he had fallen hopelessly and irretrievably in love with Lily Rose.

Which meant he had a decision to make. Did he get out of Eureka now, before his infatuation grew even more? Not for a moment did he fool himself into thinking he could make her his. He couldn't continue lying to her, but to tell her the truth would only seal his fate. Once she found out he wasn't her long-awaited missionary but a two-bit gambler and a fugitive, she'd be so disgusted, she'd probably spit. She might even consider him worse than Abernathy.

The possibility stung.

But Lily deserved better. She deserved Forbes. Yet, with Forbes laid up, there'd be no one to protect her from Abernathy if Grant left now. Swallowing the hard knot in his throat, he made his decision. He'd remain in Eureka long enough to ensure Abernathy didn't snare her, and then he'd bow out gracefully, leaving Forbes with a clear field.

For once in his miserable life, Grant would do the right thing. No matter how much it hurt.

Chapter 24

Light stabbed through a gap in the curtains, and Carter closed his eyes against the pain. Why hadn't the drapes been closed all the way? Were they trying to torture him? He gulped against the nausea rising in his throat.

Thumps, bumps, and conversation from the rousing household made it impossible for him to go back to sleep. That, and the tangled confusion of his thoughts. They were fractured into a thousand shards that splintered further upon his attempts to examine them.

The squeak of the door hinges told him someone had entered the room. The sound of footsteps, punctuated by the jingle of spurs, made him suspect it was the reverend.

He opened one eye and confirmed his hunch. At least he hadn't lost his ability to decipher clues.

"I've got some breakfast for you," Crew said.

"Mmph."

"The doctor said you should eat."

Carter opened his other eye. "What happened last night?"

Crew's brows pulled together in a frown. "They burned down the school."

One of the fractured images in Carter's mind coalesced, and he nodded. "That's right. The fire. You heard my signal?"

"I heard it. But it was too late by the time I got there. You'd been hit over the head."

"I don't remember that."

"Doc Paul says that's to be expected."

Carter pushed aside his covers. "I need to examine the site for clues." He sat up and groaned, holding his head between his hands to keep it from falling off.

"I don't think you're supposed to get out of that bed, Forbes." Crew put a strong hand on his shoulder. "The doctor says you need rest."

"It's just a bump on the head. I'll be all right."

Crew shook his head in resignation. "Nothing I say is going to make you lie back down, is it?"

"Nope." Carter gritted his teeth against the pain that shot through his temple.

"You're as bad as Miss Rose." Crew walked across the room and picked up something from a chair. "Here are your pants." He tossed them over.

Carter reached out reflexively, stifling another groan as his garment landed on the bed beside him. Fumbling, he managed to get one leg in.

Crew crossed the room and opened the curtains the rest of the way. Carter winced, almost ready to agree to stay put. The thought of burrowing beneath the covers, his aching head cradled by the soft pillow, was mighty tempting. But he couldn't. He needed to examine the site of the fire. If he could find proof of the culprits, he could force the sheriff to do something about the vandalism.

Without looking at Crew, Carter swallowed his pride and said, "Help me with my shirt, would you?"

It took Carter twice as long as usual to descend the massive staircase, and he cursed every step as it jarred his body and sent pain jolting through his skull. Upon alighting the bottom stair, he breathed a sigh of relief, only to have Miss Rose accost him, wagging her forefinger in his face. "You have no excuse for being out of bed, Mr. Forbes. The doctor prescribed plenty of rest, and that's exactly what you're going to get."

Beside him, Crew snickered, then whispered under his breath, "Now you're in for it."

That was an understatement. She was so fired up, it'd be downright funny, if Carter didn't feel as if he'd been run over by a stagecoach. "Miss Rose, I appreciate your concern. Truly." He spoke slowly and gently, for her benefit as well as his own. "I won't lie to you. I feel about a hundred kinds of terrible. But I'm physically able to do my job, and right now, that's more important than my personal comfort. If the arsonists left any clues behind, I must examine the site while there's still a chance of finding them."

She blinked a few times—not the fast fluttering of lashes that so many women seemed to think was comely, but the slow blinking of someone in deep contemplation. "I know your job is important to you, Mr. Forbes, but—"

"This isn't just a job. The fire is personal. That schoolhouse is the only project I've seen through from beginning to end in years. It's important to me, and to every single Wiyot who wants to be treated like a human being by the citizens of Eureka. If I don't investigate this crime, what kind of a message will that send them?"

"The wrong one." Miss Rose looked from him to Crew. "What do you think, Reverend?"

Crew shrugged. "I think a man knows his own body. If Forbes says he's up to it, then he probably is."

Carter could see the struggle play out across her face as she balanced her need to nurture with her desire to see justice done.

Finally, she nodded. "Very well. I'll have Joseph bring the cart around. We'll be ready to leave shortly."

"We?" Both men asked the question in unison.

"Yes, *we*." A bark of laughter shot from her lips. "You don't expect me to stay behind, do you?"

Actually, that was exactly what Carter had expected her to do. But one look at the lift of her chin and the challenge in her eyes told him he needed to revise his thinking. If he expected her to let him leave the house, then he needed to meet her conditions.

With a sideways glance at Crew, who appeared to be struggling to hold back a smirk, Carter admitted defeat. "Very well, Miss Rose. We'll do it your way."

The sky was gray and pregnant with rain, but the weak sunlight leaking through the clouds was enough to make Carter squint. With every bump and jostle of the wagon, the detective's face grew paler. Lily bit her lip. The man really should be back at the cottage, getting the rest Dr. Paul had ordered. But she understood exactly how he felt, because the same feelings burned within her. The pride of having brought the schoolhouse to completion made its destruction all the more devastating. A clap of thunder rumbled in the distance, just before fat drops of rain started plopping down. Thankful for Joseph's foresight in stowing an umbrella beneath the seat, Lily opened it and held it over Carter.

Scowling, he pushed it away. "I'm not an invalid."

"You should be resting, though."

He fussed with the edge of the broad bandage swathing his head. "Clues live a brief life, especially when you throw rain in the mix. There will be plenty of time for resting later."

The wagon came around a bend in the road, and any protest she might have offered died silently. A group of Wiyot were clustered in front of the still-smoking ruins. Not one of them cried. If anything, they looked resigned, as if they believed the fire had been inevitable. But they were there, standing in a silent vigil.

When the cart came to a halt, Lily lowered herself down. Without the constraints of bulky hoops requiring her to calculate her every step, she was free to move naturally and to think about the situation at hand. She wove among the Wiyot, offering a word of encouragement here, a pat on the arm there.

A thin wail caught Lily's ear, and she turned around. Reverend Crew knelt before a young Wiyot girl whom Lily had often seen with her mother at the building site. Only about five or six, she hadn't yet adopted the adults' stoicism. All she knew was that the building she'd witnessed go up, where she'd been promised she would go to school with the other children, had been destroyed.

Lily watched as the reverend spoke in low, soothing tones to the girl, who snuffled, popped her thumb in her mouth, and nodded. With a smile, Reverend Crew pulled a square of fabric from an inside pocket of his jacket. "That thumb can't taste very good," he said. "Tell you what. If you promise to stop sucking on it, I'll bring you a stick of sugar candy when we come back to rebuild the school." He held out the handkerchief. "What do you say?"

The girl's eyes were as round as a full moon. "You'll build us another school?" Her words were slightly garbled, since she spoke around her thumb.

"Yes, of course we will."

She pulled the thumb out of her mouth, snatched the handkerchief, and blew her nose into it.

"Good girl." He ruffled her hair.

"I will tell Mama about the new school." She turned and scampered away.

Lily had never seen Reverend Crew quite as open before. There was something so honest about him, so caring. He was such a selfless man. So then, why did Lily feel suddenly uneasy?

The reverend stood to his feet and turned in her direction. Their eyes locked, and for a moment, she wondered if he knew what she'd been thinking. He took a step toward her, but one of the Wiyot men approached him. Duty called. She no longer had the reverend's attention.

It didn't take long for Lily to discover the cause of her anxiety. Her heart pounded against her chest from the exhilaration of her brief exchange with Reverend Crew—and from disappointment that he'd turned his attention to someone else. It wasn't right. None of it was right.

She had fallen in love with a man of the cloth. A man for whom she would never, ever be good enough.

～

Carter left Miss Rose and the reverend speaking with the Wiyot. People weren't his strong suit. Finding evidence was. And at least the rain had slowed. That should keep any potential clues from being completely destroyed. He walked slowly around the burnt-out husk of the schoolhouse, his eyes roving the ground for anything unusual or out of place. The muddy field had been trampled by numerous boots. Footprints would be of no use, even if the rain hadn't begun washing them all away.

Carter made one circuit of the building. Then another, slightly wider. Nothing.

He wasn't going to give up, though. There had to be something. No man-made fire could have burned so quickly without some sort of additional fuel. The arsonist must have left some clue.

Behind him, Carter heard Lily ask Crew to pray over the building and the Wiyot.

There was a pause, and then the preacher's voice came, soft and hesitant. "Lord, I…we ask that You would give us wisdom. Help us to know what to do next. And…and provide a way for this school to be built and to flourish."

Carter paused in his search out of deference to the prayer, staring into the blankness of the cloudy horizon. Blankness. Emptiness. Of course. If nothing else, he knew that Marsden hadn't set the fire. The man had been too pickled to stand. Even if he had been the one to ignite the blaze, there was no way he could have disposed of the evidence. But maybe he had seen something.

The rattle of wheels concluded Crew's prayer, and Carter turned, bracing for trouble. One wagon came into view, and then a second. Behind them, more people arrived on foot. Every one of them had something in hand: a box of nails, a handsaw, a hammer. Trailing them was a detail of more than twenty soldiers from the fort. Lily and Crew had moved in front of the Wiyot, as if expecting trouble. Now they wore looks of surprise that no attack could provoke.

"That was some good praying, Reverend," Carter said as he joined the two.

A quick count revealed that more than fifty people from Eureka made up the delegation.

At the end of the procession, Lily's parents smiled from their finest carriage, which, Carter couldn't help but note with envy, had a roof and doors to keep them dry and warm, despite the rain. Mrs. Rose looked downright smug. She emerged from the carriage, the picture of grace, and strode toward her daughter. "Lily-belle, you should smile, dear. We're here to help."

Chapter 25

Lily couldn't quite seem to lift her jaw off the ground. "Mama?"

"Honestly, dear, I can't imagine why you're so stunned. I simply informed a few people of the need, and everyone clamored to help."

"Only you could turn this into a fashionable undertaking." Lily stepped forward and planted a kiss on Mama's cheek. "Thank you for coming."

Mama squeezed her hand. "I know I can be hard on you, Lily-belle, but I'm not entirely coldhearted."

"I know."

For the first time in what seemed a very long span, Mama looked her in the eye, rather than focusing on her dress or her hair. They shared a tentative smile, like two youthful playmates being introduced. Then, Mama sniffed. "Well, I'm here to help, so tell me what to do."

Lily glanced around. Papa had already assumed the role of supervisor. Men were shoveling the charred remnants of the schoolhouse into wheelbarrows to be carted away by others.

Lily's attention was caught by Carter, who was trying to keep an eye on everyone, as well as on each pile of debris. His gaze swiveled this way and that, until it looked as if his eyes were rolling madly and he was about to have a fit. Her face hurt just looking at his bruises.

She turned to her mother. "Could you take charge of the ladies? All the supplies that were brought should be organized and inventoried so we can figure out what we have and what we still need. I imagine everyone will be hungry before long, too. Oh! And, Mama? Everyone should cover his or her mouth and nose with a handkerchief. It's still very smoky, and there's a lot of ash in the air."

"Just leave it to me, dear." With a final pat on Lily's arm, Mama glided away.

Lily gave her head a bemused shake. The idea that Mama actually supported her interest in the Wiyot seemed ludicrous. She couldn't imagine what had made her change her mind. Unfortunately, she had no time to dwell on that miracle. She needed to see to Carter before he caused himself permanent injury.

Despite the stiff breeze coming off the bay, he was perspiring, and his face was grayer than the ashes beneath their feet. How could she induce him to rest?

"Mr. Forbes, can't I persuade you to at least sit down?"

He shook his head. "I might miss something. There are too many people. Too much"—he waved a hand at the blackened remains of the building—"everything."

"What if Reverend Crew and I were to look, as well?"

Carter swayed slightly, and Lily moved closer, ready to brace him if he began to collapse. "You don't know what to look for."

"What *are* you looking for?"

His rough laugh sounded more like a grunt. "That's the other problem. I don't know."

The postmaster sauntered up behind Carter. "Glad to see you're back on your feet, Forbes. This whole affair was a real shame."

"Takes more than a bump on the head to lick me."

"I've heard you Pinkerton fellows were tough, and now I guess I believe it. By the by, I've got that message you've been waiting for, I think. It's down at the post office whenever you want to stop in."

"Thank you kindly, Mr. Andrews. It's been so long, I'd nearly forgotten about it."

"And thank you for coming today," said Lily.

"Oh, think nothing of it. This sort of thing's not right. These Diggers ain't been so bad. They seem like quiet, regular folks to me. We all gotta figure out a way to live alongside each other." He tipped his hat and headed off.

Lily beamed after him. If only more people approached the Indians, and even one another, with such an attitude, Eureka and all of northern California would be a safer, happier place. She looked around at the willing workers. It was a start. God seemed to be bringing something good out of the destruction.

Carter took a fumbling step, and her attention immediately snapped back to him. "Maybe I-I'd better sit, a-after all." He slurred his words and looked as if he might drop in a heap where he stood.

Lily offered an arm, and he leaned heavily against her.

They'd gone no more than ten paces when Reverend Crew appeared on Forbes's other side. The reverend bent and came up beneath the detective's arm, so it draped over his shoulder. "I've got him."

They walked clear of the bustle and let him sag to the ground on a grassy hummock. His head resting on one knee, Carter breathed as if he'd just hiked the Matterhorn.

"I'm all right. Just got dizzy. I think it was the smoke." The detective thumped the ground with his fist. "I'm not going to be able to do it, am I?"

Reverend Crew shook his head. "You don't have to. We'll be your agents."

Carter lifted a hand to probe his bandaged head. "Take a look around. Keep an eye out for anything that seems odd or out of place."

"We can do that," Lily rushed to assure him, before he resumed the notion that he was the only one with eyes.

Reverend Crew knelt, put a hand on the detective's shoulder, and looked him in the eye. "Forbes, the Lord knows we've had our differences, but I promise you we'll do everything humanly possible to help you. We're on the same side."

The detective nodded, at last, and seemed to relax a little, though his complexion was no less green. "You need to look for what's not there, too."

Lily touched the back of her hand to Carter's forehead to check for fever. As she did, she cast a sideways glance at Reverend Crew. How could they look for what wasn't there?

"No cans, or...b-bottles...o' th' ground." Carter's words were growing more garbled. "Mmmarsden di'n't set th' fire."

Lily finally realized what he'd meant. She nodded. "Don't worry about a thing, Mr. Forbes. We'll bring you everything we find, and you can tell us if any of it is important."

"Tha' wou' be...good." His eyes drifted closed.

She glanced again at Reverend Crew, who cocked his head at Joseph, digging in the ash. She nodded. They needed to get Carter home and out of the rain.

By the time they bundled the detective into the cart, his head was lolling, and he didn't awaken. Joseph promised to dose him with something to make him sleep if he should wake up before being put to bed.

When at last the Pinkerton had been dispatched, Lily turned to Reverend Crew. "Do you think there's anything left to find?"

He shrugged. "Only one way to know for sure."

An hour later, the site was clear. Lily pressed her fingers into the small of her back and pulled her shoulder blades together, trying to release some of the tension caused by stooping to examine every bit of debris distinguishable from mere ash. A rumble of approaching wheels announced the arrival of new lumber.

Reverend Crew glanced at her. "Well? Have you developed any hypotheses?"

She tilted her head to look at him. "I think the window on the south side of the school must have been smashed in before the fire. Most of the glass was inside the foundation, some if it fairly far down. They might have thrown a lit rag inside, lending to my hunch that Marsden wasn't an accomplice. Even as incapacitated as he was, he might have been able to pull a brand or a burning rag away from the schoolhouse, had it been placed on the building's exterior. But starting the fire inside would have kept him from putting it out."

The reverend raised his eyebrows. "Miss Rose, I'm impressed. If you ever tire of doing good, the Pinkertons could use you."

Lily smiled back. "I don't think the Pinkerton lifestyle would agree with me. I'd rather prevent bad things from happening in the first place than chase a culprit after it's too late. Did you discover anything?"

He nodded. "I noticed the same thing about the window, though I didn't follow the trail of logic as far as you. I think whoever was behind the fire was counting on the ball. He likely knew that was where the majority of the townspeople would be, as well as most of the Wiyot. How many people knew that the Wiyot would be staffing the event?"

Lily furrowed her brow, trying to think. "Any number of people could have known. It wasn't a secret. But I don't think we had any reason to bring it up, either."

He stared at her hard. "Could Abernathy have known?"

She looked at her sooty hands, then wiped them on her equally sooty apron. "He could have. I don't know if he did."

Mama swooped in on her. "Lily, dear, I've just had the most marvelous idea. When we get the school rebuilt, we must hold a special dedication ceremony. It will be the perfect opportunity to thank all of the kindhearted volunteers. I bet we could even compel some of them to pay for books and slates and other necessities."

"Do you really think so, Mama?"

"Oh, yes. We need to plan a proper celebration, of course. Reverend Crew can speak, and perhaps there could be a recitation by the Wiyot children. We can make some banners...oh! I wonder how long it would take the carpenter over in Arcata to build some small desks. It would certainly complete the picture if there were desks. Of course, we'll invite the soldiers again. They helped put the fire out, after all. And I don't think you were able to dance with but one or two." She walked away, still thinking aloud.

Once again, Lily was left speechless and stared after her mother. Reverend Crew nudged her with his elbow. "Looks like the good Lord answered your prayers. Anyone would think this had been her idea all along."

⁓

A bittersweet knot formed in Grant's chest. It seemed like things were starting to work out for Lily. Before long, Forbes would recover completely, and she wouldn't need "Reverend Crew" anymore.

Looking past Lily, he caught sight of an awkward figure on horseback. As the fellow came closer, Grant realized it was Reverend Marsden, looking rather ill and waxy, riding an old nag even sorrier than Grant's. Marsden all but fell off his mount and hurried toward them, his gait uneven.

"Miss Rose," he panted. "Miss Rose. Is the Pinkerton here? I need you all to know that I didn't have anything to do with the fire. I swear to you."

Lily drew him away from the main hive of activity, where men were unloading logs and staking a new foundation. "I believe you didn't set the fire, Reverend. But if you hadn't been so...inebriated, you might have been able to prevent it."

The poor fellow's eyes looked about ready to pop from his head. "That's just the thing. I didn't drink much at all. I'll put my hand on my Bible and swear before God and man. I don't know what happened, but I wasn't drunk."

Grant gave a small shrug when Lily looked to him. Marsden seemed to be in earnest, but whether that was because the story was true or because it was what he needed to believe was difficult to tell.

Grant clasped the man's shoulder to steady him, as well as to draw his fervent gaze away from Lily. "Did you hear or see anything before the fire?"

Marsden shook his head.

"No one came by or rode up?"

"Not a soul."

"We think they must have used fuel of some sort to make the fire catch so quickly. That means they must have brought it with them. They probably would have had to use horses or wagons."

Marsden clasped his hands together as if in prayer. "Nobody came around, I swear. Except for Mr. Abernathy, but that was well before the fire. Before it was even dark. He'd heard I'd be out here, and he brought me a bite of supper before heading to the ball."

Grant straightened and focused more intently on Marsden. "Was he cordial?"

"Abernathy? Friendly as could be. Like I said, he brought me some dinner. And I had a tot of whiskey with him." He fluttered a hand. "But that was the only drink I had all night. I swear it."

Grant looked at Lily to see how she was taking these details. She frowned, but more pensively than angrily. "You just had the one glass?" she asked.

"Half a glass. I told him I shouldn't drink even that much, but he said it was chilly out, which it was. So, I took it, and he didn't press me any further. He was here only ten minutes or so. No one else came by after that. It's not like he could have distracted me while the fire was set. As I said, this was a couple of hours before dark."

"Did you get suddenly sleepy?" Grant asked.

Marsden blinked. "I did. Couldn't keep my eyes open. But it wasn't because I was drunk."

No, Grant thought, meeting Lily's wide eyes. *It was because you'd been drugged*. Now they needed to find a way to prove it.

⁓

The next morning, Lily came downstairs for Sunday breakfast to find that Reverend Crew had already gone out. Mr. Forbes's bruises looked worse, but he was moving more normally. The previous night, he'd made Lily and the reverend give him a full report of their discoveries, deductions, and discussions at his bedside before he would consent to taking another drop of medicine. The detective had been intrigued, and Lily had practically been able to see his thoughts as he lay on his bed, mulling over all the implications. She'd decided then and there never to play him in chess. Right now, she suspected that Reverend Crew was on a mission for Forbes.

Reverend Crew had yet to return when they were ready to leave for church, so they set out without him. Nor did he show up prior to the service.

Mr. Abernathy was there, however, seated in the pew in front of theirs. He stood at their arrival and bowed over Mama's hand, then Lily's. "Miss Rose, the ball was exquisite. You ladies did a fine job. It's just a shame that nonsense with the Indians had to interrupt such a wonderful evening."

Lily pointedly removed her hand from his. "The *shame* is that there are people so full of hate that they are willing to destroy property and lives."

Abernathy continued to nod, as if she were elaborating on some point he'd just made. "I don't know that Reverend Marsden has been quite right since that Indian Island incident. I understand he's been hitting the bottle rather heavily, but I think we should try to extend extra grace to him, don't you?"

He was taunting her. Eyes wide, Lily bared her teeth, about to tell him what she really thought of him. But the organ bellowed its first chord, cutting her off. Mama put a hand on Lily's arm and beckoned her to sit down. Abernathy did so, his hat on his knee, his hands folded in a pious pose.

Lily fumed as she turned around and sat down in her seat. All his interest in helping the Indians had been mere pretense. She was sure of that now. And he thought her too gullible to notice. Well, he wasn't going to get away with what he'd done.

She was going to make sure of it.

Reverend Marsden took the pulpit after only the second hymn, and the congregants exchanged questioning glances with one another. He looked terrible, his eyes red and swollen, his cheeks shrunken. Lily watched him for any telltale signs of drunkenness.

He cleared his throat. "My dear church family, I have come to realize that our town is in the grip of a great evil, and I'm afraid that I…I have fostered that evil."

A murmur rippled through the congregation.

Lily could see his hands shaking, but his voice remained steady. "Last year, as you all know, a vicious crime was committed nearby. Over a hundred men, women, and children were murdered. It was not a fight or a battle, for they had no means of defending themselves. No, they were murdered. The greater tragedy is that nothing has been done about it." He dropped his gaze to the pulpit, where he had placed his Bible. "I have been a coward. I've hidden behind a bottle, trying to blot out the guilt of my complicity. By our silence and our lack of moral outrage, we are just as guilty of those deaths as the men who wielded the knives."

No one made a sound. In fact, no one seemed to be breathing. Tears burned Lily's eyes. She couldn't tear her gaze away from Reverend Marsden's face.

"Well, no more. This has got to stop. We cannot live our lives based on hatred or, worse, apathy. The Lord offers His grace to all the nations of the earth. How dare we offer less?"

Abernathy shifted in his seat and turned his head right, then left, cracking it, as if preparing for a fight. Lily snatched up her parasol and jabbed the steel tip into his back. "Don't you dare get up, and don't say a word," she murmured. She hoped desperately that he would think a gun butted against his spine.

Out of the corner of her eye, she saw Mama stare at her, wide-eyed, then glance in both directions to see if any of Abernathy's men had noticed. Mama folded her hands in her lap and straightened her already rigid spine.

Reverend Marsden kept speaking, apparently oblivious to the exchange. "I know I haven't been much of a shepherd to you folks this past year. I've let you down, time and again. But together we can make this right. We may not be able to bring back the dead, but we can make certain that such a thing does not happen again, and we can begin to heal the wounds that have scarred the spirit of this community for too long."

He climbed down off the platform and marched down the aisle. Everyone except for Lily and Abernathy turned in his seat to watch. Lily kept her parasol in place. She could practically feel the tension pulsing from him. If she moved, that anger would be unleashed.

She could hear the doors being flung open and Marsden calling to the Indian servants, inviting them inside. "Brothers and sisters, I ask your forgiveness. I have treated you poorly, but I'd like to make amends. Please join us."

A long moment passed before the shuffle of feet announced that at least some of the Wiyot had decided to enter the church. Marsden led them to the front row, where they sat down tentatively.

The preacher resumed his place behind the pulpit. "As long as I am the pastor of this congregation—which may not be all that long, considering the hash I've made of it—nevertheless, while I remain, you will be welcome in our services."

Evidently deciding that she wouldn't shoot him, Abernathy shot up out of his seat. Lily reared back, her parasol falling to the floor.

"I'm not standing for this." He jammed his hat on his head. "Marsden! You're going to regret this decision." Then he marched out of the church. Some twenty-five or thirty other parishioners followed his lead.

Marsden clung tightly to the pulpit but didn't call them back. When the door slammed behind them, someone began to clap. Lily turned. It was Reverend Crew. Her heart soared at the sight of him, and she followed suit. Soon the entire place thundered with applause.

Lily looked at her parents, wanting to share her joy with them. They both were clapping, but her father's face was stern, his brow drawn.

"Isn't it wonderful, Papa?" She touched his shoulder as she leaned toward him. "Things in this town are finally going to change."

He looked at her with somber eyes. "Yes, they will change. People have no choice now but to see the truth and look at their own hearts."

Her stomach clenched as Papa's words sank in. The people of Eureka would be picking sides now. A battle had been won today, but there was still a war to be fought. When would it all end? And how?

Chapter 26

Standing at the bar of The Gilded Cage, Abernathy tossed back another gulp of whiskey, relishing the burn as it coursed down his throat. How in tarnation had that band of Bible toters managed to best him?

It wasn't supposed to be this way. Things had started out so well. That milksop Marsden had happily taken the offering he'd brought on the night of the ball. Abernathy had figured all the imbibing the preacher had done over the past year had so deadened his tongue's powers of discrimination, he'd never notice the drug lacing his food and drink. And he'd been right. But that was the last thing that had gone according to plan.

When the Pink had decided to keep an eye on the pastor, it provided a perfect opportunity to eliminate several problems. The idiots who worked for Abernathy were supposed to incapacitate both Marsden and Forbes, arranging them in such a way that it appeared the preacher had attacked the detective. Then, when their bodies were found, everyone would assume Forbes had come upon Marsden's malicious act, tried to stop him, and gotten killed in the process. Whether Marsden died or survived made little difference. The man would have no memory of the night and would believe whatever he was told.

It had been a perfect plan. And none of it had worked.

Abernathy wiped his mouth with the back of his hand and slammed the empty glass down in front of him. "Another."

Eyes wide, the bartender reached for a bottle, filled the glass, then made a pretense of cleaning something at the other end of the bar.

Abernathy snatched up the glass and sneered as the amber liquid sloshed over the side and dampened his fingers. *Lily Rose.* It was her fault. Going all over town, infecting people with her charitable ways, with her message of love and tolerance for all of God's creatures.

"What a hot, heaping pile of horse manure," he muttered into his glass.

She couldn't have done it on her own, though. She'd tried for years to get people to listen to her, but the voice of one woman didn't carry too far in Eureka. Until now. She had help. The detective and that reverend had carried her cause. Didn't they have better things to do than stick together like a set of Siamese triplets?

Abernathy frowned. Something was mighty peculiar about the Pink and Crew showing up at the same time. Forbes had come to town looking for a fugitive, but his investigation should have been well over by now. Why had he decided to stay and help build a school, of all things?

He glanced at his pocket watch. The devout were still gathered inside the building, no doubt gloating over the victory they'd won today. If he hurried, he could get to the Rose Cottage, sneak upstairs, and pry some information out of the Pink, who was probably drugged to the teeth.

Abernathy pushed away from the bar, then stopped to fish a few coins from his vest pocket. He tossed them onto the scarred wood counter. "That should cover what I owe you," he said to the bartender.

The man nodded. "Thank you, sir."

Abernathy smiled to himself. He believed everyone deserved to get what they had coming to them. Something the citizens of Eureka wouldn't soon forget.

~

The Rose Cottage was as quiet as Abernathy had hoped. The only one about the grounds was the manservant who'd come to his home with Lily and Crew. It had been a pleasure to dispatch the brute with a pistol butt to the head. Using the business end of the weapon would have been far more satisfying, but a shot would have drawn too much attention. There would be time for a more lasting solution later.

As he crept up the grand staircase, he took in the décor of the space below. As finely furnished as his home was, this one outdid it. Not only was it stylish; it had a homey quality that spoke of the family residing there. An old feeling gnawed at his insides, one he'd begun denying long ago, and he pushed it away. Loving a woman, raising a family, made a man weak. If he ever did marry, it would be purely to raise his social status, nothing more. Only a fool would choose to be ruled by his heart rather than his head.

Once upstairs, Abernathy peeked from room to room until he found Forbes. With a thick white comforter pulled up to his chin, his head on a white-cased pillow, and a bandage covering half his face, the Pinkerton was nearly invisible in the bed. The thing that gave him away was his labored breathing. Abernathy smiled. His men must have damaged the detective's ribs.

In the corner of the room was a table littered with the tools of doctoring. Abernathy picked up a bottle and read the label. *Laudanum.* Perfect. The man would be pliable. He also wouldn't be able to fight should he grow suspicious.

Lowering himself onto the edge of the bed, Abernathy shook Forbes by the shoulder. "Detective." He received only a grunt in reply, so he shook the man harder and firmed his tone to say, "Detective. I must speak with you."

Forbes moaned, then rolled on his side, facing Abernathy. His eyelids opened only halfway, and he squinted to focus. "Doctor?"

Abernathy suppressed a laugh. The Pink believed him to be Dr. Paul—a truly ridiculous notion, since Paul was a mere runt of a man. But the detective was not only highly medicated; his skull had been soundly beaten.

No matter. His confusion was advantageous. "Yes, it's Dr. Paul," said Abernathy. "You sustained a severe head injury, and I need to ask you a few questions to see if your memory's been affected."

Forbes mumbled something that seemed to indicate he'd comply.

"Very good. What's your name?"

"Carter." He smacked his lips together a few times and stuck out his tongue, as though his mouth had been pasted shut and he needed to pry it open. "Carter Forbes."

"Yes. And what is your vocation?"

"Pinkerton agent."

"Excellent." Now, with a few basic questions out of the way, Abernathy could get down to business. There was no telling how long the effects of the laudanum would last, and he didn't want Forbes coming to his senses in the midst of the interrogation. "What do you remember about the night of the accident?"

"Fire. The schoolhouse. Shot off the signal."

The signal. Those gunshots that had alerted Crew and half the town about the fire. Thankfully, Forbes didn't seem to remember anything else about that night, at least nothing to incriminate Abernathy.

"Detective Forbes, what brought you to Eureka?"

Forbes frowned, squeezing his eyelids shut. "Grant Diamond. Fugitive."

Abernathy already knew as much. He persisted, his questions becoming more specific. From the detective's sentence fragments and mumbled words, he slowly pieced together a story that was fascinating, and quite useful, to boot.

"So, you believed Reverend Crew might actually be this Diamond fellow in disguise?"

"Yes. Before." The Pink's eyes were closed, and his breathing deepened. He'd fallen back asleep, but Abernathy wasn't through with him. He shook the man's shoulder again.

Forbes's eyelids opened wider this time, his eyes a bit clearer. The laudanum was wearing off.

Abernathy jumped to his feet and headed for the door, talking as he went. "Thank you very much, Detective. I do believe you'll make a full recovery." He stopped in the doorway. "One last thing. Did you ever hear back from the missionary society?"

"Letter's still at the post office." Forbes shook his head, then pressed a hand to his temple. "What…what does that have to do… Doctor?"

With a silent touch to the brim of his hat, Abernathy slipped down the hall, descended the stairs, and left the Rose Cottage through the front door. By the time he hit the last porch step, he was whistling.

It looked like things were going his way, after all.

⌒

The first sign of trouble was when Joseph failed to return to church with the carriage.

As Mrs. Rose fretted aloud about the absence of her servant, Mr. Rose looked up and down the street. Grant put a hand on Lily's arm and led her off to the side. "Why didn't Joseph stay here during the service?"

"I asked him to go back home and keep an eye on Mr. Forbes, just in case he needed anything. But he would know to be back by now." Her fingers toyed with the top layer of her skirt ruffles. "You don't think something's wrong, do you?"

Chuckling, Grant shook his head. "With Joseph? No. Forbes is probably running him ragged, asking for hot tea and cold cloths for his forehead." His casual words belied the misgiving in his gut that told him something was amiss. But there was no use adding to Lily's worries. "Tell you what. I'll ride ahead to the house and take a look."

Lily rewarded him with a broad smile. "Thank you, Reverend. I'd appreciate that very much."

As soon as Grant had gotten a respectable distance from the church, he chucked the horse's sides with his heels, urging her into a gallop. Minutes later, he arrived at the Rose Cottage. Seeing nothing odd out front, he rode around to the back, calling out Joseph's name.

The Wiyot man stumbled out from behind the barn, his palm pressed against the side of his head.

Grant pulled his mount to a sliding halt and jumped from the saddle. "Are you all right?"

Joseph squinted at him. "Been better."

"I seem to be making a habit of finding men with head injuries wherever I go." Pulling the Indian's hand away from his head, he took a closer look. Joseph would have a nasty goose egg, but there was no blood, and he didn't appear to need medical treatment.

"I don't know what happened," Joseph grumbled. "I was minding my own business, and something walloped me out of nowhere."

"Someone obviously wanted you out of the way." Grant frowned as he gazed about the grounds, as though the reason why might be waiting for him on the lawn or under a tree. "At least you weren't hurt as badly as Forbes."

The two men turned to look at each other, as the realization hit them simultaneously.

"Mr. Forbes!" Joseph exclaimed.

Grant dashed to the back entrance of the house. "Forbes!"

Through the kitchen, the dining room, the foyer, and up the stairs, which he took two at a time, he continued calling out the Pink's name, but the only response was silence. He burst into the man's room and pulled himself up short when he saw Forbes sitting on the edge of the bed.

"Will you please stop yelling?" The detective cradled his head in his hands.

"Sorry. I was afraid someone might have come here with the intention of doing you harm."

"Why would you think that?"

Grant settled on the mattress beside Forbes. As he told the story of what had happened with Abernathy at church, and then the attack on Joseph, the Pink frowned. "Someone did come here."

Grant's spine straightened. "Who?"

"I think it was Dr. Paul."

"Couldn't have been. Dr. Paul was at church." He was one of the townsfolk who had proven himself honorable by staying put after Marsden had invited the Wiyot into the church sanctuary.

"I knew something wasn't right. He asked too many odd questions. His voice was familiar, but...." Forbes rubbed the temple that wasn't covered with a bandage. "Oh, no."

"What?"

"I think it was Abernathy." Forbes looked at Grant, his eyes revealing a mixture of pain, confusion, and regret. "He asked me about why I'd come to Eureka. Then he inquired about Grant Diamond. And about you."

Grant leaned forward, his elbows on his knees, and exhaled a long breath. Abernathy was ruthless, and he was no dummy. If he'd been asking questions about Reverend Crew, it was only a matter of time before he uncovered the truth.

With a pang of sadness, Grant acknowledged the truth: he'd overstayed his welcome, and now it was time to go. Almost.

Chapter 27

Lily gazed around her, in awe of what God had accomplished in just one week. With the help of many hands, the schoolhouse had been completed in a much shorter amount of time than it had taken with only a handful of workers. A half-dozen benches stood in two straight rows before the teacher's table, behind which her mother had lined up several chairs to seat the evening's dignitaries.

With an air of reverence, Lily lowered the stack of primers she carried onto the table. She patted the top cover as pride swelled within her. She had done something good. Something worthwhile. She nudged the books so that they were perfectly square with the corner of the table.

Reverend Crew set a pile of slates next to the primers, his hand brushing hers in the process. Her eyes sought his. None of this would have been possible without him. She wanted to show him how much she appreciated everything he'd done. But there was no way to express the depth of her gratitude or the extent of the difference he had made. At least, no way that was appropriate for an unmarried young woman and a respectable cleric. About the best she could do was hope he could read in her eyes all that she felt.

With their gazes still locked together, Reverend Crew opened his mouth as if to say something. In that moment, Mama appeared before them, Reverend Marsden by her side. Looking a dozen years younger, he could have passed for someone else altogether.

"Reverend!" Lily extended a hand to him. "I'm so glad you could make it tonight."

His eyes glowed with pleasure. "I wouldn't have missed it, Miss Rose. This is an historic moment for Eureka. It's a blessing to be part of such a reconciliation."

Lily nodded. She knew what he meant. "We've reserved a seat for you up here." Lily ushered him to a place of honor by the teacher's desk. For an instant, he looked as if he would decline, but Lily forestalled him. "I think your support is very important to the success of the school. I would appreciate it if you would take this seat so that everyone may know of your commitment to seeing it through."

Lily glanced out the window and saw Detective Forbes patrolling the area outside the building, just as he had all afternoon. He moved with confidence, several yellow-green bruises the only reminder of his ordeal. Over the past couple of days, he'd insisted on returning to work on the school, despite Lily's best efforts to make him rest. He'd been overheard muttering to himself on occasion, still working through the details of the arson in his mind. Like Lily and Reverend Crew, he was certain Abernathy had been behind it. The problem was that they had no proof. And unless they somehow managed to trick Abernathy into an admission of guilt, there didn't seem to be a way of finding any. Too bad Abernathy was so wily.

Forbes had worked closely with Papa to enlist trustworthy guards to be posted all around the schoolhouse during the opening ceremony and overnight, but the detective hadn't been able to bring himself to cease his own vigil.

Lily hoped that once the school was an established fact of life, the local ranchers would grow used to it, and the remaining dissent would die off. People couldn't stay on the boil indefinitely.

A delegation of Wiyot dressed in their finest entered the building, and Lily hurried to greet them. They wore gracious smiles and held their heads high. A few of the townsfolk approached them, and Lily made introductions. Six Wiyot children had accompanied these elders, their faces having been scrubbed until they shone. They gaped about them with bright, inquisitive eyes, but remained on their very best behavior.

Anna Walters approached Lily, her arms outstretched. Her evening gown was more suited to a fete than a dedication ceremony, but as she grasped Lily's hands, she wore a genuine smile that turned her into a beauty nonetheless. "This is amazing, Lily. I so admire you. You've been tenacious in sticking to your beliefs. I don't think I could ever be so strong."

Lily's face heated with the awkwardness of accepting an unexpected compliment. "Why, thank you, Anna. I'm just glad it seems to be working out."

Mama appeared at Lily's side. "It's time, dear."

Lily nodded and moved to the front of the table, while her mother shooed everyone to his or her seat.

"You can do it, Lily." Reverend Crew's whispered support from just behind her gave her the courage to begin.

"Thank you all for coming," she started, "and for all you've done to promote the future of Eureka. Through the generous gifts of your time and funds, you have helped to establish our town as a peaceful oasis. We can show the rest of northern California how to live in harmony."

A round of polite applause interrupted her. She acknowledged it with a nod. "Now I'd like to introduce the gentleman who has been the driving force behind the building of this school, and without whom the project never would have taken seed. A man of God whom I greatly esteem—Reverend Hubert Crew."

The subsequent round of applause was slightly warmer.

Lily ceded her place to Reverend Crew and took a seat in the front row. Gazing up at him, she realized he had turned crimson at her words. Come to think of it, even with Forbes's insistent questioning, Reverend Crew had never been very forthcoming about personal details, probably due to his humble, self-effacing nature. She had no idea where he had grown up or why he had chosen to enter the ministry. She would have to make it a point to ask.

Reverend Crew cleared his throat. "I can't begin to tell you what a privilege it has been to work on building this school with all of you. The road to this day was long and…unexpected. I don't feel particularly fit for this work, and I've often wondered if God was having Himself a joke at my expense. But He's done a remarkable thing here, and I'm glad to have been a part of it, along with you."

Lily couldn't have kept the smile from her face if she'd tried. Leave it to Reverend Crew to charm the crowd. The guests were preening as if they'd championed the school from the very start. The reverend had a way with people; there was no doubt about that. And he was different from most ministers. More real. He didn't pontificate as if he were above everyone else because of his training. He approached people on the same level, as an equal.

He would make a wonderful teacher for the Wiyot children.

"Thank you for opening your hearts to this project," he continued. "I believe God will bless Eureka, and each of you, for what you've done here."

A commotion outside drew the attention of the audience.

Lily turned in her seat just in time to see Major Raines yank open the door. Abernathy ambled in, looking extremely self-satisfied. "Pink, I normally don't give my guns to anyone, but this is a special occasion." He plunked h+is weapons into Carter's hands. "I'll want those back when I leave. Oh, and you might want to stay close. I think you're going to want to see this."

With that, Abernathy brushed past Papa and the major and swaggered down the center aisle of the school. He was followed by a scarecrow of a man with thin blond hair that stretched in three narrow strands across his pate. The fellow was dressed in the same stiff, black clerical garb as Reverend Crew. Behind this unknown gentleman strode Sheriff Van Nest.

Lily stood, as did most of the crowd. Something bad was coming. And they didn't want to meet it sitting down.

Abernathy stopped almost toe-to-toe with Reverend Crew. "This here's the fellow," he said to the man behind him.

The unknown cleric peered through his spectacles. Pushed them up on his nose. Wriggled that appendage. And then shook his head. "No, sir. I can say with utmost certainty that this man is not Reverend Hubert Crew."

⌒

Even as his stomach hit the ground, Grant looked over to where Lily stood. She met his gaze with lowered brows, her head tilted in confusion. Grant closed his eyes. He'd pushed his luck too far.

Forbes came up next to Abernathy. "Who is this fellow, anyway? Why should we take his word for anything?"

Abernathy curled his lips in a slick-as-spit grin. "This here's the Reverend Elias Stanhope of Harvard University, chairman of the board that appointed Crew to come West."

"Yes. Yes, that's right," Stanhope said, his head bobbing as he patted his pockets. "I've got my credentials here, somewhere... ah. There you are." He produced a thin portfolio and handed it to Forbes.

As the detective started sorting through the documents inside, Stanhope pressed on. "I can tell you good folks that I know, or knew, Reverend Crew very well, and this fellow does not bear the slightest resemblance."

Lily's expression had been easy to read as it progressed from anger at Abernathy's interruption to confusion and then to doubt when no immediate denial sprang from Grant's lips. As her befuddlement began to give way to hurt, panic rose within him. Forget Abernathy and everything else. He needed to make Lily understand.

"On the way into town, I found a dead man on the road," he explained, his gaze steady on her. "He was a minister. I traded my clothes for his. My letters for his. Then I came into town, with the sole intention of purchasing supplies and moving on. But then I met you."

The uproar in the room was a vague backdrop. Lily's eyes had grown so huge, her face so pale, he was sure she would faint. He stepped toward her, but someone gripped his arm, stopping him.

He looked at the hand, then up at Forbes.

"You're Grant Diamond," the Pinkerton said. It wasn't a question.

Grant wanted to apologize. To make it clear that he hadn't planned on tricking Forbes. He hadn't planned on any of this. All he had ever wanted was a family of his own and a place to call home.

Forbes spoke before Grant could conjure a response. "Grant Diamond, I hereby arrest you for the murders of Sarah Grace DeKlerk and Hubert Crew. May God have mercy on your soul."

The contempt lacing Forbes's words lanced through Grant with physical pain. "No, Forbes, I told you—I didn't kill the reverend. I found his body. And I didn't kill Sarah, either."

The look Forbes gave him made it clear he thought Grant was as repulsive as rotten meat.

Having manacles conveniently at hand, Sheriff Van Nest stepped forward. Grant didn't resist as his arms were pulled behind him and his wrists shackled. All he wanted was to see if Lily had heard him. If she would try to understand.

She stood as still as if she'd been turned into a pillar of salt, and was nearly as white.

He had to get through to her. "Lily, did you hear me? I didn't kill anyone—I swear it!"

His words were swallowed up in the commotion from the crowd.

Only Lily's voice, as quiet and distinct as an automaton, penetrated the haze that hung around him. "Don't speak to me. Not ever." The command sliced through his heart. She turned her back to him as Sheriff Van Nest forced him out of the school, Abernathy leading the way, like a hunter showing off his prize trophy.

Grant didn't care. All that mattered were the tears brimming in Lily's eyes as she'd turned away from him, and the disappointment that had drawn down the corners of Forbes's mouth as he'd made his arrest.

Grant had truly cared for only three people in his entire life. The first, Sarah, was dead, and he had just wounded the other two in such a way that they might never recover. He deserved to go to jail. He deserved to hang. And, at that moment, he half wanted to.

Chapter 28

Lily touched the chipped edge of the flowerpot. The peony it once held had died, long past bloomed and spent. All that sprouted from the dirt were the dry, shriveled remains of the stem and leaves. Lily felt exactly the same way. It seemed like a hundred years ago that she had run into Reverend Crew at the mercantile.

No, not Reverend Crew. Grant Diamond. Not a selfless, caring man of God but a selfish, heartless, duplicitous criminal. And a murderer, if what they said about him was true.

A sob tore through her, and her hand slipped from the flowerpot. There had been a time when the conservatory was a peaceful refuge, a place of beauty and new growth. But Lily didn't think she would ever find real peace again.

A shoe scraped the tiled floor, and she spun around. There stood her mother, framed by the tall potted palms in the entryway. "I thought I might find you here."

"Predictable, as always." Lily's voice cracked.

Mama's smile was sad but kind. Not the type Lily was accustomed to seeing. "My dear daughter. You have proven to be one of the most unpredictable women I know. And by far the most delightful."

"Delightful?" Lily gawked at the woman approaching her. She couldn't possibly be Dorothea Rose. "I'm clumsy, impulsive, and a terrible judge of character. I see nothing delightful in any of that."

Mama laughed. "Of course, you don't. Come." She held out her hand. "Let's sit outside in the garden. You and I need to have a long talk."

Lily took her mother's hand and followed obediently as she pulled her through the conservatory and outside. The last time Lily had lingered in the garden had been the night of the ball, when Reverend Crew—no, Grant Diamond—had asked her to dance. Had that been part of his plan? To get close to her through flattery and false attention? Or had he truly wanted to take a turn with her on the dance floor? She shook her head and sighed. She would never know, and it made no difference. She would never see him or speak to him again. The thought made her feel as if a mule had kicked her squarely in the stomach.

Mama settled gracefully on a bench of intricately designed iron and patted the seat beside her. "Sit, Lily."

Lily plunked onto the seat, not even trying to emulate her mother's grace. What was the point?

Mama's posture was perfect, her hands folded primly in her lap. She looked at Lily. But, for once, she didn't scold her. "It's difficult when you discover that someone you love hasn't been totally forthcoming."

Lily reared back in shock. "What are you talking about?"

"Grant Diamond. You're in love with him, aren't you?"

Lily drew in a deep breath. "I don't know Grant Diamond."

Her mother nodded. "I suppose that's true. But you do know Reverend Crew."

"Yes."

"And you love him, don't you?"

She wanted to remain silent. To clamp her lips together and hold back the terrible truth. But she couldn't. "Yes." Squeezing her eyes tight against the tears, she dropped her chin to her chest. "I'm sorry, Mama."

"Whatever for?"

"For not being smart enough to see him for what he really was. He lied about everything for weeks and weeks."

Mama took Lily's hand in hers. "My dear girl, all that God asks us to do is to love Him and to love each other. Never apologize for doing that."

"But...but he played me for a fool."

"Really? Pray tell, how exactly did he do that?"

Lily blew out an exasperated sigh. Was her mother's knowledge limited to social savoir faire? "He posed as a clergyman and a missionary. He lied about his identity. All while staying under this very roof." She waved a hand frantically at the mansion. "He put all of us in danger."

"Did he, now?" Mama pulled her hand away and tapped her lips with one finger. "I seem to recall that Reverend Crew—"

"Grant Diamond."

"Fine. I recall that Mr. Diamond stood up for you when your reputation was in jeopardy, rescued both Reverend Marsden and Detective Forbes from a fire, and helped build a schoolhouse, not once but twice. Should I go on?"

"Please don't. He lied, Mama."

"Yes, he did. And that was wrong. But it occurs to me that he lied in order to protect himself." She paused. "Sometimes, even good people will lie when their survival is threatened."

A tremor in her voice implied there was more. Lily turned and studied her carefully. "Mama?"

"What do you think of me, Lily?"

What an odd question. She couldn't very well admit to her mother that she sometimes scared her to death and most of the time made her feel inadequate. But she could tell her the positive things. "I respect you. You're a remarkable woman. And I love you."

"Thank you, dear." Mama stared out across the garden at the well-manicured hedges, her cheeks stained crimson. "Would you think any less of me if you discovered that I've been keeping a secret from you?"

"Well, no, but...." She paused, confusion making her mind swirl. "Have you?"

"Yes."

"For how long?"

Mama lifted her chin a bit higher, then turned to face Lily. "All your life."

Lily fought to keep her expression calm and nonjudgmental. "Whatever it is, Mama, it will not change how I feel about you."

A sad little smile pulled at the corners of her mother's lips. "I certainly hope it won't. But it's high time you knew."

She held Lily's gaze but remained quiet for such a long time, Lily thought she'd changed her mind. Finally, she opened her mouth, and the words spilled out.

"I've always told you that your grandfather was a plantation owner in Louisiana. That part is true. What I didn't tell you is that your grandparents were not married. My mother was a quadroon."

Lily gasped, unable to hold back her shock. She had never met her grandmother, but she'd always pictured her being just like Mama—a proper, polished woman who followed social conventions to the letter. Not this.

"She was his mistress?"

Mama nodded slowly. "Yes. I know it sounds terrible. In truth, it is. But you have to understand her situation. Her mother was a plantation slave, as her mother's mother was. Both of them had been violated by their masters. When all three of them pooled their resources and bought my mother's freedom, she had to make a choice. Had your grandmother remained where she was, the same fate would have awaited her. So, she went to New Orleans, but, once there, she found very few options for a free young woman of mixed ancestry who had little money."

Lily shook her head. "And that's where she met Grandfather?"

Mama clasped Lily's hands in hers. "She found a sponsor who sent her to a quadroon ball. New Orleans is infamous for these balls, at which beautiful women who are one-quarter or less Negro socialize with white men. Outwardly, these events are perfectly legitimate, but the true purpose behind this exercise amounts to a slave auction. The men choose mistresses from among the young quadroons. Being entirely ignorant of the custom, your grand-mother felt helpless and trapped when she learned what she'd gotten herself into. Remember that she had been raised as a slave. Independence of thought was very new to her."

Mama sighed, and Lily noticed how drawn and pale she looked. Telling this story was costing her a great deal.

"Your grandfather was obviously morally deficient, but, to his credit, he took good care of your grandmother. He gave her a fine home and met all her needs. He also provided for me, too, when I came along."

"How good of him." Acid laced Lily's words as she imagined the kind of life her grandmother must have led.

Mama sighed. "Your grandmother was born into a terrible situation. The choices she made may not have been entirely wise, and they may not make any sense to you and me, but she did what she felt she needed to do in order to survive. Just as I did."

"You?" Lily had a sudden urge to cover her ears with her hands and refuse to hear any more secrets. But there was no stopping it now.

"Being their daughter makes me part Negro. Not much, mind you, but any fraction of Negro heritage means that, legally, I do not enjoy the same rights as white women. As far as most of the public is concerned, I should have no social standing whatsoever.

My mother knew that, and so she raised me as a white lady. She taught me proper etiquette and steeped me in social niceties. She was determined that I would be able to hold my own in any situation, with any group of people. Before my father died, he made sure Mother would be taken care of. And when she died, she bequeathed me with the means of leaving New Orleans to start a new life. Which I did."

Suddenly, Lily's entire life began to click into place—why Mama was so exacting when it came to social graces, why things had to be done just so, why she was so hard on Lily. Then, a terrible thought nearly stopped her heart. "Papa—does he know? You and he...you are...you're not...."

Mama sandwiched Lily's face between her palms and laughed. "Yes, dear heart, your father knows all about our family history. I told him before we were married."

Lily's shoulders sagged with relief. *Married.* Thank the Lord in heaven. "Of course, none of that would matter to Papa."

"No, it didn't." Mama sat back and looked toward the house. "Your father is an amazing man. He believes, as I do, that people are people. It matters not from whence they come or the color of their skin. What matters is who they are today and what is in their heart."

"But, Mama, you've always had such a dislike for the Indians—"

"No." The word cut between them like a saber. "I respect the Wiyot, and I've been concerned for their safety. And for yours. For many years, I believed the best solution for all involved was to live quietly, not creating more strife. But now...." Her voice trailed off, and she looked down at her hands, clasped once more in her lap.

"But now?"

"Now I see I was wrong." She looked up, tears glistening in her eyes. "You are so brave, Lily. You did what was right, no matter what other people thought or said. And now I see that unless we stand up to men like Abernathy, the plight of the Wiyot will never change." A tear rolled down her cheek, and she swiped it away with a lacy white handkerchief, which had mysteriously appeared as if from thin air. "Your Mr. Diamond sees that, too."

Lily's back stiffened. "Mama, I—"

"Think about it, dear. He had plenty of opportunities to flee Eureka. The man was a fugitive from the law, yet he remained in this town, sleeping in the very same house as a Pinkerton detective. Why would he do that?"

All Lily could do was shake her head.

"I can think of two reasons." Mama raised a finger. "One, because of his desire to help the Indians. And, two"—she raised another finger—"because of you."

"Me?" The word squeaked out.

"Yes. I've seen the way he looks at you, the way he treats you. The man is smitten. I'll admit that I considered the notion a mite undesirable when I thought him to be a missionary, but now...well, now it makes perfect sense."

Lily chuckled. "You believe he's better suited to me now that you know he's a criminal?"

Mama snorted in a decidedly unladylike fashion. "No, you silly girl. I believe...I'm not exactly sure how to explain this. I think he was drawn to the goodness in you. Your example helped to change him into a man who could actually *be* a missionary."

Lily's mind traveled back to that night in the kitchen. She'd nearly choked to death, but Grant had saved her. The memory of his arms around her, encircling her in warmth and safety, brought on a flush. Now she was sure he'd intended to leave that night. Had he felt the same way she had? Was that the reason he'd chosen to stay?

"It doesn't matter. None of it matters." Lily propelled herself from the bench. She needed to move. But she'd taken only a few steps when she turned back to her mother. "He lied to me from the beginning. Everything I know about him is a falsehood."

Mama shook her head sharply. "He lied about where he came from. He lied about his past. But I believe that the man he showed you was his true self. And I don't believe for one minute that he's a murderer."

Lily had to admit she had a difficult time believing that, too. None of her experiences with Grant led her to believe he was capable of committing murder. But Carter Forbes, another man she admired, who had been totally forthcoming from the day she'd met him, believed that Grant was entirely capable of committing such a heinous crime—and that he had done so.

"What do I do now?" Lily asked.

Mama stood and took Lily's hands once more. "Pray. Ask the Lord to fill your heart with forgiveness and discernment. Then, go talk to Mr. Diamond. Hear what he has to say. Only then will you know what to do next."

The back door of the house opened, and Papa strolled into the garden. "I came outside to enjoy this beautiful evening, and I found the most beautiful sight I can think of." He kissed Lily atop her head, then slid his arm around his wife's waist, pulling her close to his side. "Lily-belle, I was thinking a drive might do us good. Joseph is waiting out front with the carriage."

Papa winked down at Mama, and she smiled sweetly back at him. They had planned the whole thing. Mama had softened her up, and now, without coming out and saying it, Papa was taking her to the jailhouse. To Grant.

"Thank you. I love you both." Lily hurtled into Papa's arms, relishing the crush of his hug. Then she hugged Mama, more gently, and gave her a peck on the cheek. With Papa's hand in hers, she pulled him toward the path that circled the house.

Thinking of her parents, a wave of emotion swept over her. He knew. Her father knew all about her mother's past, but he didn't care. He saw only the woman she was today and what was in her heart. He looked at her not through the lens of judgment and condescension but through eyes tempered by the love and grace of a forgiving God.

How could she offer Grant Diamond anything less?

Chapter 29

Grant sat on a narrow cot with his head in his hands. He was alone in the jail. After roughing him up, Van Nest had taken off for a round at The Gilded Cage. Grant hoped he would take his time. He had no desire to see or talk to anyone.

The door to the police station opened, and Reverend Marsden poked his head inside. "Rev—that is, uh, Mr. Diamond?"

"Yeah?" Grant didn't bother attempting civility.

Reverend Marsden glanced behind him, then slipped inside, shutting the door quickly. "Are you all right, Mr. Diamond?"

Grant snorted. He hurt from head to toe, and he must look like he'd been trampled by a herd of buffalo. He couldn't bring himself to assuage Marsden's concern by assuring him that he'd be fine. He shifted positions and lay down, wishing mightily that the preacher would go away.

Marsden pulled his hat off and twirled it around in his hands. "I know I might not be a man you much respect, Mr. Diamond, but I just wanted to tell you that I understand how you feel, and I'd encourage you not to give up hope. No matter what's in your past, you've done a lot of good in Eureka. And I don't think you're the kind of person who murders folks. I just wanted to let you know that, and tell you I intend to keep up what you started here."

Grant lifted the arm he had flung over his face as the man was speaking. "You believe me?"

Marsden nodded. "You saved my life, when you didn't have to. When you had no reason to. That's an act of a righteous man, somebody who takes life seriously. Not one who callously throws it away."

Grant sat back up. "That means a lot to me, Reverend."

The preacher shrugged. "I've learned a lot lately, and, believe me, no matter what you've done, you're not too far removed from God's grace. Sometimes I think we're harsher with ourselves than God is."

"But I know I'm a sinner. I've lied to people and cheated them. And, though I didn't kill Sarah DeKlerk, I fled and let her killer get away with it."

Marsden pulled the sheriff's chair from behind the desk and planted it in front of Grant's cell, sitting with a thump. "And I let men get away with the murder of over a hundred people. But that's the exceptional thing about God's grace. He's willing to forgive us. And He doesn't just forgive; He forgets, even those things we cannot. He throws the sins of our past into the depths of the sea." He began talking faster, as if bursting to share the insights he'd gained over the past week. "He doesn't view us as damaged goods but as beloved sons. And we don't just assume a new identity, like we are somehow fooling Him; He *gives* us a new identity. We're new men, and the men we used to be are dead."

Grant's throat itched. Heat pricked his eyes. "So, you think there's hope, even for me?"

"If there was hope for me, son, there's hope for you." Marsden pressed his lips together, stood up, and put his hat back on his head. "Maybe you can think on that for a bit." Quietly, the reverend turned and let himself out.

Grant let his head fall back against the wall of the cell and closed his eyes. He would have expected the reverend to bring some stones to heave in his direction. He hadn't been extended so much of what they called "grace" in his entire life. In fact, he didn't think he'd known what grace was until now. Was it possible that God would be willing to grant him grace?

The door to the jailhouse squeaked open again. Van Nest must be back to pick up where he'd left off. Grant didn't bother opening his eyes until something clanged against the bars of his cell.

"Wake up."

Grant opened a single eyelid. Abernathy stood sneering at him, and the sheriff was nowhere to be seen. "What do you want?"

"Just thought you'd like to know I decided to leave the school standing this time." He bent over, laughing.

Disgusted, Grant realized the fellow was tipsy. He closed his eyes again to show he didn't fear the rancher. "Makes no difference what you decided. The people of Eureka came together to build that school. They'll protect it from snakes like you."

Abernathy's laughter turned into a snarl, and he banged the bars with the flat of his palm. "You think you're better than me, Diamond? Guess you've played the part of a preacher so long, you forgot who you really are. You're lying, thieving trash, and so are the Wiyot. That's why you like them so much. Sorry to say, after tonight, there aren't gonna be any more Wiyots for you and Lily Rose to bestow your charity on."

Grant's stomach clenched. "What are you getting at?"

"I'm resurrecting the Humboldt Volunteers." Abernathy's voice dropped to a near whisper, his lips pulling back in a gruesome smirk. "We're going to rid Eureka of every last one of them. For good."

Grant launched himself from the cot and made a grab for Abernathy, but the rancher danced back out of reach, snickering. "Save your strength, *Reverend*. Change is coming, and there isn't a thing you can do to stop it." Abernathy moved across the room, talking as he went. "In fact, I think my boys and I will toast our upcoming victory with a few rounds at The Gilded Cage." He stopped in the doorway, turned, and flicked the brim of his hat with one finger. "Sweet dreams, Diamond." He oozed out the door, not bothering to pull it shut behind him.

Grant slammed the side of his fist into the bars. He had to find a way to stop this. "God, I've never been worth a plug nickel, but please, please help me now."

"What's goin' on in here?" Van Nest stepped inside and peered into Grant's cell. "Oh, good. You're still here." His jaws wrenched apart in an enormous yawn. From the smell of him, he'd been imbibing, too. "For a minute there, I thought you'd escaped. Can't have that. Gotta keep an eye on my prisoner."

Still mumbling to himself, the sheriff settled into the chair Reverend Marsden had recently vacated. "I'm the law 'round here, you know." He fumbled to remove his tin star from his chest. It flashed, winking in the light of the single gas lamp, as Van Nest held it up for Grant to see. The sheriff swore and then dropped the badge with a clink onto his desk. He put his thumb to his mouth and sucked at a tiny drop of blood where the pin had pricked him.

Still licking his wound, Van Nest eyed Grant blearily and raised the forefinger of his other hand. "Don' you try nothin'," he mumbled. "I'm watchin' you."

For an achingly long ten minutes, it appeared that Van Nest actually did intend to watch Grant all night. His nerves jangling with the need to escape, Grant forced himself to lie down on the cot.

After an eternity, Van Nest turned his back on Grant's cell, tipped his chair back, and propped his feet up on the desk. Another lifetime limped along until Van Nest at last started to snore.

Grant bolted upright and looked around frantically. He needed to find a way out. And then he spotted it. Van Nest had the keys.

They were dangling from his pocket—and looked like they were about to fall. All they needed was a little help. Grant stretched his arm through the bars, but no matter how he maneuvered, even a dislocated shoulder would not enable him to reach the big key ring.

Though his hands shook with frustration, he forced himself to look for other options.

A broom was propped against the wall about four to five feet from his cell. Once again, his reach was too short. He pulled off his hat and stretched his arm through the bars, trying to catch the knobby tip of the handle with the bowl of his hat. On the fourth try, it worked, and the broom fell toward him. Grant grabbed it, thankful he hadn't missed, or the clatter might have awakened the sheriff.

Sweating from exertion and anxiety, Grant drew the broom to himself, then turned it so that the end stuck through the bars. Ever so carefully, he tried to hook the handle through the key ring. A little more…there. He had it.

Van Nest snorted and shifted, pulling the ring away from the handle. Gritting his teeth, Grant balanced the broom and tried again. When at last he had it positioned, he lifted gently, and the keys continued their slide from the sheriff's pocket. He was so close. The last one slipped out with a small clinking sound. But the ring wouldn't come free. Grant jiggled it, taking care not to wake Van Nest.

It was then that he realized the keys had been secured in place by the simple expedient of a rawhide strip lashed to the sheriff's belt loop. There was no way he could get that loose from so far away without waking Van Nest.

Swallowing the explosion of curses that welled up within him, Grant used his sleeve to wipe the sweat from his forehead. He peered around, searching for some other means of escape. There was no window in his cell, and the bars were all firmly anchored. If he had a set of lock picks, he could be out in seconds. Grant's eyes flew back to the badge Van Nest had dropped on his desk. Extending the broom as far as he could, he swept it along the top of the desk. The star dropped to the floor with a metallic clink. Grant held as still as stone while Van Nest grumbled something in his sleep.

Reversing the broom again so that the bristles were outside his cell, Grant began sweeping the sheriff's badge toward him. It was a frustratingly slow process, as the star kept getting caught in the gaps between the wooden floorboards. At last, it was close enough for him to reach. He snatched it up, then pulled his ivory toothpick from his shirt pocket. Thank heavens he hadn't left it in his wallet, where he usually kept it; Van Nest had confiscated that before locking him up.

Grant fumbled blindly with his makeshift lock pick. Even with such a crude instrument, it took only a moment for the clumsy old lock to give way.

He was free.

Now he had a decision to make. A tiny part of him, which clamored for attention, urged him to run and never look back. But he squashed that notion without a bit of remorse. People's lives were at stake. The only thing left to decide was, where should he go for help? From what he'd heard, Abernathy had recruited dozens of volunteers. There would be no stopping them on his own. Nor could he warn all of the various Wiyot camps of the threat. Especially when he didn't know where Abernathy would start.

He had to think.

There was only one place he could be certain they would at least hear him out and check into his allegations: the Rose residence. They'd take him seriously, for the sake of the Wiyot. Of course, they'd also turn him back over to Van Nest. Grant swallowed a lump. That didn't matter. All that mattered tonight was protecting innocent people from being killed.

He slunk past the snoring sheriff and opened the jailhouse door. Not a soul stirred outside. Within seconds, he was halfway down the street, keeping to the shadows.

Once he'd gotten a distance from the center of town, he picked up his pace. He'd taken far too long breaking out of that cell. Abernathy might have already rounded up his men and set his vicious plan in motion.

The clatter of a carriage brought Grant up short, and he dove behind a barrel of rainwater. The vehicle's lantern lit the way, as well as illumined the occupants—Lily and Mr. Rose!

Grant had never been so happy to see someone. He leaped up and rushed forward. "Stop!"

The horse reared, and Lily yelped. Mr. Rose fought with the animal to keep it from taking off at a gallop.

Grant grabbed for the animal's bridle. "It's all right." He patted its neck, calming the beast.

"Diamond? What are you doing out here?" Mr. Rose demanded. "Last I heard, you were supposed to be in jail." His tone made it clear that Grant would be going right back to his cell, if Mr. Rose had anything to say about it.

Lily was less caustic. "It isn't safe for you out here. If Abernathy were to find you, he could kill you and claim he'd done it in self-defense, that you were a violent criminal bent on escape."

"I'm not worried about myself. I had to warn you. You need to get together all the men you can trust. Aber—"

Something rigid jabbed Grant in the back. "Stay right there, Diamond, and put your hands where I can see them." *Forbes.* Grant did as he was told. There was no doubt in his mind that the Pinkerton was serious.

"Detective!" Lily sounded surprised. "Where did you come from?"

"I was keeping an eye on the prison. I figured Diamond would try to make a break for it, and there's no way Van Nest is wily enough to match wits with him. Now he's going back in the cell, where he belongs."

Hands still raised, Grant pivoted slightly toward the detective. "Carter, you can't."

"Don't tell m—"

"Listen! The only reason I broke out was because Abernathy told me he's assembling the Humboldt Volunteers again. They're going to kill all the Wiyot, and they're going to do it tonight. We've got to stop them."

Lily clamped a hand over her mouth. Mr. Rose sat back in the carriage bench with a thud. Forbes merely circled Grant, careful to keep his gun leveled, until he was looking him in the eye.

"I swear to you, Carter, I'm telling the truth."

Forbes flared his nostrils, pursed his lips, and then parted them again, as if he were about to say something. But he kept quiet. It was as if he was carrying on an argument in his head, trying to decide whether or not to trust Grant.

"Carter, I swear to you, once the Wiyot are safe, I'll give myself up. You can still see me hang."

"No!" Lily gasped.

The fear and passion in her voice gave Grant hope. Maybe she would find it in her heart to forgive him.

Carter's scowl deepened. "I get no pleasure from seeing men hang, especially...." He shook his head and cleared his throat before continuing. "All I care about is justice. Justice must be served."

"And it will be." Grant dared to lower his hands a fraction of an inch. "As soon as the Wiyot are out of danger, I'll walk back to the jail of my own accord. I give you my word."

Forbes scoffed. "You're a liar and a killer. Your word is useless."

Grant hung his head. The Pink's cutting statement stung all the more because of its truth. For years, he'd lied his way through life, using one swindle after another to protect himself. Not only had he destroyed his own credibility, but now, people would die because of his mistakes.

"This is ridiculous," Lily muttered.

Grant's head shot up at her words. Still wearing her Sunday best, she pulled and pushed at her wide skirts, fighting her way down from the wagon, causing the conveyance to creak in the process. Then she stomped in front of Grant, putting herself between him and the barrel of the Pinkerton's pistol.

Forbes growled. "What are you doing?"

"Putting an end to this foolishness. I will not stand by and allow more innocent people to die while you two quibble."

Forbes's jaw slackened, and Grant held back an unexpected smile. So, the little sparrow had transformed into a hawk. And her talons were out.

Chapter 30

Lily was angry. Not upset or frightened. Not scared or apprehensive. She was filled with gut-burning, blood-boiling anger. Lives were at stake, and these two were debating frivolities.

A muscle twitched in Carter's jaw. "Miss Rose, I'll thank you to step away from the criminal. He's a dangerous man."

"There's nothing dangerous about him, or he would have dispatched you weeks ago. He could have taken care of you in your sleep, or left you to die in that fire. But he didn't."

Papa stepped down from the carriage and stood beside her. "For the love of all that's holy, Forbes, quit pointing your gun at my daughter."

The detective remained stoic, his face frozen in hard, merciless planes. Finally, he closed his eyes and lowered his weapon. But he didn't holster it.

Lily could feel Grant's gaze on the back of her head before he spoke. "Do you mean that, Lily? Do you trust me?"

She whirled around, ready to verbally assault him for asking such a question, but she couldn't do it. Even in the dim light from the carriage lanterns, she could see the swollen bruises around his left eye, the scab forming on his lower lip, the lack of a jacket, and the torn fabric of his shirt. He'd been assaulted enough already, and by hands far stronger than hers. "Yes, I mean it. I trust you. But we can discuss that later. Right now, we need to warn the Wiyot. Do you have a plan?"

The skin around his uninjured eye crinkled. "I do, but you may not like where it will take us."

"Will it save the Wiyot?"

"I believe it will, if we all work together."

"Then, we could march through Sodom and Gomorrah, and I wouldn't blink an eye."

"Funny you should put it that way."

He looked down the street, and all three of them followed his gaze to The Gilded Cage. *Oh dear.* Everyone knew the saloon was no place for a good Christian woman. Still, if it would save the Wiyot, how bad could it be?

⌒

It was bad. The red velvet curtains hanging on the walls were faded and worn, covered in a layer of dust and dirt. The air weighted heavily with despair. At the far end of the room, one of the soiled doves stood beside a piano, singing in a clear soprano, while the man at the keys plunked out an uneven tune. Lily blinked a few times, imagining how beautiful one of the church hymns would sound coming from the young woman's lips. The hand on Lily's forearm tightened, and she looked up into Grant's eyes.

"There he is." An almost imperceptible jerk of his head directed her gaze to the bar, where Rick Abernathy held court among a group of rough-looking men.

A shiver ran down Lily's spine. Could she really do this? She looked up again at Grant, this time meeting eyes as hard and cold as granite. All she could do was nod.

He nodded back. "Let's go, then." He propelled her forward at the same time he called out, "Abernathy!"

All heads swung in their direction. The gal by the piano stopped singing, and the music faltered, soon ceasing altogether. Abernathy looked from Grant to Lily, confusion and anger on his face. He rose from his stool and sauntered over to them. "What are you doing out of jail, Diamond?"

"Van Nest and I reached an understanding." Grant's voice was smooth and easy. If he felt at all nervous, it didn't show. "See, I explained to him that I had something you wanted, and if he let me out, it would be monetarily beneficial for all of us."

Abernathy sneered. "You've got nothing I want."

"Don't be too sure." Grant looked at Lily, and she cringed beneath the blankness in his eyes. It was as though he had shut off all emotion. Is this what he'd had to resort to in order to survive over the years?

Abernathy made no attempt to hide his surprise. "You're offering Lily Rose? She isn't yours to give."

"No, she isn't." Lily wrenched her arm from Grant's grasp and looked Abernathy in the eye. "I belong to no one but my Savior, Jesus Christ. As do you, if you want to."

One of the men behind Abernathy spat in the direction of a spittoon and missed, the thick brown juice rolling down the brass side. Abernathy shook his head. "I sure hope you didn't come here expecting to save my soul."

"Can't save what a man doesn't have," Grant muttered under his breath.

"In a manner of speaking, yes." Lily gulped. The only reason she was in this saloon at all was because she'd insisted on coming. Her father, Carter, and Grant, most of all, had opposed the idea. Grant had maintained that his plan would work just as well if she remained outside. But she'd known beyond a doubt that she needed to give Abernathy one more chance to repent. She'd never forgive herself if she didn't.

"Mr. Abernathy, you can put an end to all this hatred and killing right now. Just open your heart to the Lord."

For a second, Abernathy's face softened, and Lily thought he might actually accept her invitation. Then he brayed with laughter, doubling over and holding his stomach with one hand. "Miss Rose, you are delightfully naive. Why would I want to back down now, when I'm so close to accomplishing my goals?"

"Because you're a human being," she said, "as are the Indians."

"Those Diggers are vermin," he spat out. "They're a blight on our town, and they need to be stamped out before the infection spreads."

Lily took a step backward, but Grant's palm on her back stopped her. He'd been right. There was no changing Abernathy. Not today, at least. For now, the best they could hope for was to stop him. She lifted her chin. "In that case, we have a business proposition for you."

"We?"

"Yes. Mr. Diamond and I." She looked back at Grant, relief flooding her when he took over.

"Let's get straight to the point, Abernathy. I want my freedom, and you want the social status and financial advantages that come with marrying into the Rose family. What I propose is a trade."

The crash and clatter of breaking glass came from behind the counter, drawing the attention of everyone in the room. The bartender rushed to mutter an apology as he retrieved a broom to sweep up the mess. Abernathy turned back to Grant, his eyes narrowed. "And what does the fair Lily get out of this arrangement?"

"Your agreement to leave the Indians alone," she said, finding her voice again. "No harassment, no murder. You will let them live in peace for the rest of their days."

Abernathy shook his head sharply. "No."

Lily's heart beat faster. "But—"

"No!" He held up his hand. "I'm sorry, my dear, but you're simply not worth it."

Grant's fingers curled around her arm once more. "I thought you might feel that way, which is why I have an alternate proposal." He pushed on, not waiting for a response. "You want to eliminate every single Indian, but I happen to know you can't."

"Have you bothered to look around you?" Abernathy's hand swept the air. "Most of the men in this room are with me, and there are more out there waiting for us. What could possibly stop us?"

A mirthless chuckle rumbled deep in Grant's throat. "In order to kill them, you have to find them, yet you don't know the where-abouts of all of them."

Lily whipped her head around. "Grant, no."

"This is about survival, Miss Rose," he said gravely. "It can't be helped."

She tried to pull free, but this time, he held her tight.

Abernathy grinned. "Keep talking."

"There's a hidden Wiyot camp that you'll never find. But I've been there."

Abernathy licked his lips. "And you'll tell me where it is if I agree to your terms?"

"Yes. You guarantee my freedom, and I'll give you the location of the hidden Wiyot."

"Grant, stop." Lily struggled, beating his arm with her fist until he let her go. She ran up to Abernathy, her arms outstretched. "You can't do this."

"I most certainly can. And I will."

"You intend to commit cold-blooded murder?"

"He's already committed cold-blooded murder." Grant's voice sounded from close behind her. "You were the one who killed the missionary, right, Abernathy? It must've been a shock for you when I showed up. But why bother with a harmless minister—and a white one, at that?"

"Harmless! He was coming to do everything you've done—rile up the town and get the Wiyot thinking above themselves. He was going to lead the people astray, just like you've done. Turn everybody against me and the true order of things. I did what I had to do to keep the fellow out. And if I'd known you were coming, I'd have killed you, too.

"You people are too weak-minded to see the truth. If I don't put a stop to this, the Indians will be stealing our cattle and our women and killing any homesteader trying to protect his property."

Lily shook her head. "The Wiyot haven't done any of that. They've been peaceable since white men first arrived in Eureka."

Abernathy's eyes shifted to Lily, and she saw that they were glazed over. "They're wild animals. You can't trust them. Once they get a taste for blood, it'll always be there."

"So, you're going to lead an army of men against the Wiyot and wipe them out in their sleep, even though they've done nothing to you?"

"Done nothing to me?" Abernathy's face stained with color from his collar up to his hairline, like a spilled glass of red wine overtaking a white tablecloth. "Indians took everything from me."

Lily looked at him in confusion. "I don't understand. The Wiyot—"

"Not the Wiyot. The Comanche. They killed my mother when I was just a boy." Strangled by emotion, his words were difficult to understand. "It devastated my father. Drove him mad. I found him hanging from the rafters of our barn. I was twelve years old." He poked a finger at her. "That's what Indians took from me."

For a moment, genuine sympathy twinged Lily's heart. She felt for the boy he had been, for the family he'd lost, and for a life changed forever. But that didn't excuse his actions today, or his blaming the Wiyot for his troubles. Lily needed to focus on the situation at hand. She had a job to do.

"Mr. Abernathy," she said softly, "the death of your parents was a terrible tragedy. But you can't bring them back or avenge their deaths, no matter how many Wiyot you kill or how many schools you burn down."

Abernathy growled. "I gave you a chance to save them. I had that school burned as a warning for you to stop putting notions in their heads. But you wouldn't listen." His eyes, now crazed with hatred and grief, swept from her to Grant, then back again. "If those Indians hadn't been away on some heathen ceremony last year, we would have finished off all of them on the island. It's time for them to go now, if I have to kill every last one of them myself."

A cry rose up within Lily as memories of the slaughter came rushing back. The blood, the bodies...so many people massacred. And there had been nothing she could do.

"You monster!" Lily hurled herself at Abernathy, beating his chest with her fists. There was a scuffle, and then strong hands grabbed her shoulders, pulling her away. Her tears ran freely as arms enfolded her, and she pressed her cheek against a warm, solid mass.

Above her head, Grant's voice rumbled, "Lily, it's all right. It's over."

Abernathy laughed. "Nothing's over. It's just getting started."

"That's what you think." Grant turned slightly, and Lily opened her eyes. "Forbes, did you get everything you need?"

"More than enough." From a shadowy corner of the room, Carter Forbes pushed back his wide-brimmed hat and stood to his feet. "I'd call that a confession, wouldn't you, Mr. Rose?"

At another table, Papa stood. "I certainly would." He looked over at a fellow covered in a huge poncho and slouched in a chair. "Did you hear all that, Reverend?"

"I most certainly did." A clear-eyed, decidedly sober Reverend Marsden popped to his feet, flinging aside the oversized garment. The grin spreading across his face showed just how pleased the reformed preacher was to be included in the scheme to take down Abernathy.

Around the room, additional familiar faces popped up—Hodge from the general store, Mr. Andrews the postmaster, and a half dozen other prominent citizens, including Reverend Stanhope.

Abernathy sputtered and swore. "What…? When did you all get in here?"

Lily's cheek felt the reverberations of Grant's laughter. "It's amazing what you can do with a bit of distraction." He patted her on the shoulder. Behind the bar, another glass hit the floor. The bartender shrugged his shoulders, then glared at Abernathy's crew.

Carter approached Abernathy, a pair of handcuffs dangling from his fingers.

Abernathy stepped back and reached for his holster but grabbed only air. "What the—"

"Looking for this?" Still grasping Lily with one arm, Grant held up the gun he must have lifted from Abernathy while she'd been pummeling him. Lily smiled. That scene from their little drama had been unscripted, but it had certainly worked out well.

While Abernathy struggled with the reality of the situation, Carter grabbed his wrists, locking the cuffs around them. "Rick Abernathy, as a sworn agent of the Pinkerton agency, I hereby put you under arrest for the crimes of arson, murder, and conspiracy to commit murder."

"You're not the sheriff. You have no authority here."

Carter tapped a piece of paper protruding from his breast pocket. "Actually, the United States of America has hired the Pinkerton firm as intelligence officers and endued us with police powers." He looked past Abernathy to the men who had planned to follow him. "I suggest you gentlemen disperse. You will be called on as witnesses in Mr. Abernathy's trial. And if any of you as much as considers carrying out the nefarious doings that were planned here tonight, I will personally see to it that you stand trial right beside him. Am I clear?"

A chorus of affirmations rang out, and then the men made for the door in a hasty stream.

Lily looked up at Grant. "We saved the Wiyot."

He smiled down at her, his eyes warm and familiar again. "Yes, love, we did."

Her heart melted. Right there, in the middle of a saloon, surrounded by ladies of ill repute, drunkards, and criminals, Lily had learned all she needed to know about Grant Diamond.

Chapter 31

Standing outside the saloon, Grant gulped down a breath of cool, clean air, rubbing the back of his hand across eyes gritty with exhaustion. Keeping a protective hand on Lily, he inhaled the lavender scent of her hair one last time before giving her shoulder a squeeze and then releasing her. "I've got to go after Forbes."

She turned to him, her eyes full of questions and, more important, love. There had been no doubt in Grant's heart that he loved her, but now he finally knew she felt the same. After all that had happened in the last twenty-four hours, he might even believe they could find a way to be together. If not for one remaining problem.

"I need to turn myself in." With a rueful smile, Grant headed in the direction of the jail.

Lily stayed on his heels. She could be a real bloodhound sometimes. "Grant, you can't."

His steps faltered. How he loved hearing his real name roll off her lips. But the sweetness of it only made the situation more difficult. "I have to. I gave my word."

"But there's only one cell in the jail. They can't possibly lock you up with Abernathy."

He hadn't thought of that. "I sure hope not. Maybe Forbes'll agree to take me to the lockup in Arcata. But that doesn't change anything. I have to turn myself in. And you have to go home." He strode off.

In the post-midnight hush of a sleeping town, his boots sounded excessively loud on the wooden boardwalk. But it wasn't just the steady tread of his own feet he heard. Softer, quicker steps still followed his.

Why wouldn't she let him go? Couldn't she see she was making this harder on him? His resolve to give himself up was weakening, and if Lily wasn't careful, he might ride out of town and take her with him.

He plunked down on the step outside the sheriff's office. Lily sat gently beside him.

He sighed. "What are you doing?"

"I intend to make sure you aren't locked up with Abernathy. It would be a...a miscarriage of justice, that's what." She sounded as testy as he felt. The elation of capturing Abernathy sure hadn't lasted long.

At the sound of raised voices coming from inside, they glanced sideways at one another. Grant readied himself to intervene if Carter needed help. A thump like a fist pounding a desk was followed by silence. Then came Carter's commanding voice, answered by the suddenly meeker Van Nest.

A smile tugged at Grant's lips, and he leaned back against the doorframe, pulling his hat over his eyes. "You don't need to worry about Forbes. He'll do the right thing." He peeked from beneath the brim at Lily.

She glared at him, her arms crossed, her jaw jutting out pugnaciously. He'd seen that look before. There was no point repeating his suggestion that she go home.

After a few minutes, Forbes opened the door, shaking his head. He stopped short when he saw them. "What are you doing here, Diamond?"

Grant pushed his hat back and stood. "I told you I'd turn myself in. Though I'd be obliged if you'd put me somewhere other than Abernathy's cell."

Forbes nodded and scratched the back of his neck.

"Detective, couldn't he stay at our house again?" Lily inquired. "You'll be there, too, if he should get it in his head to run away. But I believe his act of good faith in coming to you would suggest that forced confinement isn't necessary."

Forbes stifled a yawn with the back of his wrist. "All right, Miss Rose. I'll take you up on that offer."

Grant didn't know if it was kindness or fatigue that had influenced the Pink's decision, but he was thankful. "Much appreciated, Forbes."

Mr. Rose had driven many of Abernathy's would-be volunteers home in his carriage as a means of ensuring they dispersed, so the three of them started back to the Rose Cottage on foot.

Forbes fell into step beside Grant. "You said you didn't murder Sarah DeKlerk."

"I didn't."

"Convince me."

Grant's stomach churned. It was time to put all his cards on the table.

⌒

Lily glanced over at Carter, trying to catch his eye. Grant was obviously exhausted and in pain. Surely, an interrogation could wait.

"I owe both of you an explanation." Grant ran the palm of his hand quickly over Lily's back. Her desire to intervene waned at the same rate her curiosity rose.

"I grew up in an orphanage in New York City. When I was fourteen, they signed me on to apprentice with a gardener."

"That's how you knew so much about the flower when we first met," Lily surmised aloud.

He smiled over at her. "Yes. My ambition in life was never to be a gambler but a gardener. And I was a good one, which is why I was hired on at the DeKlerk estate.

"If I do say so, I turned their garden into the prettiest in New York. After a couple of years, I became the head gardener. One day, I came upon their daughter crying her heart out beneath a big old evergreen, a distance from the house. I offered to get her mother, but she refused. Said all her family did was try to control her feelings and dreams."

Grant's voice sounded so faraway, and Lily realized with a jolt that he'd loved this girl.

"She didn't want to be trapped by other people's expectations but to chart her own course. I'd felt the same way at the orphanage, so we began talking. From there, we became friends. She'd come to visit with me while I worked. Soon, our friendship turned into something more."

"You loved her," Carter said.

"Yes. I fell in love with her fire and her wit—two traits no one else seemed to realize she possessed. I never did figure out what she saw in me."

A sharp pang shot through Lily's heart. She knew exactly what Sarah had seen.

"Her parents would never allow a match between us. So, being young and foolish, we decided to elope. We figured once the deed was done, they'd have no choice but to accept it. We planned to meet in the garden at midnight, but when I showed up, Sarah wasn't there. I was scared she'd changed her mind, but then…I saw her…on the ground…."

His words stumbled to a halt, and Lily saw the bob of his Adam's apple as he swallowed once. Twice.

"I knelt down to try to help her, but she was already gone. There were dark bruises on her throat."

Lily's stomach turned.

Carter nodded. "She'd been strangled."

The three walked in silence for a few minutes, until Carter encouraged Grant to continue. "What happened next?"

"There was a commotion at the house, and I heard someone yelling about one of the gardeners. I knew if they found me with her like that, they'd never believe I hadn't killed her. So, I started running." He pressed his lips together grimly. "I've been running ever since."

Forbes eyed him speculatively. "The family told the police and our office that you'd abducted her. The theory was that she'd struggled, and you'd been forced to kill her. No one even hinted that she'd been in love with you."

Grant snorted. "Doesn't surprise me. They couldn't believe a DeKlerk could stoop to have feelings for a laborer like me. But think about it. If she didn't want to come with me, why was she out in the garden, fully dressed, in the middle of the night?"

Forbes nodded. "I'll admit, that part never did make much sense. But if the two of you were eloping, why didn't we find any luggage?"

Grant's shoulders slumped, and he looked about as lost as he must have felt back then. "Whoever killed her must have taken it. I tell you, Forbes, I loved Sarah. I never would have hurt her. I had no reason to."

Lily followed the conversation as she would a tennis match, her attention swiveling from one man to the other, in her desperation not to miss a word. Impulsively, she put a comforting hand on Grant's arm.

Grant covered her hand with his. "I'm sorry, Lily."

Her eyes brimmed with tears.

Forbes cleared his throat and motioned to the telegram in his pocket. "I've been ordered to report to Washington, D.C., immediately."

Lily turned to him, one brow raised at the seemingly unrelated comment.

Forbes took no notice of her questioning glance. "One more thing I have to know, Diamond. How did you end up with such an outlandish last name?"

Grant chuckled. "That's the thing you need to know?" He shrugged. "It's simple. No one at the orphanage knew anything about me—when I was born, where I came from…. When I was about nine, the nuns let me pick my own last name. A diamond was the most expensive thing I could think of, and I picked it to shock them. Looking back, I think it was also an attempt to force somebody—maybe myself—to see that I had value."

They arrived at Rose Cottage and started around the back to the gardens.

Forbes gave a satisfied nod. "Well, that answers one question that's been bothering me since I first heard about your case." He clasped Grant's shoulder and turned to face him fully. "I wish I could take the time to get to know the real Grant Diamond, but I've got to take this morning's steamship down to San Francisco."

Grant's eyes narrowed. "What are you saying?"

"I'm saying I believe you. Sarah DeKlerk's murderer was never in Eureka."

Grant blinked, his jaw hanging open, apparently incapable of speech. Lily had no such hindrance. Words spilled out of her. "Mr. Forbes, that's wonderful! And what of the poor missionary? Is Grant still a suspect in that case?"

Carter shook his head. "No, Miss Rose. I examined that body myself, and, given what Abernathy said tonight, Mr. Diamond is cleared of all charges. I already spoke to Van Nest and made sure he knows."

"What about Sarah's murder? Does Van Nest still think me guilty of that?" asked Grant.

"No. I informed him I was mistaken on that score, too. And it seems Reverend Stanhope will be taking the same steamer to San Francisco this morning. After what he heard last night, I don't think it will take too much to convince him that Abernathy was on a witch hunt, and I was overly zealous in labeling you a murderer. The worst you're guilty of is fraud by assuming another man's identity and profiting from it, in the shape of room and board." He looked at Lily.

It took her only a second to realize the implication. "I decline to pursue any charges of fraud."

"Well, then." Carter grinned. "I guess that means there are no other legal issues to worry about."

Lily couldn't help herself. She embraced the detective. "Thank you, Mr. Forbes. Are you certain you must leave so soon?"

"I'm afraid so. I wasn't bluffing about the Pinkertons having the U.S. government as a client. We're needed to help with this war."

"And Sarah?" Grant asked.

"I'll keep up the search for her murderer whenever I'm able. For now, I've got just enough time to grab my things and be on my way." The detective started inside, then paused and turned back around. "Diamond, I'm giving Friday to you. She's a big step up from that old nag you rode into town, and, for some reason, I think she likes you."

A deep belly laugh rolled out of Grant. He approached the detective in two long strides and clapped him fiercely on the back. "I might even miss you, Pink."

Lily extended her hand to Forbes. "Thank you again. For everything."

"And you, Miss Lily." He enfolded her hand in both of his and bowed slightly. "The experience has been a pleasure and a revelation." He looked past her and grinned at Grant. "In more ways than one."

Then Carter disappeared inside the house, Lily and Grant waving after him.

The sky had lightened to a soft dove gray, and the air around them was plush with dew, as night gave way to a new day. For the first time since learning Grant's true identity, Lily was alone with him.

Grant removed his hat and looked down, toeing the ground. "I owe you an apology, Lily, for trespassing on your trust and hospitality." He raised his head to meet her eyes. "I never meant to hurt you."

She took his hand. "I know. It hurt to discover that you'd lied to me, but I understand now why you did. Not to excuse it, but I think I was mostly upset to have my idol dashed."

"Can you forgive me?"

"I already have." She grinned. "I prefer the flesh-and-blood man to the idol, anyway."

He groaned and then drew her to him, his fingers tangling in her hair as he cupped her face and brought his lips to meet hers in a sweet, warm kiss.

When finally they broke apart, Lily stood with her shoulder tucked beneath the crook of his arm, her cheek resting against his chest, as they watched dawn break over the far horizon. It was a perfect moment, as round and beautiful as a pearl and full of promise.

"Breakfast is ready!" The cook's indelicate announcement broke the spell.

They looked at each another and laughed, then turned and walked toward the house, hand in hand.

They still had so many things to talk about and work through, but one thing was foremost in Lily's mind. "Now that your name is clear, do you plan to stay in Eureka?"

"Yes, love, I do." Grant pulled her close, tucking her arm under his and raising her hand to his lips. "I think the role of minister really took hold of me. How would you feel about my becoming a real preacher? Though I won't have any fancy degree from Harvard."

"I think you'd be good at it. The Wiyot still need a teacher, too." She paused. "Did you notice the young woman singing in The Gilded Cage? Her eyes looked positively haunted. She clearly needs help, and I know there are others like her, at The Gilded Cage as well as at the other saloons in town."

Grant laughed. "You're a born crusader, Lily Rose."

"Just call me Joan of Arc."

Their laughter mingled as he motioned for her to precede him into the house. Only one of the French doors was open, and before she knew it, she'd become wedged in the doorframe. "Oh, drat." She pressed and tugged at her crinoline hoops.

Grant squeezed her arm. "Hold on. Let me help."

With a smooth movement, he opened the other door, releasing her.

Lily faced Grant, her heart swelling with joy as he took her hand again. She would never be perfect, but this man somehow loved her in spite of, and maybe even because of, her imperfections. God had turned her mourning to gladness.

Grant glanced toward the dining room. Her parents' voices carried out in murmurs. A frown creased the skin between his eyes. "I love you, Lily, but I'm a reformed gambler, with nothing to offer except a promise to do all I can to become the man God wants me to be. Is there any chance for us?"

Yes, they had challenges ahead, but Lily had never been more certain of anything in her life. She rose up on tiptoe for a quick kiss, then whispered in his ear, "I love you, too, Grant Diamond, and I'm willing to take a gamble on you."

About the Authors

Jennifer AlLee and Lisa Karon Richardson are a dynamic writing team. Jennifer believes the most important thing a person can do is find his or her identity in God, a theme that finds its way into all her work. She has published numerous novels, short stories, devotions, and plays. Over the years, she has enjoyed being part of church drama ministries and worship teams. Jennifer lives with her family in Las Vegas, Nevada. Readers may visit www.jenniferallee.com to find out more about her and her writing.

Lisa Karon Richardson has led a life of adventure—from serving as a missionary in the Seychelles and Gabon to returning to the States and starting a daughter-work church—and she imparts her stories with similarly action-packed plot lines. In addition to writing and ministry, Lisa manages medical malpractice litigation for two major health systems in Ohio and Indiana. She lives in Ohio with her husband and their two precocious children. Readers may visit her website at www.lisakaronrichardson.com.

Both Lisa and Jen can be found at www.inkwellinspirations.com.